The Lines of Torres Vedras

Book 7 in the Napoleonic Horseman Series

By
Griff Hosker

The Lines of Torres Vedras

SWORD BOOKS

Published by Sword Books Ltd 2019

Copyright ©Griff Hosker First Edition

The author has asserted their moral right under the Copyright, Designs and Patents Act, 1988, to be identified as the author of this work.
All Rights reserved. No part of this publication may be reproduced, copied, stored in a retrieval system, or transmitted, in any form or by any means, without the prior written consent of the copyright holder, nor be otherwise circulated in any form of binding or cover other than that in which it is published and without a similar condition being imposed on the subsequent purchaser.
A CIP catalogue record for this title is available from the British Library.
Cover by Design for Writers

Contents

The Lines of Torres Vedras i
Spain and Portugal 1810 1
The Lines of Torres Vedras 1809 2
Chapter 1 3
Chapter 2 13
Chapter 3 24
Chapter 4 35
Chapter 5 50
Chapter 6 65
Chapter 7 79
Chapter 8 89
Chapter 9 100
Chapter 10 108
Chapter 11 120
Chapter 12 136
Chapter 13 145
Chapter 14 156
Chapter 15 168
Chapter 16 177
Epilogue 187
Glossary 189
    Fictional characters are in italics 189
Historical note 190
Other books by Griff Hosker 192

The Lines of Torres Vedras

Spain and Portugal 1810

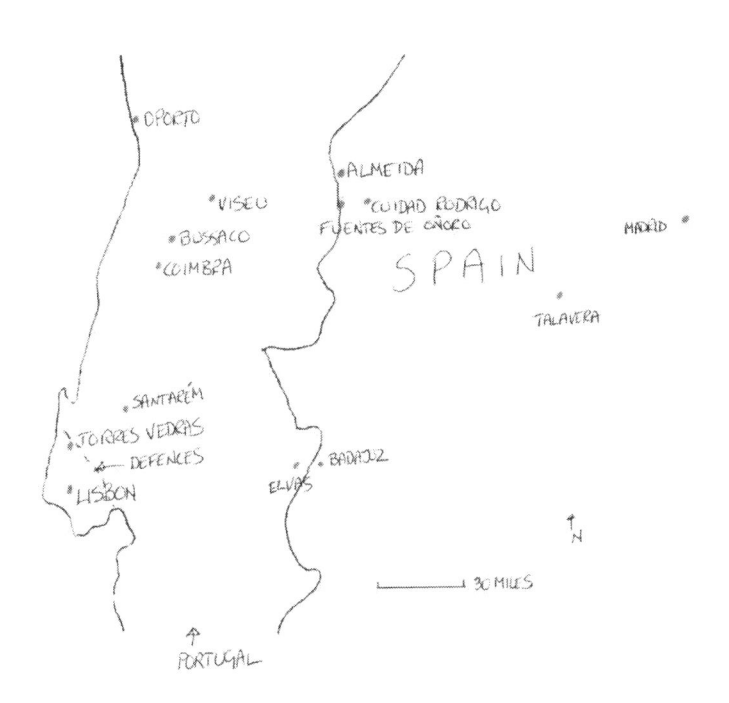

The Lines of Torres Vedras 1809

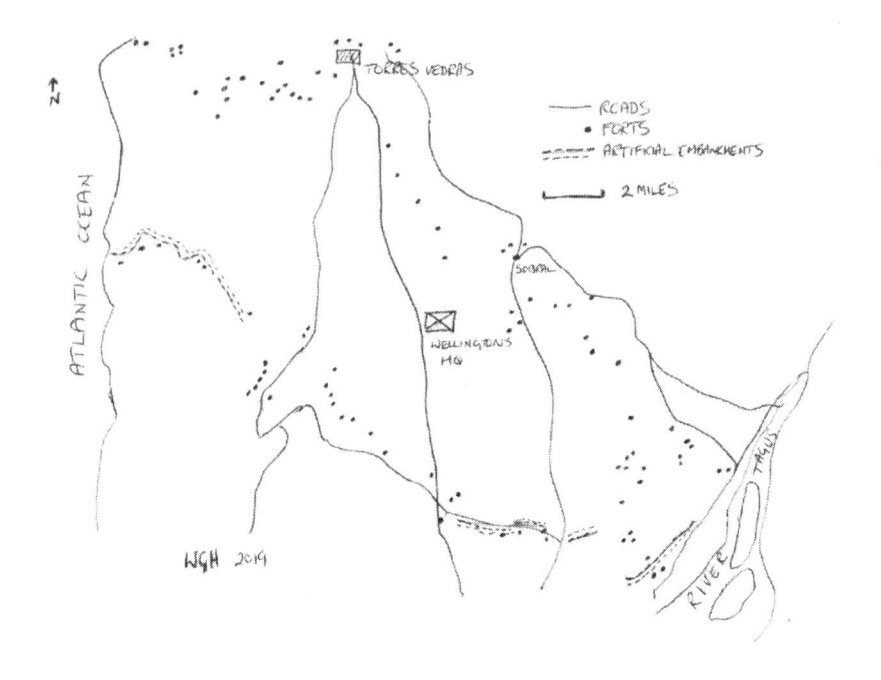

Chapter 1

Life in Lisbon should have been good for my soldier servant, Sergeant Sharp, and me. We had been with Sir Arthur Wellesley, now titled Viscount Wellington, when he had defeated the French at Talavera and we had both acquitted ourselves well. However, what should have been a great victory was diminished when our Spanish allies were heavily defeated. The army had been forced to pull back to Portugal and Talavera abandoned to the French for General Wellesley did not want extended lines. We were accommodated in Lisbon close to the staff of Sir Arthur Wellesley where we had good quarters, fine food and a life free from French musket balls and cavalry sabres! There had also been other dangers not endured by most of the British Army stationed in Portugal. A French spy, Mrs Turner had almost killed me and had killed a dear lady who had befriended Sharp and I many years earlier. The death of Mrs Turner did nothing to assuage the grief at Donna Maria's death.

I am Major Robbie Matthews of the 11th Light Dragoons although I have served for longer on secondment than I ever did with my own regiment. I was not born an Englishman. In fact, there is, as far as I know, not a drop of English blood in me. My mother was Scottish and my father a French aristocrat executed during the terror. It was the fact that I was fluent in both languages which attracted the attention of General Wellesley's spymaster, Colonel Selkirk. I also had the ability to speak Italian, Spanish and Portuguese somewhat well and so, albeit reluctantly, I was regularly sent behind enemy lines as a spy. For his sins, my former officer's servant Alan Sharp, now a sergeant, had to endure the same dangers as I and he had become skilled in languages and in my other specialism, killing the enemies of England. Those same enemies were also doing their best to end my life! Joseph Fouché who was Colonel Selkirk's French counterpart hunted me at every opportunity and I knew that it was only a matter of time before I was caught.

I had been slightly wounded by the French spy, Mrs Turner or the Black Widow as Sharp referred to her, and so I was allowed a brief time to recuperate. However, Sir Arthur was not one to allow such inconveniences as a superficial wound to stop a soldier from serving his country for long. He deemed my recovery was done and so Sharp and I were summoned from our quarters in Lisbon to travel thirty miles north to the defences he and his chief engineer, Sir Richard Fletcher, were building a series of defences to hold up the French who, although still in Spain, would soon be able to invade Portugal. Sharp and I knew the area well for we had travelled the land as scouts for the General. We left the city to travel through the tortuous Portuguese roads.

As we were so often called upon to travel behind enemy lines Sharp and I did not wear the uniform of the 11th Light Dragoons. Instead, I emulated General Wellesley and wore the blue uniform of the 23rd Light Dragoons with whom we had served at Talavera. My hat was the same as the French used and Sharp wore a forage cap. We had run foul of certain Portuguese and British officers who could not identify our uniform but they tended to ask questions first and once we spoke, we were able to convince most people of our identity.

"If I was a gambling man, sir, and you know I am not," I laughed for Sharp was typical of every British soldier and would gamble on anything and everything. He shook his head at my laughter and sniffed, "as I said, sir, if I did bet, I would put a month's pay on his lordship sending us behind the French lines again!"

"And you are probably right, although as we have been pushed out of Spain, it seems unlikely that we will be far from the British lines this time. We will just do what we are ordered and try to stay alive."

"Will they be sending the regiment out here, sir? There are damned few light horse regiments and we need them." Like me, Sharp had been in the 11th and he had strong connections to Sergeant Major Jones and the rest of the regiment. There had been some bad officers, like Captain de Vere, but they had left and it was a happy regiment.

"I suspect they will but we both know that logic and the war office do not often share the same place! They will probably send them to the West Indies where they would be of no use whatsoever!"

"Aye, sir, you have it there." He nodded to another wagon driven by Portuguese carters. We had passed dozens of them as we headed north. They were laden with all sorts of tools, building materials and labourers, "Do you reckon old Beaky is building a fort, sir?" Beaky was the affectionate nickname for General Wellesley. Napoleon was Boney and the Viscount was Beaky.

"I wouldn't let Sir Arthur catch you using that name. He will be building something but I am not sure it will just be a fort. Speculation is idle, Sharp, for we have but another five miles to go and we shall discover the reason for our summons."

The last time we had been on this road north it had been a quiet and peaceful region. Even the fortress of Torres Vedras had appeared as though it was a sleepy backwater. The closer we came the more we saw the extent of the work; now the whole of the land was in turmoil as engineers both Portuguese and British toiled to make redoubts, forts and every conceivable defence. I recognised some of the engineers who

The Lines of Torres Vedras

waved cheerily as they worked in the hot sun to make an impenetrable barrier. As we made our way through them to the Viscount's Headquarters, I reflected that if the French knew what the General planned, they would make all haste to get to Lisbon before he could finish the formidable defences. With the exception of Marshal Beresford in Andalusia and Viscount Wellington here in Portugal, the French-controlled the rest of the Iberian Peninsula. True, there were Spanish armies but they had yet to defeat the mighty French war machine.

We had to wait, of course as that was Sir Arthur's way. Sir John Moore had been almost as good a general but he had been warmer and more approachable than Sir Arthur. And yet men were equally willing to die for the dour Irishman!

The Coldstream Guards' sergeant outside the house nodded to me as I approached the headquarters building with the Union Flag flying. "I will let the General know you are here, sir. If you would wait in the orderly room, sir."

I nodded, "Sharp, I am guessing we will be spending the night here, see if you can get us a room." I handed him one of the French coins we had acquired when we had completed a secret mission for Colonel Selkirk.

"Righto sir," he took the coin and Donna's reins.

The Coldstream sergeant grinned, "I can see that you are an old hand, sir."

I smiled, "As the alternative would be a tent and it is getting a little chilly at night, sergeant, then the coin will be well spent."

The orderly room had a corporal and a sergeant who were checking figures. They snapped to attention when I entered, "At ease."

I had learned when I worked for Napoleon Bonaparte that it paid to keep your eyes open all the time for there was no such thing as useless information; there was just information which you had yet to find a use for. I saw maps and diagrams pinned up on the walls. Some of them were the defences which were being built but I also saw a map of Spain and upon it were towns circled in red: Almeida, Badajoz, Elvas, Cadiz, Ciudad Rodrigo. I deduced that they were fortresses. Badajoz was where he had left the army which had won Talavera but was too battered to take the offensive. Someone had put crude French flags over most of the map. The little red dots were the only resistance to the French war machine. As Napoleon had just had another victory in Austria it seemed highly likely that sooner or later, he would return to Spain and finish what he began. That would be interesting, a battle between the two living generals I had served and more than that, the two best generals anywhere! Who would win?"

"Major Matthews? The General will see you now."

He took me up a narrow staircase to a room which had, obviously, once been a bedroom. The bed had been removed and there were papers scattered all over the table which had replaced it. I saw Sir Richard Fletcher, the man who had designed the defences; I had met him once before and liked him. He was a true engineer and enjoyed the challenge of building. He would be challenged in this rocky part of Portugal. He nodded towards me, "Good to see you, Matthews! While you are occupying his lordship, I shall take the opportunity to grab some food." He gestured towards the Viscount, "The man does not even think about food!"

Without looking up Sir Arthur said, "Fletcher I do but only at mealtimes. It seems to occupy your whole day!" He looked at the Lieutenant, "Mountshaft, see that we are not disturbed."

"Sir!" The young Lieutenant looked to be extremely nervous and I guessed that he had only recently arrived in Portugal.

Sir Arthur looked at me, "Recovered?"

"Yes, sir."

"Good, I need your mind and that most elusive of qualities which you seem to possess in abundance, luck!" He took a map from a leather document case. I recognised it as a more detailed version of the map I had seen in the orderly office. "This is for you. Make a copy of it and then return it to me by tomorrow!"

"Sir."

"You have a military mind, Matthews, and I like that. More, you understand discipline although you do not have breeding, I prefer you to some of these young jackanapes who have been giving the army such a bad name in Lisbon!"

He referred to the officers who had gone to the theatre drunk and then proceeded to go onto the stage to join the actors. There had been outrage in Lisbon and some officers had been sent back to England in disgrace.

"I need you to go on a little ride to the land east of Cuidad Rodrigo and Almeida. Those fortresses are the key to the defence of Portugal. I need to know who is in command now and where the enemy is gathering." He looked at me and I recognised the expression. He was allowing me the opportunity to ask a question or two.

"When you say head east, sir, I am assuming that you mean keep going east until I find the French?"

"Of course. Since Talavera, I have no idea which marshal the Emperor Bonaparte has put in command. The orders will have come from Paris and not Madrid. His brother is a fool and I thank God for that particular piece of nepotism!"

As it is winter, sir, Sharp and I will not be able to travel as quickly as we might in more clement weather."

He waved a dismissive hand, "The French will not move until spring, I know that. Like us, they will be in winter quarters but the difference is that they will have reinforcements and, since the disaster at Walcheren last summer where 7000 of our men died of malaria, it is unlikely that we will be reinforced for a while." He poured himself a glass of wine, "The thing of it Matthews is, that we know the quality of the French. They have damned fine cavalry who are disciplined, artillery which is better than ours and infantry who will keep coming so long as they are led. I can plan for those eventualities but the marshals who lead them? That is something altogether different. Colonel Selkirk has compiled a dossier for me and once you tell me who leads them then I can plan."

"Sir, this seems, to me, something that the Colonel could discover easier than I."

"And he is doing his part, even as we speak. He is in Naples and using his Italian connections to discover as much as he can of Bonaparte and his plans. However, you will bring me confirmation soon, of that I am certain." He waved a hand and I was dismissed.

That he had confidence in me was one thing but the task he had set me was a hard one. I was not surprised that the Colonel was in Italy. It was where I had met him and been recruited. When I reached the orderly room Lieutenant Mountshaft handed me a purse. The General said that you might need expenses, sir."

I took it and said, "Thank you, Lieutenant", noting the question in his eyes. That the General had not told him what I was doing was obvious and I guessed that the young officer would speculate. I was an enigma for I was not a Colonel Selkirk. I also served in the line and I had participated in battles. Indeed, Sharp and I had distinguished ourselves at Talavera when helping to extract the 23rd Light Dragoons when they had made a disastrous and ill-advised charge, tumbling into a hidden gulley.

Night had fallen since I had entered the headquarters building and there were lights in the buildings around the square. The Coldstream Sergeant pointed to a tavern across the square from the headquarters, "Your Sergeant said to tell you, sir, that he has found rooms for you there." He smiled, "A nice little billet, sir. Good food and they don't water the wine too much!"

The first thing a British soldier did when he came to a new town was to find the best places to drink. The Guards were particularly good at it!

The Lines of Torres Vedras

Sharp had a table ready for us and he had ordered a jug of wine. I had been with Sharp for a number of years and we knew each other well. He understood my tastes and almost anticipated what I might need. He smiled when I sat, "I tasted the wine before I ordered a jug, sir. It tastes like the d'Alpini wine you like."

I nodded and took the proffered beaker. I had connections to the d'Alpini family in Sicily and, indeed, I enjoyed an income from the estate. I tasted the wine and he was right; I liked a wine that you almost had to chew and this was just such a wine!

"I ordered the food, too, sir. The owner reckons it gets busy later on."

"Good man and we need an early night. We leave first thing in the morning."

He nodded and drank some wine. "East, sir?"

"East, Sergeant."

He nodded, "Thought so." He would ask no more questions until we were alone. He was every bit as good a spy as I was and I knew that if I could not carry out the mission then he could complete it. The food came and proved to be a tasty rustic stew with chicken, seafood and spicy sausage. We spoke of what we might need for the journey. Had anyone been listening then they would have struggled to know where we were going. We had brought one spare horse with us. There were two others but we had left those in the stables at Donna D'Alvarez's home in Lisbon. She had left all of her property to me in her will for she had no one else to leave it to and her husband had been rich. She was a kind-hearted soul and taken it upon herself to clean and look after the royal palace when the royal family left for Brazil. The gesture of the house and her property touched me but knowing that she had no family I found sad for when her husband had died, she had lived alone. Now was not the time for I was in a war with no end in sight but when it was over then I would have to marry for I wanted a family.

Once we were in the room, we were able to talk for the tavern had filled up and the soldiers who were eating and drinking made noise enough to cover the sound of a twelve-pounder battery! I told him our mission as I made a fair copy of the map I would have to return before we left the next morning. He nodded, "Then I take it we play at being Frenchmen, sir?"

Although my French was fluent as I had been raised speaking it, Sharp's was learned. We had developed a character for him to play. The servant he played had been born in the Spanish Netherlands and learned his French later. It explained his accent. He also spoke as little as possible. To that end, the items of a personal nature which we would carry were French rather than English. We had found them on the various battlefields so we had French tobacco tins, French coins. I had a French timepiece. Our Baker rifles were left in Lisbon for they would mark us as British soldiers. Our pistols, we had four each, were a mixture of British and French. That was normal although it meant we had to carry balls of different calibres. The sword I would take had been obtained from a dead French Cuirassier while Sharp had one taken from a French Hussar. The danger would be if we came upon Spanish guerrillas who tended to shoot first and ask questions later! I finished copying the map which I would drop off at the orderly office before we left. We would ride before dawn and before the trumpet blew reveille as I wanted no one to see us leave.

Sleep was slow to come. Firstly, because I had the mission running through my mind and secondly, until the tavern emptied, we were kept awake by raucous British soldiers. All of this meant that I woke early and although I was not refreshed, I was ready to ride. The tavern owner and his staff were up for they served food from before first light. We ate bread, cheese and ham before we paid our bill and left. We had bought a ham from the tavern keeper and some cheese and bread, as well as sausage from the local shops the night before and we would be self-sufficient on the road. While Sharp went for the horses I went to the orderly room. As I had expected Lieutenant Mountshaft was already there. An aide for General Wellesley earned his pay but the reward would be a promotion if he did not die on the battlefield and performed to the high standards set by the General.

He gave me a wry smile as I handed him the map, "I can see, sir, that you are well used to Sir Arthur and his ways."

"I was his aide once, Lieutenant, and I have a suggestion, make sure you have a good horse for when the General is on the battlefield his aides have to move as fast as possible!"

"Thanks for the tip, sir."

We headed first for Badajoz as the army was still there and I knew that they would have had scouts out themselves. Before we ventured further east, it was as well to know what we might come up against. This was November and while not as bad as November in England it was still wet and cold. The mountains had snow on them and the roads were churned up and muddy. I was grateful for the heavy-duty oiled cloaks we both wore. Sharp had bought grain for our horses but we paid for grazing as we headed east. We were lucky that few regiments had marched this road. When General Wellesley moved the army then they would find grazing hard to come by. Badajoz guarded the southern gateway to Portugal, which along with its sister fortress, Elvas, was garrisoned by the Portuguese. Marshal Beresford had trained them to operate in the British manner and they were almost the equal in terms of discipline.

They could never match the rate of fire which British redcoats could manage. I knew that the French were mystified at the ability of the British to fire, in one minute, five volleys when they could barely manage three.

I did not think that the Viscount would keep men in the field in winter. It was unnecessary as no one fought battles in winter unless it was absolutely necessary. Even as we headed into the camp, I saw the first wagons and companies heading westward towards Portugal and winter quarters. It was typical of General Wellesley that he had not told me that he was bringing his army closer to the new fortifications he was building. Sharp and I paused, partly to allow some wagons up the slope and partly so that I could use my telescope to examine the fortress of Badajoz. Like all of these frontier fortresses, it was an impressive structure and was intended to withstand modern warfare and artillery. Having said that, there was not a fortress which had been yet built which could withstand a determined assault by Napoleon's twelve-pounder cannons and his mighty siege guns which needed a team of bullocks to pull them. I knew that the General just wanted the Portuguese fortress to buy him time. His defences at Torres Vedras would stretch from the border to the sea and I doubted that they would be easily overcome.

The last wagon having gone, we spurred our horses down the slope to the camp. I spotted the cavalry camp and headed there. Most of the cavalry had already been withdrawn closer to the coast for the horses had suffered badly in the battle and in the heat of Spain. It looked to me like they had left a brigade made up of troops from the regiments which had fought at Talavera. That made perfect sense. Spying the standard of the 23rd we headed for it. I suppose we should have sought out the camp commander but it was coming on to dark and in my experience, the officer would probably be lodged in Badajoz itself and would be enjoying his wine and a hot meal.

We were seen by Corporal Groves who gave a cheery wave to Sergeant Sharp, "Sergeant! are you rejoining us?"

Sergeant Sharp gestured with his thumb, "Major Matthews!"

"Sorry, sir, I didn't see you there. I will tell Captain Minchin that you are here!"

Troop Sergeant Fenwick came over and his face had a huge grin across it, "Major, Sergeant, it is good to see your faces. We have spare tents if you are staying the night for we have been given orders to leave for Lisbon on the morrow and for that we are grateful. Here is as cold as a witch's…" He flushed, "Sorry sir."

Sergeant Sharp nodded, "Let us put our war gear in the tent and then sort out the horses. I take it there is food?"

The Troop Sergeant lowered his voice and said, conspiratorially, "It is our last night and when the patrol was on the road, we found a sheep which was lame. It was a mercy we found it and put it out of its misery! There will be a fine stew this night and you are more than welcome to join us."

"Sergeant Sharp, give the Troop Sergeant half of the sausage, it will enrich it."

"Aye, sir."

I was left alone and I looked at the tents of the troop. Captain Minchin had been an impoverished and bullied lieutenant when I had first met him. While the Battle of Talavera was the undoing of some officers it was the making of him and he was now a confident and capable captain. He was just the sort of officer you wanted here in Spain.

The Corporal brought the Captain back and he was obviously happy to see me. "I thought I might see you in Lisbon, sir, and this is a happy meeting for we return to Lisbon tomorrow."

"I know but you shall not see us there for some time, I fear. I need to pick your brains."

"My brains sir?"

"Yes, Ned, you see Sharp and I are off behind enemy lines and you have been as close to the French as any. Whatever you can tell us will help."

He nodded, "I have a bottle of Spanish brandy, sir, it will take the chill off the night and I can tell you all that I know."

There was a large fire and the troopers were seated around it. There was no rain but they were all wrapped in their cloaks. Sharp had brought a couple of jugs of wine and he was sharing them with the NCO's. Captain Minchin and I were given space and we sat apart as the mutton stew enriched with Portuguese sausage bubbled away. The smell was making me hungry. Captain Minchin poured us both a mug of the powerful local brandy.

"Cheers! Here's to absent friends and the lads who did not make it!"

"Cheers Captain!"

"I am not sure how much use this will be but I shall try. We never went any further east than Merida. There is a regiment of French Light Cavalry there and a company of infantry. They discouraged us from getting too close."

"What was the cavalry?"

"The 10th Chasseur à Cheval."

I could not recall having served with them but the Chasseurs were good horsemen and knew how to use carbines.

"And the infantry?"

He shrugged, "We never got close enough to identify them, sir, but they looked to be a company. The had one four-pounder there."

"And I take it there has been no probing of our lines?"

He suddenly looked up from the mug of brandy, "That's right, sir, I had not thought of that but they were always chasing us off and never even came close to the camp or Badajoz. What do you think it means?"

"I think it means that, for the moment, they are leaderless and concentrating on easier enemies than us. The Spanish will be bearing the brunt of their wrath."

Lieutenant Frayn approached, he had obviously been on piquet duty, "Major Matthews, what a pleasant surprise."

"And it is good to see you, Lieutenant. How is life in the Troop?"

"Couldn't be better, sir, for the troopers are as fine a bunch of men as one could hope to command."

"Good."

I saw the question on his face as he took in my nondescript uniform and mud-spattered boots. He was wondering what we were doing out here. I would let Ned Minchin satisfy his curiosity. For myself, I enjoyed sitting with the sergeants and corporals as they spoke of the trivialities of camp and troop life. I could sit and listen; I could be relaxed but once we left the camp then Sharp and I would be living on our wits and sleeping with an ear and eye open.

Chapter 2

When we left the next morning, I did not bother going to Merida as there would be nothing to be gained from such a visit. I doubted that we would learn very much while there was a great risk that we could be captured. Merida was the front line and the men there would be wary. Instead, I headed north and east towards Talavera. For the French, the town and the area were now safe and secure and it was there we might learn more. The rain had ceased but the wind was still from the north and was bone-chillingly cold. Our route was off the beaten track and we used the smaller roads which would not risk French Cavalry patrols. They were not good roads!

When we stopped to give our horses water and to take food ourselves, I examined the copy of the map I had made. If the French had a regiment of horse at Merida then they could cover a large area. The next outpost would be Trujillo as that lay more than fifty miles from Merida. This was the effective border for it ran almost north to south and there would be some point on the road which the horsemen would use to meet and exchange information. If there were riders with messages they would be handed over. At some point, we would need to get across that road and then we could head to Talavera. Although the Spanish were sympathetic to us, we could not risk staying in Spanish homes for while they would willingly protect us our very presence would put their lives at risk. The French had a draconian policy. They would hang men, women and children for the slightest breach of their security. For their part, the Spanish guerrillas would inflict the most hideous of punishments on any Frenchman they found alone.

Our camps were fireless and cheerless. We used whatever shelter we could whether that was the cover of an overhanging rock or an improvised hovel. Our cloaks often doubled as tents hung between the branches of trees. By the second day, our uniforms no longer looked like uniforms for mud and dirt clung to them giving us both a brown hue. Our hats were the only sign that we were soldiers.

It was on the third day out of Badajoz that we saw the French cavalry. There was a section of Dragoons and they were patrolling the road ahead. It was either a very much depleted troop or a section sent on a specific mission. We were lucky in that the little road we had used to descend from the ridge to the plain below twisted and turned down the steep slope. Scrubby trees clung to the rocks and afforded us some shelter and, along with our mud-stained appearance, made us harder to see. I saw the movement and we halted. Taking out my telescope I looked at the ten Dragoons who were heading on the road towards Merida. They were veterans for they had their muskets across their saddles and they looked to be vigilant. They were more than a mile away but I recognised that they were led by a sergeant. As in the British army, they were the backbone of the army.

Once we had left the camp of the 23rd we spoke French at all times rather than English or Spanish. It would help Sharp and it was a good habit to get into. I did so now, "We will wait here, Sharp, until they have passed."

"Sir."

We had not been seen and if we remained still then we would not be discovered. The Dragoons were seeking enemies closer to them. When they stopped, about half a mile after I had first spied them, I began to wonder if we had been spotted. We were still almost a mile away from them and if they had spotted us and chose to follow us then we would be able to outrun them however, that would alert the French to our presence and also lose us time as we would need to find another way into the heartland of French Spain. They dismounted and I breathed a sigh of relief. They took food from their saddlebags but two of the Dragoons remained mounted. It confirmed that their sergeant knew his business.

The attack, when it came, surprised even me and I had seen the guerrillas operate at close quarters. One moment the French were eating and the next moment fifteen Spaniards had risen, apparently from the ground, and were using their short swords and wicked knives to butcher the unsuspecting Dragoons. The Dragoon sergeant was one of the first to be targeted and I saw him fall. The two vedettes fired their muskets and then spurred their horses to head back towards Trujillo. As the muskets cracked the other horses fled. I saw the flaw in the Spanish attack as they had had no one to grab the horses. Had they done so they might have been able to run down the two fleeing Frenchmen. The two Dragoons would bring the wrath of their regiment down upon the guerrillas. Perhaps that was in the guerrillas' minds for two of the Dragoons were still alive and the guerrillas tortured them while the horses were recovered. The screams of the Frenchmen carried all the way to our lofty vantage point.

I dismounted for we could not move until the road was clear and then we would have to ride as quickly as we could so that we could avoid the French who would come to demand their retribution. "We might as well save our horses, Alan."

He dismounted too. I kept my glass on the road. I saw the Spaniards take everything of value from the Dragoons' bodies. Their boots, belts, guns, swords and ammunition would all be useful. When the horses were recovered, I saw that there were just six of them. Two had evaded capture. When they placed two bodies on the horses and as they wore no uniform, I knew that they had suffered losses. They moved off southwest. It was away from the road and, more importantly, away from us.

"We can mount. Let us not be tardy!"

We moved down the road as quickly as we could. I saw the crows and other carrion gathering near the roadside feast. We crossed the road half a mile from the squawking, squabbling birds but I looked not south but north towards Trujillo. By my estimate, we were eight miles from that town. The two Dragoons would be bringing help and we needed to be across the road and lost in the pine forest I could see on the slopes of the next range of hills. We had barely made the eaves when I heard the sound of thundering hooves. Once more we stopped and turned. This time it was a full squadron of Dragoons. We had barely made the trees and I deduced that the squadron had been closer than Trujillo than either we or the guerrillas had expected. When they reached their comrades, the officer sent half of his men to the west of the road. They must have seen the signs left by the guerrillas and their horses. Leaving fifteen men to bury their fallen comrades the rest took off after the guerrillas.

"I reckon they will find those Spaniards, sir. If they had all been mounted, they might have escaped but those Dragoons know their business."

I knew what Sharp was saying but we could do nothing about it. This was a dirty war, not that any war was clean but at least in a battle such as the one in which we had fought at Talavera, there was some compassion for the wounded. I had watched French and British soldiers sharing the same stream in the middle of the battle of Talavera. The war between the French and the Spanish guerrillas just escalated with atrocity piled upon atrocity.

We reached Talavera four days later. We had not seen a single Frenchman for we had taken the smallest of roads crisscrossing the rocky hills which lay to the south of Talavera. I had no doubt that we were seen by Spaniards but they were not guerrillas and so we remained unmolested. I had taken us to the east of Talavera and we camped on the southern bank in a stand of trees. There were no roads close by and I had not seen a farm for two miles.

"So, sir, what is the plan?"

"We eat, and we rest. As soon as it is dark, we ford the river. I intend to enter Talavera from the east. We have to get into the town and we need to speak to people. If we come from the east then we will arouse less suspicion as they will assume we come from Madrid or Toledo." I had chosen the place we would cross the river carefully. There was an island in the middle of the Tagus which meant we had just thirty paces to cross to reach the island and then thirty more to reach the other side. Of course, it also meant we had to cross the Rio Albreche for that river fed into the north side of the Tagus but that was also just thirty paces wide. I remembered both rivers from the battle when I had ridden across the land for Sir Arthur. "We will dry off and try to clean our uniforms as best we can on the other side of the Albreche. You can wear the French forage cap and we will say that we are being sent to join the Chasseurs at Merida. But if no one questions our presence then we say nothing!"

The crossing was wet but as we were already soaked from the rain it mattered not. The river actually cleared some of the mud from us. By the time we led our weary horses from the Albreche, dawn was a few hours away and we took our horses to the shelter of some trees. We would be able to see the road through the thin foliage. I knew, from my time in Talavera, that the road lay just half a mile north of the river. We needed to arrive in the town at midmorning for any earlier would look suspicious and there would be more people arriving later in the day. We took off our saddles and cleaned up the horses as best we could. That done we cleaned our pistols and prepared them to be fired. We would not prime them yet but that was not a long job. If we had to leave quickly then a brace of pistols could cause much confusion, especially in a confined space. That done we began to clean our uniforms and boots a little. We waited until I saw a pair of wagons heading into Talavera before we saddled our horses and, after ensuring that the road from the east was empty, we headed towards the road.

We had decided to say that we had come from Toledo. As that was just forty miles from Talavera we could have, legitimately, broken our journey just fifteen miles from Talavera. We rode slowly along the road. If we hurried then it would look suspicious. As we neared the town I saw, although there were still many units there, most of the army had left. Where had they gone? Were they, even now, gathering to invade Portugal as Sir Arthur feared?

What I did notice was that the bridge across the Tagus had the gendarmerie at each end and that there were many wagons and troops marching across it. My route had avoided the scrutiny of the bridge. I hoped that two riders approaching from the east would not interest a French officer and so I adopted a bored expression as we passed a couple of sentries at the edge of the town. I could see the marks of the battle were still in evidence. There were the marks made by musket balls and the scorching of exploding howitzer shells. I reined in next to the corporal and private of the 24th line. As I recalled they had been part of General Ruffin's division and had been in square when we had charged them. They had been badly cut up and it explained why they had been relegated to sentry duty. They would be awaiting replacements.

I waved over the corporal, "Which is the best inn in the town?"

"That would be the Cockerel's Crest, sir. It is just off the main square. The ones in the square are all full."

"Thank you, Corporal, you have been most helpful." He nodded and we rode off. The fact that I had spoken to him first would put his mind at ease and so we slipped into the town far more easily than I had expected.

I remembered the inn and he was right about it being a good one although it catered more for the rank and file than officers. As we neared the centre, I saw that the French were moving the army south and not west. There was a Spanish army in the south and a British presence too at Cadiz and Gibraltar. Was our job over already? I had done this too many times to be complacent and I would do the job I had been sent to do and leave speculation for the General when I gave him my report. We rode through the busy town square and headed for the tavern. The Corporal had been correct and there were rooms available. That they were an exorbitant price was also to be expected. The Spanish had no love for their French masters and there was little could be done about it. Had this been the British army then I would have reported to the general in command but it seemed to me that there was much confusion in the town and I would take advantage of it.

"Sergeant, take our bags to the room and I will go for a drink to get the road from my throat." The words were spoken for the benefit of the tavern owner. Sharp would stay in the room until I returned. It was better not to put his French to the test too much.

"Sir!"

I headed for the square. It was approaching lunchtime and I knew that officers who were not on duty enjoyed a long lunch. It would not seem out of place if I was there ostensibly eating and drinking but, in reality, listening. I had been one of Bonaparte's bodyguards for a while and knew how senior officers operated. I intended to use that knowledge to my advantage.

I selected an inn which although not full was already filling with officers. Despite the apparent egalitarianism of the French army, there would be some inns reserved for officers and I chose the most expensive-looking of the ones I saw. I asked for and was given a table for one. It was between two tables of four one of which was already occupied. The four officers at the occupied table were infantry officers and the most senior was a Captain. I had a Colonel's insignia sewn on to my uniform and when I handed over my cloak the four officers stood to attention, I smiled, "Sit, gentlemen. This is not the parade ground."

The Lines of Torres Vedras

I received smiles and I assiduously avoided them as the waiter brought me a menu. I saw that it had been badly translated! "Bring me a jug of your best red wine."

"Yes, sir!"

While studying the menu I listened to the officers who were infantrymen, speaking. It soon became clear that the whole army was moving south to try to take Cadiz from the Spanish and British. I could have left there and then for that was all the news that Sir Arthur needed. There would be no winter attack on Portugal! However, there was nothing to be gained from leaving. I ordered a beef stew although I doubted that the meat would be beef. In all likelihood, it would be salted horse for many animals were killed in the battle. The inn began to fill up and the four neighbouring officers were forced to raise their voices so that they could hear each other. It was from them that I learned that Marshal Jourdan had been recalled to Paris. He was obviously being blamed for the defeat at Talavera. I also learned that Marshal Soult was now the Military Commander of Spain. Napoleon's brother, King Joseph, had also disgraced himself and Napoleon had punished him by taking away the command of the army. Soult was not a bad leader but if he was in charge of the forces in Spain then he would not personally lead the army in Portugal. Who had replaced Jourdan?

A Dragoon major and two Light Cavalry colonels walked in and were directed to the table next to me. We nodded to each other and I saw the hint of a frown on the Colonel of the 11th Hussars. My wine arrived and that gave me the opportunity to taste it and listen in. Sadly, they were just talking about the menu and how poor it was.

My food arrived at the same time as their wine and the Dragoon leaned over and said, as I took my first mouthful, "What is it like?"

I shrugged, "What can you expect in this land? It is passable but I am guessing that it is horse and not the beef it states on the menu."

He nodded, "I fear you are right and we are spoiled for we have come from Toulouse and there the food is much better than here." He smiled, "I am interrupting your lunch, my apologies."

I smiled and ate. The three officers seemed more at ease now that they had spoken to me and I learned more from them than the more junior officers. I discovered that there was to be a new marshal who was to take over the Army of Portugal but that he would not be appointed for a few months. The three men did not come out with it in that way but they went through and discussed the marshals and generals who were already in Spain, Ney, Junot and Reynier were all dismissed as commanders of the army because of their involvement in the Talavera defeat. That was interesting for it bought Sir Arthur even more time. I had just lit my cigar when I learned the most worrying fact; Napoleon Bonaparte was now master of Northern Europe. He had won the battle of Wagram and having defeated everyone, his vanquished foes had sued for peace. It meant he had huge reserves of reinforcements he could send to the Peninsula. The four men were cavalrymen and their greatest complaint was the lack of cavalry in the Peninsula. They had lost so many dragoons that they were cobbling together squadrons from different regiments to make a scratch regiment. Perhaps that was what the 23rd had seen near to Merida. There were no heavy cavalry units and that was important news for Sir Arthur although worryingly they spoke of Imperial cavalry being sent south. That sounded like a rumour but a worrying one. We, too, had fewer horsemen but that was made up for by the superior quality of our infantry. As I finished the bread and the cheese and quaffed the last of the wine, I reflected that Sir Arthur was doing the right thing. If we could draw the French onto prepared positions then our superior soldiers would prevail.

I waved the waiter over for the bill and overpaid with the French coins General Wellesley had given to me. As I stood the Colonel of the 11th Hussars said, "Excuse me, Colonel, but don't I know you?"

I smiled and shook my head, "I have never had the honour of serving alongside the 11th, Colonel."

He was like a dog with a bone, "I know you, not as a colonel but it is your face and voice I remember. Were you ever in Egypt?"

I stood and shook my head, "I am afraid not, Colonel, as I never served in that campaign. I must go, Colonel, as I have bags to pack. Good luck with your next posting."

I strolled out of the tavern when I wanted to run. I did not recognise the Colonel but I had been in Egypt with Napoleon and I had been part of his Consular Guards. I thought that I had changed but he had seen and heard something which triggered a memory. We would head north as soon as possible for I had learned all that I could. The General had asked me to look at the northern fortresses too and I would do so but first I had to get out of Talavera before the Colonel remembered where he had seen me.

I did not think I was being watched but, just to make certain, I walked in the opposite direction to my inn and headed, instead, to the bridge. I took out another cigar and smoked it while leaning against a wall and watching a regiment of infantry tramp across it; they were heading south for Andalusia. This was the army which we had beaten but it, in turn, had beaten the Spanish. As they were marching to defeat the last of the Spanish generals they were in a confident mood. I moved when I heard a regiment of Dragoons heading towards me. The Colonel of Hussars had had a memory awoken and horsemen would remember me. Perhaps some of these had been in General Ruffin's division when I had helped to rescue the 23rd Light Dragoons. I had pushed my luck enough.

I heard many accents and foreign languages. The Confederation of the Rhine, as well as soldiers from the former Spanish Netherlands, were in Talavera. Bonaparte's army was, indeed, polyglot! I used side streets and back alleys to reach the inn. Sharp was in the room and he saw, on my face, my concern. He locked the door and I told him what had happened and what I had learned. This was our normal practice. If anything happened to one of us then the other could take the news back to our lines.

"We could go now, sir."

"French, Sharp!"

"Sorry, sir."

"The horses need the rest and I do not want to walk into that Colonel. If he saw us leaving then he would be even more suspicious. We will leave the same way we came, early tomorrow morning, and then head north." My plan was simple. If we were spotted leaving then I wanted any pursuers to think we were heading for Madrid. I knew the hills north of Talavera quite well and there were many places where we could evade pursuers. The hard part would be getting away unseen.

"Sharp, go and have some food and then buy some for us to eat here in the room. I will stay here and out of sight."

"Sir, are you happy for me to go out there? What if someone sees through my disguise?"

"There are lots of foreign soldiers and lots of accents. There are some places to buy food close by and you were not in Egypt; the Colonel might remember me but not you."

He went but he went reluctantly. He pulled his cloak up over his forage cap and left. I locked the door again. While he was gone, I wrote down what I had learned and I added to my map. I was beginning to become worried about Sharp and when he gave our coded knock, I was relieved. He rushed in with a piece of cheese and some bread. He shook his head. "The Gendarmerie are looking for someone, sir. I think it might be you. I heard one of them say they were looking for an officer. That is why they let me slip by although I came back here by a circuitous route in case I was followed."

"If they come here, we are done for." I cursed myself as I had not scouted out the escape routes before we booked in. "I will go down and pay. The last thing we need is for a disgruntled innkeeper to set the dogs on us!"

I took off my jacket before I went down in just my shirt and overalls. It just changed my appearance a little and removed the evidence that I was an officer. The inn was full and I had to wait to get the innkeeper's attention. I felt exposed and expected to be caught at any moment.

He turned to me when he had finished serving his customers, "Yes sir?"

"Something unexpected has come up and we will need to leave in the morning. I would like to pay my bill." Just then the door was thrown open and two Gendarmerie troopers stood in the doorway.

The innkeeper saw my face and said, "If you would like to come to my office, sir, I will make it up for you."

We went through a curtain into a room with a desk and a small metal box. I heard one of the French soldiers shout, "Where is the owner?"

For a moment I thought that I had been brought into the room to trap me and my hand went to my boot for the stiletto. The innkeeper shook his head and shouted, in Spanish, "What is going on?" He hurried out leaving me alone in his inner sanctum.

I listened to the conversation. The man could speak French for he had spoken to me but he spoke in Spanish and the French trooper had to answer him in the same language. It was a clever move.

"Have you any officers staying here?"

"I have a sergeant of the hussars."

"Which is his room?"

"I will send Maria for him. Maria, fetch the sergeant from room two."

"Yes, Miguel."

"What is this all about?"

"There may be a spy masquerading as a French officer. We are checking all of the inns in Talavera. If he is here, he will not escape us."

I heard Sharp's boots as he came down the stairs. "What is going on? Can a man not sleep, innkeeper?"

The Trooper said, "What is your rank and your regiment?"

"Sergeant Albert of the 3rd Dutch Hussars."

"Why are you here and not with your regiment? They left for the south two days' ago."

Sharp was quick thinking. "The Colonel asked me to wait here in case a letter came from his wife. She is due to have a child. I was awarded a medal in the battle and this is a little reward. Were you in the battle?" He adopted a slightly aggressive tone of voice.

It was just the right tone and the Gendarmerie trooper blustered, "No need for that, friend. I was just asking and I can see that you aren't an officer. You do not fit the description. Come on Jean, let us try elsewhere. Landlord, if you see an officer behaving suspiciously then let us know!"

"Of course."

I heard the door slam shut and then the curtain opened. I said, in Spanish, "Thank you."

He smiled, "I remembered you from when the English were here. You passed my inn with your General. I recognised you straight away. Will your General return?"

"Perhaps but it will take some time as he has an army to build. I am in your debt."

"And when you have freed us from French tyranny then the debt is paid. I would suggest you stay indoors until morning. How will you manage to evade them?"

I shrugged, "At the moment I have not got any idea but I will come up with something."

He handed me a jug of wine, "This may help you to think!"

I headed up the stairs with Sharp and it was as I poured out the wine that the idea came to me. I knew how we could escape if not unseen then with a head start, at least. Sharp helped me to refine my plan and we used Miguel to finalise the details. We left in the middle of the night. There was a curfew, as one might expect but that was intended, largely, for the Spaniards. Soldiers could move around. The streets were empty for the French camps were along the river. We walked our horses to the eastern end of the town. I gambled that it would be the same regiment who had been on duty when we arrived. If we had not needed horses then it would have been simplicity itself to escape but horses could be heard and so we used my plan. We tied the horses to the trail of a gun damaged in the battle. The barrel had been taken but the broken trail had been abandoned. I took off my cloak and hat. My two pistols were in my belt and ready to cock and I headed through the back alley to come around the other side of the two sentries and their brazier. The brazier would destroy their night vision but Sergeant Sharp would be the main distraction. I heard him singing an obscene French song in a drunken voice as he staggered along the main road holding a jug in his right hand. As I hurried along, I took out the two pistols and heard the French sentries demand that Sharp stop.

"Now don't be like that, my friends. I have a jug of wine to finish and my messmates have gone to bed. I need some company!"

"Get back to your bed, Dutchman! You will be whipped for this."

The fact that they thought he was a Dutchman told me that he was close enough for them to see his uniform.

"Only if you tell anyone and I think you will enjoy this one for it is like the wine from the Rhone."

I heard a voice say, "Let's just have a taste, eh Brigadier, and then we can send him on his way. It will keep the chill from our bones!" He used the word Brigadier and that meant it was a corporal who was in charge of the roadblock. The sergeant was probably sound asleep.

I had now managed to get to their side and I slipped around behind them. Pressing a gun in the centre of each of their backs I said, "I do not wish to harm you so lay your guns on the ground and then lie down with your hands behind you."

The Brigadier looked around and found himself staring down the barrel of a French pistol. He looked fearfully at me as he said, "Do as he says, Henri! This is the spy they were seeking!"

Sharp laid down the jug and took the cords we had prepared. Within a short time, he had tied their hands to their feet. He hurried off for the horses and I poured some wine down their throats. When they were discovered it might be assumed that they had been drinking. I took out my stiletto and tapped it on the buttons of the soldier's tunic. "Now, my friends, you will wait until you cannot hear our horses' hooves and then you can shout for help. Do so while we can hear you and you will die. Do you understand?"

They nodded and I poured more wine down their throats.

"You can say that we knocked you about and rendered you unconscious."

Sharp brought the horses and we mounted. I could not rely on them obeying me and I had no intention of killing them. I counted on the fact that when they shouted it would be men on foot who came. By the time horses had been saddled and they came after us we would be more than a mile away hiding in the dark. We would not stay on the road.

Chapter 3

The shouts followed by the trumpets were so far in the distance that I knew the two soldiers had obeyed me. I wondered why. Perhaps I was more chilling to others than I thought. We were far enough down the road for us to risk leaving the road and head north. I had slowed to a walk and was looking for somewhere to leave it and I found it in the form of a wrecked house. It looked to have been shelled in the build-up to the battle of Talavera and we picked our way through the rubble. Once we had passed the burned-out farm, I found a track which led up into the hills, towards the Cerro de Cascajal to the northwest. I knew that the area was riddled with arroyo and dried up river beds. It was the perfect place to become lost. I did not want the sound of galloping horses' hooves to carry through the night and so we walked and picked our way along the trail. It also minimised the risk of an accident as we could ill afford to lose a horse so far from safety. We were about a mile from the burned-out farm when I heard the sound of hooves on the road. If they slowed or came closer to us then I would consider riding faster but they carried on east and faded.

I knew that we were about an hour from the first hint of dawn and the sun would appear in the east. By then we needed to be above Talavera close to the scene of the fatal cavalry charge led by Colonel Hawker. Many brave men had died that day and many others, like Captain Wilberforce, who should never have been officers. Such was life.

By the time the sun came up we were hidden from the south by a ridge and we rested in the Arroyo de la Cabra. This was not a dry river bed; at this time of year, even the dry ones had water in them from the rain. We let our horses drink and I studied the map. I still thought that the French would come through Badajoz as their army was in the south but we had been asked to check on the beleaguered garrison of Cuidad Rodrigo. There were two routes; one a loop to the north and another, a loop to the south. Between them lay the Sierra de Gredos. I liked to involve Sergeant Sharp, not least because he was a clever soldier and often saw the flaws in my plans which were not obvious to me.

"We will take the northern route as it takes us further from Talavera and the Colonel who recognised me."

"Sounds like a good plan to me, sir. Did you not recognise him from Egypt, Major?"

I shook my head, "He might have been the same age as me. He was not one of the Consular Guides, I know that for a fact but as I was always seen with Bonaparte then he might have been in one of the other regiments and if he saw me with the Emperor then he would remember me. General Junot I knew, as he was General Bonaparte's ADC. If he had walked in then my goose would well and truly have been cooked! I am afraid, Alan, that my past may well come back to haunt me. One of these days I will meet someone who recognises me immediately!"

I had thought to disguise myself by growing facial hair but that would have done little as I had had the moustache and pigtails of a hussar when I had served in the French army. I thought that age had changed me but there was obviously something about me which had been identified. Then I realised what it was. Although I had been brought up as the son of a lord's concubine, because I was his son, the Marquis had insisted on me being taught to speak French properly as became the offspring of a lord. My French was always grammatically correct and I pronounced my words correctly. Jean and the others who had been in my first regiment had laughed at me and called me, lord. That must have been it. There was a fine balance between playing a French officer and a French officer who would be remembered. My experience in Talavera was a lesson. The Colonel and the Corporal had both been wary of me but for different reasons. If I was to continue to do this then I needed to be more careful.

There would be few places for us to find shelter and the weather grew colder as we climbed the trails which crisscrossed the Sierra. Even our thick uniforms and heavy cloaks could not keep the cold from seeping into our bones. We were forced to light a fire. We took every precaution. We used dead ground and we did not use damp wood. We used our saddles and baggage to shield the fire but I knew that if anyone was close then they would smell the smoke and see the fire. The first couple of nights were uneventful.

After we had crested the ridge we spied the road to Cuidad Rodrigo below us. The sun was dipping in the west and I knew this would be our last camp in the hills. By my estimate, we were thirty miles from the fortress and if we rose early, we could do it in one day. As we had descended from the heights of the sierra, we had glimpsed the road from time to time and we had seen little evidence of the green of French horsemen. Of course, we had only seen the road intermittently and the French could be patrolling it but the fact that we had not seen any thus far heartened me and made me think that they did not have large numbers there and that meant there was no imminent attack on the fortress.

"We will make one last camp here and then ride hard for the fortress. There, we may well be given a bed and hot food."

"Aye, sir, I have forgotten what it is like to be warm."

Perhaps we had grown complacent or, more likely, we were just exhausted but whatever the reason we were surprised in the night. I woke and I knew not why. Even as I sniffed the air and smelled garlic my hand was sliding down to the pistol I kept close by.

The Spanish knife was almost touching my throat when a voice hissed in my ear, "One move and you die!"

They were guerrillas and I wondered why we were not dead already. Then I heard a laugh and a familiar voice said, "You can let him up Antonio, it is milord! You have heard me talk of him."

The pressure from the knife disappeared and I stood. In the glow of the embers from our fire, I saw Juan of La Calzada de Béjar. He had saved my life before and we had used him as a messenger and as a spy before the battle of Talavera. I held out my arm, "Juan, it is good to see you."

"Antonio spotted you a couple of days ago as you began your journey. He sent for me for he wondered why French Dragoons were chasing a French officer. I thought, from his description, that it might be you and your Sergeant Sharp. Apologies for the rude awakening. What brings you here?"

His men had begun to stir the embers of the fire and I saw that they had brought food and were preparing to cook some ham. That, alone, told me that we were safe.

"Sir Arthur has sent me to find out the French dispositions."

He shook his head angrily as he spoke of the Spanish generals who were so despised by the guerrillas, "They are chasing those fools of generals who cannot do as your Sir Arthur does and defeat the French. Antonio here was at the battle of Arzobispo where that fat fool Cuesta ran! Antonio and many of his comrades joined us and now we have an army here which keeps the French fearful."

I nodded and smelled appreciatively the ham which had begun to fry, "That is good news to take back to Portugal."

"Your general does not bring an army here to chase the French away?"

I would not lie to this man for he was clever and would see through the falsehood. I had learned that the truth was always the best route to take. I shook my head, "He does not have the troops yet. England is far away and there will be reinforcements but not for six months at least. I am afraid we can do little to alleviate the French yoke."

"You are honest and we can trust you. The weapons you gave us last time have been put to good use. Miguel particularly likes the Baker rifle you gave to me and he said if we meet again, he would ask for one for himself."

"And I will try to get him one. Where is he?"

"He now leads his own band and they are to the south, closer to Badajoz. He follows the troops as they head south to Cadiz. There will be far fewer when they reach there."

His men brought us the ham. They had some stale bread and we ate breakfast in silence. We were all soldiers and food was something to be taken seriously.

When I had finished, I said, "Is the road to Cuidad clear?"

"It should be but as I said, Antonio did not slit your throat on the first night because he wondered why you were being hunted. The French horsemen who sought you are still out there, somewhere."

I saw Antonio grin and then shrug, "I am sorry, milord, it would have been a shame but the more French officers we kill the sooner this war will be over!"

"They are still hunting us?"

"They found where you left the road. The two men who climbed the trail were killed by Antonio's men and now they have a squadron of Chasseurs. They know the direction you have taken but if you ride hard then you should be at the fortress by dark."

The sun began to peer over the Sierra de Gredos. I stood and held out my hand, "You are ever a friend, Juan. The General and I will be at Torres Vedras in Portugal if you need to get a message to us."

He shook his head, "I fight for Spain and not Portugal but you, I think, will be here again. Antonio now knows you but if you continue to dress as a Frenchman then you can expect to be in danger."

"Thank you for the advice."

Sharp and I saddled our horses and, in the time it took us to do so, the dozen or so guerrillas had disappeared. Sharp shook his head, "Like ghosts they are, sir. How did they get here?"

"I am guessing they have horses. Remember those horses that were captured before we reached Talavera? I think that there will be more like that. They are an army, Sharp, but a better-organised one than the real Spanish army. We had better get to the road as quickly as we can. I do not like that we are being hunted."

As soon as we reached the road, I saw evidence of traffic. There were piles of horse dung littering it. None was fresh but Juan was right. They were hunting us. Our horses had endured a hard time and they needed a period of rest. I had hoped to have two days, at least, in Talavera, to help them to recover. They had had less than a day. Donna was in the best condition of the three but even she needed a rest. So, when I spied the six French Hussars on the road ahead, my heart sank.

"That is a problem, eh sir?"

The Lines of Torres Vedras

I looked around and thought of taking the road back up into the hills but, as I did so I saw another group of horsemen galloping along the road from the east. We were trapped, "Let us try and bluff our way out. Have your pistols ready."

Our four pistols were always loaded and as we rode slowly towards the six Hussars who were galloping down the road to us, I primed my pistols. Donna would walk with my reins wrapped around my saddle and it was the work of moments to have four weapons ready to use. Sharp had the packhorse and he had to do it one-handed. He took longer. He had just finished when the French Sergeant reined in and pointed a pistol at me.

"My Colonel would like a word with you, Englishman!"

"Englishman? Do I look like an Englishman? Sound like one? I was born in Breteuil!"

He laughed, and nodded to his Brigadier, "The Colonel said he was a tricky one. I have never heard a Roast Beef who could speak French well but this one is good. I will enjoy it when you are shot!" I heard the hooves behind us and knew that I had left it too long to make an escape before the rest arrived. Cuidad was just a heartbeat away but it might as well have been on the other side of the world. I would have to do something dramatic when they were least expecting it. I knew that when I made my move Alan would follow for we had an understanding.

I heard the Colonel's voice from behind me. "It took me some time Englishman but I finally remembered that you were the traitor who murdered Colonel Hougon. You will be taken to Paris for there are men there who wish to question you and I shall take you there! Who knows there may be a reward from the Emperor!"

I had noticed that, now that we were surrounded the French had relaxed. Their pistols were pointed down at the ground and that was always a mistake. Even as I began to turn, I was drawing my two pistols.

"There has been some mistake!" I fired my pistols at point-blank range. One threw the Colonel from his saddle with a hole in his chest and the other hit a trooper in the shoulder. I heard a double bang and knew that Alan had fired. I dug my heels into Donna's flanks as I holstered my pistols and then drew a pistol from my saddle holster. I fired at the Brigadier who was raising his own pistol. My ball hit him in the chest. Five pistols fired in close proximity make an immediate fog and Sharp and I were through the shocked troopers and heading down the road before they knew it and had time to react. Sharp had let go of our pack horse and he fired behind him with his saddle pistol. The French horsemen who had pistols fired them but they were firing through the smoke at two men who were laid across their horses' necks and their balls missed. We both had one pistol still loaded but there was little point in wasting it. I could only guess how many Hussars had been neutralised but I had to hope that it was five, at least. Perhaps with the Colonel and Sergeant killed or wounded they might lose heart. Then I heard the crack of a pistol and felt the passage of an aimed ball close by me.

It was now a race but their horses were in better condition than ours and I knew that they would catch us. I glanced under my arm and saw that there were eight Hussars spread along the road behind us. Whoever had fired his pistol had wasted his ball for they were more than forty paces behind us. A pistol had to be much closer to stand a chance. Suddenly I heard the distinctive crack of a Baker rifle. There were no Rifle companies in Spain. I turned and saw a French trooper falling from his horse and the Hussars looked around. It had to be Juan and the guerrillas. Sharp had turned too.

I shouted, "Turn and draw your sword! Let us help the guerrillas!" It was neither bravado nor was it heroics. The French were catching us and if we had allies then we could turn the tables on them.

I drew my heavy cavalry sword. It was not curved and it was longer than the ones carried by the Hussars. We had taken them by surprise. They had pistols drawn and most had already been fired. When Sharp and I had fired our horses had been still. These Hussars were galloping. The pistol balls zipped around us but none hit and I brought my sword to sweep into the chest of one Trooper as the Baker fired again. This time I saw the puff of smoke from behind a farmhouse wall two hundred paces from the road. One of the Hussars clutched his leg. Juan had become skilled. I saw eight of the guerrillas on their horses racing from the farmhouse. The Hussars knew that they were beaten but two of them kept fighting while the rest turned their horses and fled.

Sergeant Sharp had become far more skilled as a swordsman; it had been forced upon him by our adventures but he was fighting a skilled Hussar. The Hussar I fought was also skilful but I had a sword which was so long and heavy that when he tried to block my strike my blade shattered his sword and tore into his shoulder. He had the presence of mind to throw the broken hilt at me as he turned his horse to gallop away. The Baker sounded again and the Hussar fighting Sharp looked up as the ball hit his back. He threw his arms in the air and fell from his saddle. The guerrillas chased after the fleeing Hussars.

Antonio reined in, "Well, milord, you bear a charmed life! It is fortunate that Juan decided to follow you. If you get Miguel a rifle then I beg you to consider one for me for it is a truly magical weapon."

"I will try."

By the time Juan joined us his men had returned. They had a fruitful haul with seven horses, muskets, swords, boots and French coins. They were pleased for they had aided us and become stronger in the process. The French Army was becoming the guerrillas' quartermaster. After our packhorse was recovered, he escorted us until we could see the mighty fortress of Cuidad Rodrigo.

"Farewell, my friend."

"Farewell, Juan, and I am, once more in your debt!"

We parted and we walked our horses towards the fortress and safety. Cuidad Rodrigo rose from the plain and I could see why it was important and also why Sir Arthur would not risk a battle close to it. It would suit the French for they could use their larger numbers of cavalry on this plain. It was getting on to dark by the time we reached the fortress and the Spanish there were suspicious of us. I told them who we were but we were not admitted until a British liaison officer, Captain Fletcher, came to vouch for us. I did not know the officer but he recognised me.

"You look like you have a rum tale to tell, sir. I dare say that Lieutenant General de Herrasti will wish to speak with you but I expect you would like to clean up first."

"Yes, Captain. If you could have someone show my Sergeant to the stables. Our horses are worn out."

He looked surprised, "Of course sir."

I smiled, "Captain, I have learned that caring for your horse is as important to a soldier as keeping his weapons sharp."

"Sir."

I saw that Captain Fletcher was a Grenadier Guard. As they were deployed in Lisbon then he had to have asked to be seconded. The Captain craved action and that was obvious as he questioned me on the way to my quarters. He led me to a barrack room which was obviously for officers. I dropped my bag on a spare bed and dropped my cloak there too. The Captain waved over a servant, "This fellow will see to your needs. Half an hour eh, sir?" He waved over the Spaniard and pointed to me. The Captain could not speak Spanish.

After he had gone, I said, in Spanish, "What is your name?"

The old man smiled at my use of his language, "Carlos, sir."

I took out a couple of coins. "If you would take the worst of the dirt from the uniform and clean the boots then I would be grateful." I handed him the coins and his look told me that this was not a common occurrence.

"Of course, sir. There is water over there. I can heat it up for you if you wish?"

"As I only have half an hour, I shall have to forego that pleasure but thank you for your consideration." Having been brought up amongst servants I knew how to speak to them. I took off my boots and uniform. I knew that I stank of horses and sweat, not to mention blood, but there was little I could do about that. A bath and a clean uniform would have to wait until Lisbon or Torres Vedras.

I looked a little more respectable when the Captain came for me. He said, "The General's English is not the best, sir, you will have to make allowances for him."

The Captain's attitude was not unusual. He could probably speak a little French but that would be as far as his linguistic skills went. "Don't worry, Captain, I can speak a little Spanish. Tell me, Captain, is Sergeant Sharp accommodated?"

"I believe so, I had my fellow take him to the non-commissioned mess."

I would seek him out later and ensure that he was comfortable.

The Lieutenant-General was a good officer and a fine general. I had met General Cuesta and did not rate him at all but the commander of the 5500 men in the garrison was a different man and it was obvious to me that he would fight the French until the last ball had been used. 5500 men sounded a lot but the truth was it was a renaissance castle and the ordnance, 100 guns, was not the most modern. I think General Herrasti knew that. I met him in his office with his senior officers.

He began to speak in English and I could tell that he was struggling to find the right words. "I can speak Spanish, sir, if that is easier for you?"

He beamed and his attitude changed in a heartbeat, "Thank God for that! An Englishman who speaks our language. I understand you have been behind enemy lines." He was suddenly aware that I was standing and he said, "Sit, Major. Give the officer some wine and we can hear his tale."

The wine was good and most welcome but food would have been better. I had eaten nothing since the ham cooked in the early hours of the morning! I told him all that I had learned and finished with our encounter with the Hussars. I did not tell him of my connection with the Colonel and Bonaparte.

When I had finished, he lit a cigar and gave me a shrewd look, "A most interesting and entertaining tale but you have not told me all." He held up his hand, "I understand for you are a spy and a spy must have secrets. That the French are heading south to Cadiz makes me feel a little more secure here but the fact that Bonaparte has dealt with his enemies in the north fills me with dread. When last he came, he drove your army to the sea!"

He was right and I would not try to argue with him. It had been a disaster for I had been there but Sir John had managed to save most of the army and in that, I saw victory.

"And now you will return to Sir Arthur?"

"Yes, sir. He will be eager for my news."

"Then when you see him, I beg you to ask him to remember us. I know that we guard the back door to Portugal but I also know that we are somewhat isolated here. You look to be an officer who has experience." I saw the disparaging look he gave to his British liaison officer. "And so I know that you understand that our garrison and our guns cannot hold out for long against the monster that is the French army. Their artillery is the best in Europe."

"I will plead your case, sir, but you must know that the General has less than 35000 British, Portuguese and German troops at his disposal. There will be reinforcements but we have many men still in the colonies and the West Indies. If Sir Arthur were to be defeated then the whole of Spain and Portugal would be lost."

He smiled, "I know that better than any but he has yet to be defeated by a French Marshal and I have hope. Whatever he does I shall do my duty and if the French do take this fortress then it will be at a greater cost to them than to us!"

He was a brave man and I did not envy him.

Sharp and I stayed two days in the fortress before I deemed that our horses were fit to travel and we rode the twenty miles to the Portuguese fortress of Almeida. If Cuidad Rodrigo was important then Almeida was vital for this was the last obstacle before Portugal. I noticed that there was a place which could be defended should Cuidad fall. The road rose and passed through a small village, Fuentes de Oñoro and then headed towards the narrow river, the Côa. Sir Arthur could slow an enemy down. Almeida was Portuguese and looked strong enough. Although Portuguese it had a British Commander, Brigadier General William Cox. Like many British officers who served in the Portuguese army, he had been given a much higher rank. He was actually a colonel. I told him what I had told the Lieutenant General and like Herrasti General Cox was not optimistic. I was asked to take back the same message that Almeida should not be abandoned.

I was actually more confident about Almeida for the border and Portuguese armies were less than twenty-five miles away and Almeida could be supported. We stayed for two days again but this time it was not out of choice. A storm of Biblical proportions hit the mountains and the roads were impassable for a day and a night. Even when we did leave it was still a treacherous journey. The bridge over the Côa was incredibly narrow and I saw a funnel which could hold up the French. We had two hundred and fifty miles to travel through a Portuguese winter. We were lucky that we were able to find inns along the way and, while we rode, I used my eyes for who knew when we would be fighting here again. When we reached Torres Vedras, Sir Arthur was not there. He was in Lisbon. I did not blame him for it was now December and the city would be both warmed and more enjoyable than the bleak mountains thirty odd miles north of Portugal's capital.

We were lucky for Sir George Murray, Sir Arthur's Quartermaster General, was in Torres Vedras and he arranged for us to share a house with some other British officers of the Engineers. Work was still going on but it was now in the hands of Portuguese labourers and soldiers supervised by British officers. I liked Sir George as did Sir Arthur. He was a bluff Scotsman and while he was Quartermaster, we rarely went short.

When he saw me, he tut-tutted, "Major Matthews you look like a scarecrow! You are almost as bad as Sir Thomas Picton and his bare and ragged staff. There is a tailor here in the town. I will arrange for him to make you a decent uniform and suit of clothes." He gave me a shrewd look, "If you are to carry on gallivanting behind enemy lines then perhaps civilian dress might be the order of the day, eh?"

I laughed with him for he was right. As Sir Arthur would be spending Christmas in Lisbon, I wrote a report for him. We spent a quiet Christmas in the new defences and I felt my spirits restored. We were also accorded a tour of the defences by Sir Richard Fletcher who was proud of them and quite rightly so. When I saw them, they were unfinished but their purpose was clear. Between Villa Franca in the east and the estuary of the Zizandre in the west, there were a series of redoubts, small forts and strong points. There were more than seventy of them and they guarded every road and pass which led from Spain to Lisbon. Supported in the rear by the British and Portuguese armies they would stop the French for the simple reason that they were self-supporting. There were so many of them that if an enemy attacked one there would be four or five others which would attack the attackers. I had never seen anything like it.

However, it was not the war nor the French which made problems for me. As Sergeant Sharp had once said to me, "The French and the enemies of Britain are not a problem for you, sir, but a whiff of perfume and a pretty face can prove fatal!"

The Lines of Torres Vedras

When Sir Arthur returned to Torres Vedras in January, he brought with him some politicians who had been complaining about the expense of the war. One of them, Sir Godfrey Smithson, brought his daughter, a widow who had lost her husband at Roliça. Emily Smithson was a beauty and when she arrived in Torres Vedras, my life was thrown into disarray.

Chapter 4

I discovered from Lieutenant Mountshaft that there were many Members of Parliament who believed that we had lost the battle of Talavera and that the war in Spain and Portugal was an unnecessary expense. William Cobbett, the famous rabble-rouser, had suggested that we would be as well pulling out of Spain as the Spanish armies were patently incompetent. The result was that Parliament had sent a delegation of members to come to Portugal and to see for themselves. It explained the lengthy absence of his lordship as he could not afford for parliament to withdraw the subsidy for the Portuguese army. There were four Members of Parliament in the delegation but only Sir Godfrey had brought his daughter for she wished to see where her husband, who had served with Sir Arthur in 1808, had died. I did not meet her until the second day when Lieutenant Mountshaft came for me, "His lordship needs a word, Major."

I knew Sir Arthur well enough to know that he would not be happy about having to pander to four MPs and I was right. "We do not need this, Matthews! What a waste of all our time. We should be addressing the issue of an impending invasion by the French and I should be focussing all of my energies into the defences I am building!" In a rare fit of pique, he banged the desk and then rearranged the papers which had moved. It was an unusual action from the general who normally controlled his emotions. He smiled, "By the by that was an excellent report you wrote for me and confirms much that I already knew. As it happens, I know that the marshal who will lead the army of Portugal will be Masséna. Do you know him?"

The General had to be aware of my background as he had been briefed by Colonel Selkirk many times. "He is a capable general, sir. Not as headstrong as Ney and a better mind than Junot."

"And if they come, they will come through Cuidad Rodrigo. We need these defences finished before the summer! Bonaparte wants results and the sacking of Jourdan is a warning for the rest of them!"

I nodded for I knew he had not brought me here to listen to him rant. He nodded as though he was clearing his mind. "Tomorrow I will take these chaps and their lady to inspect the defences which I hope will impress them and show that the money which parliament has grudgingly provided, will be well spent. I hope to be rid of them by the end of the week. You are a passably good-looking chap and, as I recall, that Mrs Turner or whatever her name was found you attractive. I would use Mountshaft but he looks as though he has barely started shaving!"

I was confused, "Use me for what, sir?"

"Why to keep this Mrs de Lacey amused and to keep her safe." He said it as though it was the most obvious thing in the world.

"But sir…"

"No, buts, Matthews. I can't be pestered by women. Keep her amused and her pater will be a happy man and that will be a quarter of the delegation on my side. Two of them are fond of port and Sir George has arranged for us to visit a bodega. Once they are happy, they will clear off back to England and let us get on with winning this war. There is no discussion here, that is an order!"

"Yes, sir."

He nodded and waved a hand at my new uniform, "I am glad to see that you have smartened yourself up."

"Can she ride, sir?"

"What?"

"The lady, can she ride, and if so can she ride like a man? If she can't ride then we will need a carriage and if she only rides side-saddle then we will have to procure one."

"Damned good question! You know I hadn't even thought of that. Good fellow. I will get Mountshaft to find out. He must be good for something!"

With that, I was dismissed. I went back to find Sharp and we headed for the stables. We had a couple of horses and the spares would be suitable for a civilian if she could ride. I told him what we had to do and he took it better than I had. "Easier duty than going behind enemy lines, sir. Just you remember Mrs Turner though, sir! I shall keep a close eye on you this time!"

The good news was that Mrs de Lacey could ride and would not need a side-saddle however, there was also bad news. I discovered that her husband had not died at Roliça. We had had so few losses in that battle that I would have remembered an officer being killed. I did not know all of the officers at the battle but de Lacey stirred a memory. It was Sharp who recalled the man. We were finding a soft saddle in the tack room of the stables where our horses were housed when he suddenly stopped and stared at me, "Sir, I remember now Lieutenant de Lacey, he was in the 9th, the East Norfolk Regiment, he died not in the battle but the night before. You must recall the incident, sir, he was drunk and on piquet duty. A sheep wandered close and when he pulled out his pistol to shoot it, thinking it to be a Frenchman, he caught it in his belt and shot himself in the stomach. It took him all day to die. The sergeants in the regiment were harsh, sir and said it was good riddance."

It all came back to me. Sir Arthur had been furious about the unnecessary death for we had lost very few men that day. "That is right, Captain Gromm and Colonel Cameron covered it up. He was buried at night and barely a handful of people knew about it. It was done to protect the regiment, the officer and the officer's lady.

"The NCO's knew, sir, but we kept quiet because the Norfolk's Sergeant Major told us that he had a young wife. We closed ranks and no more was said."

It made perfect sense now. With a father in law who was an MP, the Colonel of the regiment would not wish scandal to mar a victory. The taste of the retreat to Corunna was still a bitter taste. I viewed the young woman in a different light. Fortunately, we were many miles from Roliça and she would never see that her husband was not buried with the other dead from the battle.

It would have been impossible to take the party to visit all of the defences and so Sir Arthur had us escort them to those defences around Torres Vedras. The other forts and fortlets were built to the same design and so it mattered not. The escorts, a squadron of Portuguese Cavalry, were already waiting, when Sharp and I arrived. They had the horses of the MPs and I saw Lieutenant Mountshaft examining them with a critical eye. As a young gentleman, he would have an eye for such things. However, he was looking for horses with spirit. I was not certain that the middle-aged politicians from England would appreciate such horses.

Sir Arthur hated to waste time and he and Sir Richard, along with his aide, Lieutenant Rice Jones, arrived promptly at 8.30. He looked up at the sky and saw that it was cloud-free. We would be cold but once we began to ride then we would warm up and, in addition, viewing the defences in the rain would put anyone off. Sir Arthur needed to win the approval of the politicians for there were too many enemies in Parliament; it seemed that they were like pigs with their snouts in the trough and Sir Arthur was taking their feed from them. As we were outside the hotel used by the politicians, they should have been already there but they were not. Sir Arthur gave them an impatient fifteen minutes and then snapped, "Mountshaft, tell the visitors from Westminster that they have five minutes to present themselves otherwise we leave without them!"

"Sir!"

It was bravado for the only reason to ride to the defences was to show them to the visitors but Sir Arthur was being diverted from his real purpose and he did not like it. When the Lieutenant returned, five minutes later, he had with him just the one visitor, Mrs de Lacey. That meant that the General had to be polite. We all doffed our hats.

"Good morning, Mrs de Lacey, this is Major Matthews who will be your escort this morning."

She was slightly older than I had expected but she was as thin and delicate as I had anticipated. She looked as though a good breeze would knock her down. However, she had eyes which made her whole face look like a spring morning. They were the bluest blue I had ever seen.

"Good morning Major, I hope that I will not inconvenience you too much. I am sorry, Sir Arthur, but the other gentlemen were keen to finish their breakfast; they enjoy their food. My father is chivvying them along now."

Sir Arthur forced a smile, "No matter, my dear. Major, if you please."

I waved over Sharp who brought Sunflower, the horse we had chosen for her. She was a golden colour and had the gentlest of dispositions. We rarely used her for she was too small for Sharp and I and could not carry as much as our other horses. It was the smallest horse we had and having seen the size of Mrs de Lacey, I was glad. I took the lady's hand and saw that she was wearing thin leather riding gloves. She had done this before.

"Sunflower is a gentle horse, Mrs de Lacey, but if you wish I can lead her for you."

"That will not be necessary, Major. I have ridden since I was ten years old. My father and I are both competent riders. If you please."

I cupped my hands and, placing her riding boot in my hands she grabbed the reins and the saddle and pulled herself into the soft leather. I was ready to put her boot in the stirrups for her but she managed that easily. She settled herself and then, after nodding to me, dug her heels in and galloped Sunflower around the square.

I saw Sir Arthur look in horror and then grin, as she showed her mastery of the mount, "By Gad, Matthews, the lady can ride."

She reined in as the four men emerged from the hotel. It was quite obvious that only Sir Godfrey was a rider as the other three were overweight and unfit. Had Mrs de Lacey not been there I might have enjoyed the amusing sight of the three overweight MPs trying to mount.

Mrs de Lacey looked down at me, "She is a delight. I cannot, however, see her as a horse of war."

Sharp brought over Donna and I mounted her. We towered over Mrs de Lacey and Sunflower, "No, Mrs de Lacey, Donna is the horse I ride to war."

"And she is magnificent!" She laughed as Mr Hugo Bentinck fell from the saddle. "I think, Major, that this will be a long day!"

Sergeant Sharp nudged his horse to the other side of Sunflower as Mr Bentinck finally mounted his horse.

Sir Arthur said, "Let us ride for we have much to see."

I knew from the Lieutenant that lunch would be at Cortada, the westernmost town on our tour. It was eight miles away and I wondered, as the three overweight MPs struggled to keep up with us, if that had been a little optimistic. The Portuguese had built a road to enable the defences to be built and we rode along that.

The small earthen forts did not look much but Sir Arthur had chosen the sections which already had their artillery in place and were manned by Portuguese soldiers. It was costing the British government £2,000,000 a year to maintain and Sir Arthur was showing that it was money well spent. We spent longer at the first fort than the others as Sir Richard wanted to explain how they worked for they were simply made of earth and wood.

He dismounted and stood on the banquette next to the eight-pound artillery pieces, "You see how there is a twenty-foot ditch before the fort. The steep glacis means than an enemy can get in easily enough but cannot get out. The rounded berm is hard to climb and the guns have embrasures through which they can fire. We have raised the level of each banquette by thirty feet. There is a talus which descends to the interior of the fort. The French have good artillery, gentlemen, and lady, but they would find it hard to dislodge the men who defended this fort."

I leaned in to explain to Mrs de Lacey the technical features mentioned by the engineer. "The berm is the rounded part just below the places where the guns poke out, the embrasures. The guns themselves are on a raised platform called a banquette and the talus is just a slope leading down from the banquette to the interior of the fort."

She smiled, "Thank you Major. Now it makes sense!"

Sir Godfrey was the one who appeared to have the better military knowledge and he was the one who made the pertinent observations, "And there would, of course, be infantry to defend the walls."

"Of course, they would be Portuguese units and they are fine soldiers. However, we have units of the British army in camps just behind the lines." Sir Richard smiled and pointed to the south, "The 5th Division is camped there. If you have been in Northumberland then you may have seen the Roman version of this although there it is a continuous structure. Here we defend the passes and the roads."

When we reached Sao Vincente then they became really impressed for there were three forts, 20, 21 and 22. The three of them dominated the road leading to Torres Vedras and they covered 360 degrees. Here there were Portuguese troops and they must have been primed by their officer for they were all stood to with smart uniforms and polished brass. Even I was impressed for the last time I had been here with Sir Richard it had been a pile of earth. They had worked hard.

As lunchtime approached, we headed for Cortada and the lunch which awaited us. I rode just behind the Portuguese Cavalry with Mrs de Lacey safely between Sharp and myself. "Tell me, Major, is this your normal line of work?"

I smiled, "This is a most welcome task I can assure you."

She laughed, "Very diplomatic I am sure, but you strike me as a soldier. I have noticed that despite the fact that we are, ostensibly, in friendly territory, you and your sergeant have been scanning the road for danger and I see that you have pistols loaded in your holsters."

"You have good eyes, Mrs de Lacey, for they are loaded but not yet primed. You are right, Sergeant Sharp and I have survived as long as we have by being careful." As soon as the words were out of my mouth, I regretted them. "I am sorry, I meant nothing."

"No, you are right, Major. My husband was young when he died and he was excited to be serving in a war. I am pleased that there are soldiers who survived. The main reason for my presence was to see how Geoffrey might have turned out. He came as a raw Lieutenant and progressed no further. Who knows, he may have ended like you, a gallant Major whom everyone lauds."

"I do not know about that."

"You do yourself a disservice. When we ate last night there were many officers talking about the gallant Major Matthews. Indeed, Colonel Cameron and Captain Gromm mentioned you when they brought me the news of my husband's death. I am honoured that you escort me."

"The honour is all mine."

As we headed for the tavern which had been hired to cater for the party, I realised that I was falling under the spell of this lovely lady. I was mindful of my experience with Mrs Turner, the Black Widow, but that had been lust and I felt no such desire for Mrs de Lacey. I just enjoyed her company for she was witty and clever. I also liked her father for, of the four, he was the one I could respect. The others had little interest in the defences and were just looking for their next meal and jug of wine. To them, this was a junket and the opportunity to travel at the Government's expense.

The food in the inn was excellent fare but it was somewhat rustic. The most refined part was the white bread although I suspected the normal customers would have eaten rye. I enjoyed the seafood and I know that Mrs de Lacey did too. Mr Bentinck and his two friends just concentrated upon the wine. The Portuguese drank to enjoy their wine.

The three politicians drank to consume as much as they could. The Portuguese were good hosts and they kept refilling the glasses.

I saw Sir Arthur breathe a sigh of relief as we left the inn to head back to Torres Vedras and his headquarters. We would be able to return in far quicker time than we had taken to reach Cortada as we had finished the inspection of the forts and he and Sir Richard, along with Sir Godfrey rode with the Portuguese Cavalry. The three drunks were with the aides Sir Richard and Sir Arthur had brought. We were approaching Sao Vincente when disaster struck. Mr Bentinck was not a good horseman and he was using his hands to gesticulate and point to the north. His horse's head whipped around and all might have been well had not the politician panicked and dug in his heels. The horse was a cavalry horse and thought it was being commanded to hurtle down the steep slope. Even worse, as the MP careered down the steep slope, clinging on for dear life, the horses of the other two politicians followed suit so that the three of them were heading for the river which lay down the valley side. The aides took off after the three of them and I saw that Sir Arthur had seen what was happening and had halted the column.

I turned to Alan, "Sharp, you had better get after them or all this morning's good work will be undone."

"Yes, sir."

Mrs de Lacey shook her head, "They are drunk and they are a disgrace. My father only brought them as they represent the main opposition to the prosecution of this war. I hope they get a good soaking!"

I could not help but smile and I had every sympathy with her point of view. When the General saw that there were enough soldiers to catch and rescue the politicians, he waved his arm and the column moved forward. I confess that I was enjoying my conversation with Mrs de Lacey too much and did not notice that we were becoming isolated on this lonely stretch of the road. As we watched Sharp and the officers grab the reins of the wild horses and lead them up a zig-zag path, I was aware that Donna was becoming agitated. As much as I was enjoying the conversation, I was still a soldier with a soldier's instincts. I took out my pistol and began to prime it.

Mrs de Lacey was quick-witted, "Is there danger?"

"Donna thinks there is, Mrs de Lacey. Stay close."

I had just primed and cocked my pistol when a ragged figure in the remains of a French uniform leapt at me from the rock which towered above us. I turned and fired instinctively and hit him in the chest. I dropped the pistol and drew my sword as Mrs de Lacey's horse reared. It was then I realised what a good horsewoman she really was for Mr

Bentinck would have been dumped unceremoniously to the ground while she stood in the stirrups and controlled her mount easily. A Portuguese bugle sounded for they had heard the pistol and Sir Arthur had seen the danger. My sword was barely out when my attacker's three companions came from behind the rock. They had the short swords favoured by the French Artillery and like their dying companion wore the vestiges of a French uniform. I slashed down with my sword and hacked across the neck of one of them. A second tried to grab the reins of Mrs de Lacey's horse but she whipped her mount's head around and being a cavalry horse, it snapped and bit at the man who pulled back. I brought my sword down towards the head of the third man but he had already slashed at my leg. My sword split his head in twain but his sword had laid open my breeches and leg. Ignoring the blood, I spurred Donna at the Frenchman who had tried to grab Mrs de Lacey's reins. In trying to jerk out of the way he lost his footing and tumbled down the slope. For a brief moment I thought that Sergeant Sharp, who was hurrying to my aid might capture him but when I heard the Frenchman's head strike a rock and crack open like an egg then I knew he was doomed.

Sir Arthur and Sir Godfrey reached me first as the Portuguese Captain led his men up the slope to search for companions of the four Frenchmen.

"Emily, are you hurt?" I heard the concern in her father's voice. She was his only child and more precious than gold.

She shook her head, "Thanks to the gallant Major, no!" Then she saw my bloody leg, "But you are wounded!"

I climbed off Donna's back and took the belt from one of the dead men. I tied it around the top of my thigh, "There, that will halt the bleeding until we reach home."

Sir Arthur was scowling and he pointed down the slope, "Your peers, Sir Godfrey, almost cost you your daughter!"

"It might have been better if your men had let them fall into the river." He pointed to the dead men as I tried to climb back on to Donna's back. "Where did these four come from?"

Sharp joined me and shook his head. Ignoring his admonition, I answered, "My guess is that these were left behind when their army retreated last year. From the looks of their uniforms, they were artillerymen. I suspect they became bandits. Until Sir Richard began building the defences there would have been few soldiers here. They must have been desperate. I suppose they saw the chance to steal two horses and get across the river."

Sir Arthur nodded his agreement, "Quite, now let us get back to the fortress and have Major Matthews wound seen to. A one-legged cavalryman is not much use to anyone!"

Both Mrs de Lacey and Sharp fussed over me all the way back. Luckily, we did not have far to travel but Sergeant Sharp insisted upon loosening and then tightening the tourniquet frequently. I was taken directly to the doctors. I told Sharp to stay with Mrs de Lacey until they were back in their quarters. The wound was more serious than I had thought and I had to endure a painful cleansing of the wound with vinegar. When the orderly showed me the dirt and fibres on the swab then I knew that I had been lucky he had been so scrupulous, "That could have cost you your leg, sir. This will need stitches. Shall I fetch the doctor?"

"Can you do it?"

He grinned, "Aye sir, but you being an officer I thought you would want the doctor."

"Just stitch it eh?

"Aye, sir, and as neat a piece of stitching you never will see."

"Then there will be a silver shilling for you orderly!"

He kept his word and I gave him two shillings. He had just finished when Sharp arrived, "Next time, sir, I will let the fat politicians drown! Every time I take my eye off you…"

"And how is Mrs de Lacey?"

"Worried sick about you, sir, and singing your praises like you are Ajax or Hector, sir! Still, they will be away back home in a couple of days and we can get back to normal!"

The fates, or rather the Iberian weather conspired against us and a snowstorm descended which made the roads impassable. It turned out that Mrs de Lacey and I had longer to get to know each other.

The weather might have prevented civilians from travelling on the roads but Sir Arthur had me accompany the squadron of Portuguese cavalry to see if there were any more remnants of the French army. I was chosen because I spoke Portuguese and also because I spoke French. Sir Arthur wanted prisoners rather than corpses. The four dead Frenchmen's bodies had revealed nothing except that they were French artillerymen. The Portuguese Captain was a young man of a noble family and he did speak a little English. My Portuguese was improving but his few words helped us to communicate.

We began by backtracking from the ambush site. The snow had covered up any tracks they might have left but, in their place, the snow showed us the trails, both animal and human, which led down to the river. The Captain and I reasoned that they had to have a hideout within four or five miles from the ambush site and that it had to be somewhere which was relatively inaccessible. Once again, the snow came to our aid for we saw prints in the snow and I recognised them as the prints of French boots. As these were in the snow, they were not made by the four men we had killed. Leaving ten men to watch the horses, Sharp and I accompanied the Captain and twenty of his men to follow the tracks in a long line. I had with me my Baker rifle which I had not used since Talavera. I carried it primed and cocked. I wanted it to encourage the French to surrender. I thought it highly unlikely that they had either musket or powder; the Portuguese only had swords and I wished to avoid a bloodbath.

It was Sharp who spotted their lair. The footprints were joined by some coming from the west and he saw that they led to what looked like a cave although the leafless bushes before it made it hard to see as the branches were covered in snow.

I turned to the Portuguese captain, "Captain, have your men spread out in a long line and we will approach and ask for their surrender."

"They are up there?"

"It seems likely." He nodded and we moved along the trail. I saw that it twisted to our right and then double-backed. I shouted, in French, "This is Major Matthews of the 11th Light Dragoons. I have soldiers with me. Surrender and I guarantee that you will be fed and housed."

There was silence.

Sergeant Sharp shook his head, "I know what I would choose, sir. You have a chance of escaping if you have a full belly. What do these poor sods have to eat?"

I nodded and shouted, "It is possible that you will be exchanged for English prisoners captured at Talavera. If you stay here you will starve to death. We buried your four friends. Do not make us bury you."

A voice shouted, "We will come out with our hands raised. If we are murdered then God will punish you."

"I gave you my word."

The four men who followed the grizzled old sergeant looked more like scarecrows than members of the army which had conquered most of Europe.

I nodded to Sergeant Sharp, "You have done the right thing, now give your weapons to the Sergeant here. You will not need them again."

The Portuguese were not happy but I had the five men ride double for it might have killed them to walk. I handed them over to the Provost Marshal and asked him to treat them well, "It is not their fault that they were trapped behind enemy lines."

"Right, sir, and they look weak enough for a strong breeze to fell them."

I had learned on the journey back that they had been based at Cortada and they had manned a battery which guarded the estuary. When the French fell back they were forgotten and the Sergeant had managed to keep his gun crew together for a year by scavenging and hunting. I admired him. He was typical of the men I had fought alongside when I had been a Chasseur. They had done nothing wrong and yet had been punished by the land and nature itself.

The snow stopped the next day but the roads were still in a sorry state. Sir Godfrey discovered that the 9th, his son-in-law's regiment, was just down the road with the 1st Division. He managed to gain an invite for his daughter and himself to the mess where a dinner would be held for Sir Godfrey who was MP for King's Lynn. Once again Lieutenant Mountshaft said that Sir Arthur had asked Sharp and me to be their escorts. He added, confidentially, that Mrs de Lacey herself had made the request. I did not mind an evening in her company.

Sir Godfrey asked, "And how is the wound, Major?"

"Healing, sir, it is good of you to ask."

"You saved my daughter's life and I am indebted to you."

"Those men were to be pitied, sir, for they were abandoned and hungry. I do not think they would have harmed your daughter. They wanted the horses."

He shook his head, "The men were fools! There was a troop of cavalry close by!"

"And that troop, sir, was moving on. It was a bold move, I grant you, but they saw just one horseman and two horses. If they had dealt with me and unhorsed your daughter then they could have been across the river before any would have been able to stop them."

Mrs de Lacey smiled, "You are a strange man, Major. Anyone else would have been angry for you were wounded."

"I am a soldier, Mrs de Lacey, and my body is covered in old wounds. I have been fighting since I was but sixteen."

"Major, my name is Emily, I pray that you use it for I owe you my life. Even if you are right and I was not in danger of losing my life, you still risked your life for me."

"While I am on duty, I am afraid I must be more formal and call you Mrs de Lacey. I am sorry but Sir Arthur is quite clear on such matters."

She nodded, "I understand for you are a gentleman."

We reached the camp. The regiment was well aware of the importance of their visitor and the welcoming parties were in their best uniforms. They would not thank us for the visit for the ground was muddy and after we had gone their uniforms would necessitate some serious cleaning. It was a young lieutenant, the Regimental Sergeant Major and the colour party who greeted us. They snapped smartly to attention and I returned their salute.

Dismounting I said, "We will wait in the guard-room until you are ready to leave."

The Lieutenant said, "Oh no, sir, you are invited too. The Colonel insisted!"

"But I have not come dressed for the occasion."

The Sergeant Major said, "Sir, you are a soldier. I saw you at Roliça and Talavera. You could go in rags and the real soldiers would not mind. We will look after Sergeant Sharp for you."

There was a camaraderie amongst good NCOs. I handed my reins, hat and cloak to Sergeant Sharp and said, "Very well."

I saw the delight on Mrs de Lacey's face and she linked her father and me. The 9th had taken over a farmhouse and converted the barn into a mess. They had made a good job of it and it was warm and inviting. I saw that all of the officers had turned out and were all in their best uniforms. From the smell of the food being prepared in the kitchen, it was a roast pig. The regiment was honouring their local MP. They began to applaud as we entered. I recognised Captain Gromm and Colonel Cameron but many of the other officers had changed since Roliça. I had not had much to do with them at Talavera. There were seats for Mrs de Lacey and Sir Godfrey on either side of the Colonel and the adjutant, Major Arkwright, was on the other side of Sir Godfrey.

Captain Gromm said, "Here, Major, I have the best seat in the house between the lovely Mrs de Lacey and the dashing Major Matthews. We look forward to hearing about your latest exploits."

Although my mission to Talavera had been secret, I knew that word had leaked out. There were despatches arriving from the border fortresses all the time and my involvement with the guerrillas and the French Hussars would have enlivened many a mess. Mrs de Lacey glanced at me having heard Captain Gromm's words.

The attention was diverted from me when Sir Godfrey began to speak to the Colonel about his son in law's death. I knew that the Colonel was making up the story of the death but he did a good job of it. The senior officers had obviously discussed it. Emily de Lacey frowned when she heard it for although her father believed it, she, having heard the colonel's words, was questioning in. She was a clever woman and I had seen that in the conversations we had had thus far.

Then the Captain turned his attention to me, "I heard you were recently in Talavera! Right in the middle of the French camp."

I could not deny it and so I made it sound far simpler than it was, "You know yourself, Captain, what it is like in a town where there are lots of troops coming and going; there is confusion. I slipped in and slipped out. The General just needed to know what the French were up to."

"But weren't you chased by Hussars and rescued by the guerrillas?"

"Guerrillas, Captain, what is a guerrilla?" Mrs de Lacey looked intrigued.

"A Spaniard who fights the French, Mrs de Lacey. They are tough men, isn't that right Major?"

"They lead a hard life that is certain, Captain Gromm, and they keep many of Bonaparte's men tied down."

One of the young officers lower down the table had been listening and he said, "But, sir, it isn't war is it? There is something distasteful about these fellows sneaking around and slitting throats."

The Colonel snapped, "Lieutenant Pemberton, there is a lady present!"

"Sorry, Mrs de Lacey, sorry Colonel."

"Lieutenant, in 1805 the French were going to invade England and but for Admiral Nelson they would have succeeded. Suppose he had taken over our home would you have accepted that!" I did not mean to raise my voice but I thought of Juan and the other guerrillas living in the harshest of worlds.

"Of course not, sir, I would have fought on!"

"Even though the army was defeated and you were with a few comrades who had also survived?"

Doubt crossed his face but he said, "We wouldn't lose! We are better soldiers!"

A few of the younger officers banged their hands on the table in approval. Captain Gromm said, quietly, "The men we left in the mountains when we retreated to Corunna might tell a different story. Major Matthews is quite right, Lieutenant, and I for one would be a guerrilla if the same thing happened in my country."

The discussion prompted other discussions amongst the officers. I heard the name of Sir John Moore mentioned and the talk was of Sir Arthur. Mrs de Lacey looked at me and said, "Major, I can see now that Sir Arthur chose his best as my guardian and I am grateful."

Captain Gromm swallowed his food and wiped it with his napkin, "You are right there, Mrs de Lacey. In any battle, you will always find the Major where the action is the thickest."

I was glad when the conversation moved on from me. By the time we left the skies had cleared and the ground was treacherous with heavy and thick ice. Had Mrs de Lacey not been a superb rider then I would have been concerned. While Sir Godfrey said goodbye to the Colonel and Sharp held the reins of his horse, I helped Mrs de Lacey on to her mount. As I handed her the reins she said quietly, "How did my husband die, Major and do not say it was in battle for I know a piece of fiction when I hear it? Captain Gromm said you are always in the thick of the action and the story that was concocted tonight suggested that my husband was in the thick of it too, yet that was not Geoffrey!"

"That was almost two years ago, Mrs de Lacey, and I was too busy fighting to notice who was dying. It is the story I was told and, therefore, I believe it."

"You are an honourable man but I do not believe it. That does not sound like my husband. I loved him dearly but he would not willingly put himself in harm's way. You do and you are a different man. I can see the difference."

We rode back in silence and the next time I saw her was when I was sent with the Portuguese cavalry to escort the delegation back to Lisbon. Sir Godfrey, it seems, had again asked for me. Mrs de Lacey and I were apart from the politicians who discussed, as they rode, what they had seen. Mrs de Lacey seemed keen to talk and, in truth, I enjoyed it. This time she spoke of her home in England. Her father was rich, as were most MPs, and he had given her and the Lieutenant a cottage in King's Lynn and it was clear that Emily adored it.

"When you are next on leave you must come and visit me. The cottage is lovely and overlooks the sea."

"Would that be appropriate, Mrs de Lacey, for you live alone?"

"It is Emily and I have servants. Would you not wish to visit with me?" She sounded disappointed.

"Of course, but I am a gruff old soldier and..."

"There is nothing old about you, Major, and as for being gruff. Do you not like me?" She was flirting and I knew it but it made me uncomfortable.

I found myself blushing, "But of course I do... I, er."

She laughed, "I apologise, Major, this is unfair of me. It is clear that you do not understand the world of ladies. If you wish to please me then visit my father's home. It is much grander and he lives not far from me. That way I can show you my home and yet you will not have your honour compromised."

"It is your honour I worry about."

She looked sad, "I am now a widow without even a child to show for a brief six months of marriage to a husband who was abroad for five of those months. I have a bleak future, Major, for as the heiress of my father's estate, then every man who calls upon me I see as someone who sees a pot of gold and not Emily de Lacey. If you came to visit then I would know that your intentions were honourable."

"You barely know me!"

"You learn much about a man from what others say of him and thus far you have lived up to my expectations. Would you write to me?"

"Of course, but I am no letter writer!"

She laughed, "That I can believe. It matters not for if you write to me then I can write to you and that activity will fill some of the empty hours I will have to endure alone."

When we parted I thought that this would be the last that I would see her. I was wrong.

Chapter 5

By February the news reached Sir Arthur that the whole of Southern Spain, with the exception of Cadiz held by the British, had fallen to the French. When senior officers were summoned to Torres Vedras, I knew just what the end of Spanish resistance meant; the French could bring their forces north and now that winter was drawing to a close then the French could send reinforcements to finally rid Bonaparte of his Spanish ulcer! I anticipated either another mission behind enemy lines or a commission in a regiment of cavalry. Either way I needed saddle furniture renewing and weapons maintained. Sharp and I had not been idle since Mrs de Lacey had left. The local tailor recommended by Sir George knew his business and we both had some civilian clothes made up as well as spare uniforms for Spain and Portugal were hard on them. If we were to go behind the lines then civilian clothes would be a better disguise especially now that the French had news of my identity. I had been recognised and the French would seek me out.

It was the end of March when I was summoned, once more, by the General. He took me along the defences for he was never one to waste time and he inspected them while he briefed me. The first line of defence was almost complete and work had now begun on a second line from the Atlantic to Alverca. Sir Arthur was a cautious man. He nodded in satisfaction at the formidable line of forts, fortlets and redoubts. "You know, Matthews, that the French are coming?"

"Yes sir, now that Spain is under their boot, they will come north and take either Cuidad or Badajoz."

"Or both but as they do not know about these defences, I am expecting them to come through Cuidad Rodrigo for it gives them access to Coimbra, Oporto as well as Lisbon. They can surround it and pound it to pieces. They will think that I will bring my army to the aid of the Spanish, but I will not." I nodded. "For that reason, I wish you to go to Lieutenant-General Herrasti and tell him so. I would not have him suffer unnecessary casualties because he expects me to go to his aid. You must make it quite clear to him that I will not be doing so."

"You want him to abandon the fortress, sir?"

"Good God man, no! I want him to fight but there will come a point where fighting will be useless and would result in a pointless loss of life. Then I would have him surrender for Almeida is a strong fortress and is manned by the Portuguese. By that time my defences should be in place."

I knew that he would not tell me his plans for it was not his way and I might be captured. I could work them out, however. He would move his army north to the River Mondego and Coimbra. Whoever led the French would take Cuidad Rodrigo and then would have to come through Coimbra and cross the river. By funnelling them through that town he would slow up the advance and when they reached his defences the French would have a rude shock!

"I also want you to scout the land between the Côa river and Cuidad Rodrigo. You have a good eye for such matters and I would value your opinion of the area as a place we could slow up a French advance. You will report to me at Coimbra."

"Sir!" As ever Sir Arthur was terse and to the point. I liked that in him for you were given the fewest words and there was no room for misinterpretation.

We had made friends in many of the regiments and we arranged for the 9th East Norfolk Regiment to take our spare horses and equipment with them. We would use our civilian clothes for if the French had left Southern Spain then we could run into their patrols and scouts. We left Torres Vedras and headed north. We had completed this journey before and we knew both the road and the places where we could be accommodated. The weather was more clement than when we had returned south from Talavera.

When we reached Cuidad Rodrigo I saw that the garrison had swollen a little and there were nearer 6000 men in the garrison. Upon meeting the Lieutenant-General he explained the increase, "When the French defeated our men many of them made their way here and I have employed them. More of them, however, joined the guerrillas. The French will find that will make their lives difficult." He looked at me, "However, Major, I think that you bring equally unpleasant news for me. You have a face which is easy to read for you are an honourable man!"

I nodded and he took me to his inner sanctum. I told him my news but I added more of an explanation than Sir Arthur had given to me. "General, he has less than 30,000 British troops. We both know that he can expect to face twice that number when he battles the French. The plains around here do not suit Sir Arthur's style of warfare."

He smiled, "Ah, yes, the reverse slope and the ridge. I can see how that would suit but I cannot abandon my post for now that we have lost Andalusia, the Spanish people see me as their last hope."

"But my general urges you not to waste lives. If you feel that you are going to be overrun then save lives and surrender. We have Almeida which is not far away and that can slow up the French advance. The more time we buy then the more reinforcements can come from Canada and the West Indies."

"I understand, Major, for I am a soldier but I am disappointed."

I was not happy when I left for I sympathised with both generals and could see both their points of view. If Parliament was not full of corrupt politicians then the money and men would have been made available and Sir Arthur could have met the French with parity of numbers and saved Cuidad Rodrigo. I had not been given orders to go to Almeida for that was Portuguese with a British Commander and Sir Arthur did not need to offer his apologies. However, courtesy demanded that I do so.

Sharp and I rode towards the Côa. We rode up the slope to the plateau close to the sleepy village of Fuentes de Oñoro. Its narrow streets could hold up an enemy. We passed Fort Concepcion, an abandoned Spanish defence which could also be used and then we reached Vale da Mula which guarded the road to the Côa. As we descended to the river, I saw that this was perfect country for an ambush or a withdrawal which would slow up an enemy. Steep, rocky sided valleys provided perfect places for small groups of men to hold up an enemy. More importantly, it was closer to Coimbra and help could be brought more quickly. Heading along the river to Almeida, we found a small village, Junca, and I spied a road which led to the Côa. When we followed it down the steep slope, I saw that there was a narrow bridge which crossed it and I remembered it from our return from Talavera. As the bridge was almost equidistant between Almeida and Cuidad Rodrigo, it would be the perfect place for Sir Arthur to place men to slow down the French. We rode the area for most of the day and then headed for Almeida where we could spend the night.

The Brigadier General was in a good mood for the garrison had managed to acquire more gunpowder and shot for his cannons. The arsenal being too small, they had used the cathedral to store it. As we left the next morning he said, "Tell General Wellesley that even if Cuidad falls the ground here does not favour the French and we can hold out for much longer."

That he was proved wrong was not his fault. Many men might have called it an act of God. Sir Arthur called it incompetence.

By the time we reached Coimbra, a month had passed since we had left and the army was beginning to gather. Sir Arthur had learned that the Marshal who had been given command of the Army of Portugal was André Masséna. He was an imaginative general and Sir Arthur knew that he would have his work cut out to defeat him for he was clever; I had told him that. Spanish guerrillas were keeping watch on the army as it gathered north of Madrid.

Sir Arthur still did not entirely trust the guerrillas and, sadly, did not give them as much credit as he should. He made me spend a long morning with him while he annotated his map and his questions would have caught me out had I not been thoroughly prepared. When I had finished, he said, "Then we use Crauford and his Light Division. 3000 men should be enough to slow down an advance on either Almeida or Coimbra. It will take him a while to get there. I would like you and your fellow, Sharp, to go with him, General Crauford is a stout fellow but he has the heart of a wild Scotsman. You have a certain standing with my senior officers and I believe you two knew each other during the retreat. I will see him later and give him his orders."

"Yes, sir."

"Good, then it is settled. Send Sharp back if anything requires my attention. I know that he can be discreet! You have one day to sort what you need. But remember, I do not wish the Light Division to be risked. If Masséna comes then General Crauford must fall back. I am relying on you to be my eyes and ears."

We went to the East Norfolks to retrieve our war gear and uniforms and then went to the tent we had been allocated. Sergeant Sharp was whistling as we changed into our uniforms. "What is making you so happy, Sergeant Sharp?"

"Just that this will be more like proper soldiering, sir. You know, face the enemy, shoot them before they shoot you. Standing with your mates. Proper soldiering."

"We can still get killed quite easily, you know!"

"Aye sir, but when we are behind the enemy lines it is like the whole world is after us. At least this way we will be with our own lads!"

I shook my head but knew that every British soldier felt the same. Having your own countrymen close by made you feel, somehow, stronger.

We went into Coimbra to buy supplies which we knew we might need. We also went to the quartermaster for more powder and ball. We dined that night with the 9th. This was a more casual and informal affair and I sat between the Colonel and Captain Gromm who had just bought a majority. I was pleased for him for he was not a young officer.

"Congratulations, Major."

He nodded and smiled, "Took me some time to find the necessary funds but it will be worth it."

The Colonel said, "Lieutenant de Lacey's wife was a little different to what I expected, Matthews."

"How so, sir?"

"He was younger than she was and I thought that she must have been some spinster desperate for a marriage." I thought that it was a little unfair and ungracious of him.

"Love is a funny thing, sir."

Major Gromm said, quietly, "It was not love of the lady which prompted Lieutenant de Lacey to marry the young woman but rather the love of money and land."

"Major, the gentleman is dead and cannot defend himself."

Colonel Cameron said, "And he was no gentlemen. When we covered up his death it was nothing to do with the man, you understand, but out of respect for his widow. The Lieutenant had gambling debts. Had he got his hands on his wife's money then goodness knows what might have happened. As it was, he died owing other officers money. That money remains unpaid! I know not what the young lady saw in him for, from what we saw, she was a beautiful and intelligent young woman."

"Perhaps she saw something in him which you did not."

Major Gromm nodded, "You could be right, Major, for he was good looking and had a ready wit about him. He was a good dancer too but he hunted Sir Godrey's daughter as though she was a twelve-point stag."

I felt angry when I heard that for I had been somewhat sympathetic thinking the young man had been unlucky. Now I saw that this was almost divine intervention. I knew there were such bounders and I had met them. De Vere, one of the officers in the 11th had been just such a one. Captain Rogers of the 23rd Light Dragoons also shared some of those vices. Poor Emily! She could never know and yet she grieved for a man who did not deserve her tears. We put him from the conversation and spoke instead of the French. The officers were interested to know my thoughts on the coming campaign. Without revealing too much of what Sir Arthur had told me I told them what I knew of the land and the enemies we would fight. All of them were confident that Sir Arthur could beat any Frenchman, save Bonaparte. As none of them had ever fought in a battle against the master of Europe they were just using his reputation as the basis for their opinion. I knew that the Emperor had yet to meet a foe as skilled as Sir Arthur. I had fought under him and seen him close to. He could be beaten!

We were summoned early the next day to Sir Robert Crauford's headquarters. His aide took me into his tent where he was busy reading the muster. "Ah Matthews, glad to see that you are still alive although, with the line of work you have chosen, I cannot see that continuing." He said it with a smile upon his face and that was rare for Black Bob rarely smiled. "Still, we have a chance to avenge Sir John, eh? We'll show these Froggies. We have some cavalry with us, Light Dragoons and German Hussars but I want them behind us. You will liaise with them. You know the Côa?"

"Yes sir, I scouted it for the General. It should suit the Light Division."

"I fear no Frenchman, not even Boney but I do like some rough terrain!"

I used the map before him to explain what I had seen and to offer my opinion. He concurred. "I can tell you have an eye for terrain. Aye, this place close to the bridge looks ideal. You can take some of the 14th Light Dragoons to scout out the enemy. From the intelligence gathered thus far, it looks like they are still some way away. We have time."

In the end, it was April by the time we were ready to leave and began the long march east. Sir Arthur now had almost 50,000 men at his disposal made up of British, Hanoverians and Portuguese. Colonel Selkirk's spies in Madrid sent the message that there were at least 60,000 Frenchmen heading our way. We had to hope that Cuidad Rodrigo and Almeida could do their job and slow down the French!

We were just leaving the town when a corporal raced up to us with a document in his hand, "Sir, you have a letter. The mail packet docked yesterday and this came for you. I was told to get it to you before you left."

"Thank you, Corporal." I put the letter in my jacket without even looking at it for I had rarely had a letter and I would read it once we reached our camp for the night. I needed no distractions as I was leading a squadron of the 14th as scouts. We had with us some Portuguese Cazadores but they were not mounted and I would have to use my experience to look for danger. I knew that even if the French were still on their way west, they would have their Chasseurs out to scout out the land. It was still early April but the weather was becoming hotter and I knew that grazing, while not a problem at the moment, would become one as high summer approached. Not only did I need to find a good defensive line, but it also had to be one which gave us grazing. If not then the three regiments of horse would have to wait beyond the Côa.

That first night found us twenty-five miles from Coimbra. I estimated it would take us four days to reach our destination. I used the Light Dragoons to form a piquet line as the regiments marched into the area I had chosen as our camp. They did not bother with tents. This was the Light Division. I knew I had taken it easy on the first day and Black Bob was not slow to reprimand me.

"Major Matthews, this is the Light Division and not some Fencible regiment made up of farmers and clerks. We can march forty miles in a day and still fight a battle at the end of it. If you cannot make good speed then I will find someone who can! I want to be beyond the Côa in two days! Do you understand me, sir?"

"Yes General!"

I saw sympathetic smiles from his aides. They had all had to endure his caustic tongue too. My consolation was that I got to read the letter and it was from Emily de Lacey. She had asked me to write to her and I had not. Even as I used my stiletto to cut the wax seal, I felt guilty at my omission.

Sunrise Cottage,
King's Lynn
Norfolk
March 1810

Major Matthews,

I hope this missive finds you well. I have been presumptive and written to you first. If this offends you then I do not apologise for since my husband's death I have learned that life is too short to wait upon another making a decision which could have a profound effect upon my life and my future! If I am considered a lady who is forward then so be it!

Firstly, I wish to thank you again for all your efforts on my behalf. Although you were under orders, I gained the impression that you were quite happy to do so and for that I am grateful. It could have been one of the many dreary officers that I met while in Portugal. I pray that you do write to me for I am genuinely interested in you and my life in England is dull! If that appears forward then all that I can say is that I sensed an interest from you. If I am mistaken then tell me so in your reply for I have a life ahead of me which I wish to enjoy. I hope that you might be part of that life but I understand that some men, often military men, avoid entanglements with ladies. If you are thus predisposed then let me know so that I may find another object of my affections.

My father does not know that I write this letter. One reason he took me with him, apart from to visit the land where my husband died, was to keep me close to him for he believes that I make poor decisions where men are concerned. As you might imagine from my words, he did not approve of my marriage to Geoffrey for he thought my husband was a chancer who sought my fortune. He may have been right but I had lived a dull life before then. Norfolk is not the most exciting place in England and when I met the dashing young Lieutenant, he won my heart. He dazzled me with his swordplay and his wit made me laugh.

My father, however, may have been right and, having met you, I can see that he was not a real, what was it Captain Gromm said of you, warrior? Was I looking for a knight to sweep me off my feet and to fight dragons for me? Probably?

I beg you, Major, your Sergeant told me your name is Robbie and I will use that from now on for I like the way saying it makes me smile, Robbie, to write to me. If nothing comes from this exchange of letters then I will, at least, feel attached to the real world and if you reject me then I can begin my life again.

I will pray that God keeps you safe,
The one who would be your friend,

And more,
Emily
xxx

I found myself lost both for words and for thoughts. There had been ladies in my life but none had ever shown any interest in me and yet this lady seemed to seek me as a husband or was I reading more into this than was intended? For the first time in my life, I needed a best friend. Sergeant Sharp was the closest that I had and yet I could not confide in him. I would have to wrestle with the demon myself. For the time being, I could do nothing about it for, not only did I not have a pen and paper, I would be away from the means to send a missive back to England. I re-read the letter four times more and then secreted it in my jacket. I knew that Sergeant Sharp wondered what was amiss but I kept my thoughts to myself and, when I slept, I dreamed of Emily and I had never yet allowed a woman to creep into my thoughts.

We had crossed the bridge when the Spanish rider found us. It was fortunate that I was there for he could speak no English and the Captain commanding the Light Dragoons could speak no Spanish.

"Cuidad Rodrigo is under siege, Major! My General said to tell your general that there are more than 60,000 men there. They have far more guns than we do and they have surrounded the city. Unless you come to our aid then we are doomed."

I nodded, "Thank you. What will you do now?"

He grinned, "Why return and join my comrades! We will fight to the end!"

With that, he whipped his horse's head around and road north. I turned to Sergeant Sharp, "I am afraid you have a long ride ahead of you, Alan! Tell General Crauford the news and then ride to Sir Arthur! I believe we will be close to Junca."

"Yes, sir." As he wheeled his horse around, he said to the Troop Sergeant, "Harry, keep your eye on the Major, will you? He needs me!"

I shook my head and the Troop Sergeant grinned, "Will do, Sarge!"

I had the Light Dragoons form a skirmish line. I did not believe that the French would have got this far so soon but it paid to be diligent. Sir Robert left the column to join me with his aide. "So, the French have moved quickly, eh, Matthews?"

"Looks like it, sir. I have the troop out as skirmishers but tomorrow, with your permission, I would like to take them closer to Cuidad Rodrigo. I do not doubt the Spaniard's report but it is always better to use the judgement of your own eyes."

"I quite agree."

That night I studied the map I had made when I had scouted the area. The road to Coimbra led through Vilar Formosa to the south. We would need men to watch the road but we also had to guard one of the roads which led to Almeida. However, that road was a longer one and the shorter route led through Junca. I waited until the General had his headquarters set up and then I took my map to him. He agreed with my assessment of the situation.

"I will keep the Horse Artillery in reserve. Ross is a fine fellow and he and his battery can reach anywhere along our defences quickly. I want the cavalry close to Vilar Formosa but I want you and your troop to get as close to the French as you can. I will have my lads in the hills to stop their skirmishers getting too close. I want you to spot any major troop movements."

Captain Wilson and I had an understanding. He was a good officer but he had bought his commission and he was young. He had realised early on that he was out of his depth and he deferred to me, in fact, he asked for advice on almost everything military. For that I was grateful; I did not want a battle with him. We left before dawn had broken to head south and east towards Cuidad Rodrigo. I rode next to him and spoke as we rode the first few miles in the cold air before dawn.

"John, the French have the best cavalry in the world. Their Dragoons can fight as line troops and their Chasseurs are simply the best. How good are your chaps with their Paget Carbines?"

The blank look gave me my answer. I nodded, "Then when we are in camp have them practice for this is not a war of slashing swords and brave charges; we fight Frenchmen and do not hunt foxes. We have to deter the French from getting close to our lines." I pointed to the hills to our left, "We can't go there. That is for the Light Infantry and Rifles so we keep this road British! Listen to me and learn."

"Yes, sir!" In his voice, I heard the worry that the purchase of a commission would not give him the glory he sought. It might bring his grave just a little closer.

I had my Baker rifle slung across my saddle. I had drawn some strange looks from the officers in the camp as I had done so when we had left. In their eyes, a rifle or a carbine was for the other ranks and not an officer. I had Sharp just behind me and he also had his rifle at the ready. The road, which was far from straight, meant that we could not see a long way ahead. I doubted that there would be any ambushes but this ground and road invited chance encounters and when that encounter involved two groups of armed men then there was always danger. We rested our horses and watered them at Vilar Formosa. I wanted to examine the place a little more closely. This was perfect country for cavalry. The tiny town had no wall and no strongpoint. This vital crossroads could easily change hands in any battle. After we had watered our horses and headed towards Cuidad Rodrigo I realised that Sir Arthur did not have enough horsemen and here, on these plains, cavalry would rule the day.

Sharp's eyes spotted the French Chasseurs in the distance, "Sir, the French!"

I saw them and heard the Captain say, "Bugler sound…"

"Bugler do nothing!"

Captain Wilson looked at me with a shocked expression on his face, "But there are Frenchmen up there and we should charge them!"

"Captain, you will obey orders. Have your men form a skirmish line and draw their carbines. On my command and my command alone, they will open fire and they will aim for the French horses!"

He looked shocked, "Aim at the horses, sir? That is ungentlemanly!"

I had no time for this and gave the command myself, "The Troop will form a skirmish line, draw their carbines and when I give the order you will fire and you will aim at the horses!"

The Troop Sergeant bellowed, "You heard Major Matthews!"

As I primed my rifle I said, "The reason we will aim at the horses, Captain, is your fault. You do not know the ability of your men and I need them to have the largest of targets. That will be the horses. I will be aiming at the officers, as will Sergeant Sharp for we hit that at which we aim."

He looked crestfallen, "Sorry, sir!"

"Don't be sorry, just do the job for which you are paid! You are an officer and that means you lead!"

French cavalry always believed that they were better than their English counterparts and generally they were right. The English were led, in the main, by officers who thought they were on a fox hunt and the French were the foxes. The Chasseurs rode at us confidently, expecting us to charge them for English cavalry normally did and when they charged the French, they normally came off worse! Even as they came down the road they spread economically into an easy line. It confirmed my view that this was perfect country for cavalry.

I sensed that the troopers were nervous as the Chasseurs gradually increased their speed and I knew they expected us to do one of two things: either counter charge them in a ragged line or break. They did not expect us to fire at them. "Troopers, the French are of the opinion that British horsemen are poor cavalrymen. We will prove them wrong. We will give them one volley and then we will draw sabres and engage them. Bugler, listen for my commands." I knew from Sergeant Sharp that British soldiers liked to be led and I made my voice as confident and commanding as I could.

Sergeant Sharp and I had trained our horses well and I rested my left forearm on Donna's neck while my right elbow was anchored on her saddle. I shouted, "Aim low for your barrel will rise when it is fired. Prepare!" We would be sending thirty-four balls in the direction of the French, if just five struck anything then I would call that a victory. However, the thirty-four balls would go close enough to the horses and riders to make some flinch and some baulk. I needed the French disordered. Without speaking to Alan, I knew that he would go for the Chasseur Sergeant and I would aim for the officer. The Baker was so accurate and we were such good shots that when we fired, at a range of less than seventy paces, we would hit that at which we aimed. The Baker, like the Paget carbines, were attached to our saddles by a sling on a swivel. As soon as we had fired, we could drop our guns and draw our swords.

As they neared us, I sensed the nervousness amongst the troop. In many ways, I did not blame them. The Chasseurs were riding hard and their sabres flashed in the air. The ground was shaking with the thunder of their hooves. As this was the first time they had faced an enemy in battle conditions it was worrying.

"Ready!"

I aimed at the head of the French officer's horse. My ball would not hit the head but, I hoped, would hit the rider's chest. My Baker would also rise when I fired.

"Fire!"

The sound of thirty-four guns was deafening and the French Chasseurs disappeared in a fog of powdery smoke. Some of the Light Dragoon's horses had bucked and reared. That all had kept their saddle was a miracle but showed me that they were horsemen. They were not yet cavalrymen but that would come. I drew my sword and shouted, "Bugler! Sound the charge!"

It would not be a charge for they were too close but we would be moving in the right direction, forward. As we charged through the smoke, I was already swinging my sword from behind me. When I saw the riderless horse of the officer, made distinctive by a white blaze, then I knew that one lead ball had found its mark. As luck would have it my swinging sword found the chest of the standard-bearer. I felt no guilt at the fact that he had no sword drawn for this was war and the NCO tumbled from his horse clutching the standard. As the smoke cleared and I was able to look around I saw more empty Chasseur saddles than Light Dragoons. The senior French NCO was the Brigadier and I heard him shout, "Fall back! We have done enough! Fall back! Someone pick up the standard!" I watched a rider lean from the saddle and pick up the standard by the flag.

I heard one Light Dragoon shout, as the Chasseurs disengaged, "After them boys!"

The Troop Sergeant roared, "Anyone who follows the Froggies is on a charge and will be cleaning up horse shit for a month! Secure the loose horses. Dixon, see if any of our lads are wounded." He smiled at me, "Nicely done, sir! That was straight off the training ground." He shook his head and added quietly, "Not that this shower of ladies has had any such training."

I looked around and saw that Captain Wilson looked almost shell shocked. I saw three embarrassed looking troopers who had been unhorsed, running after their horses. We had two men down while the French had lost five including their officer, standard bearer and sergeant. We had been lucky and the accuracy of two Bakers had saved the day. If we were to survive here then the captain needed to become better at his job.

After riding over to the standard-bearer and ascertaining that he had expired, I waved Captain Wilson over, "Have the men search the French dead, Captain. Any kind of papers might be useful."

"Sir."

"And Captain."

"Yes, sir?"

"You were lucky today. You lost a couple of men. The rest need to be trained to use their guns and their horses need to be acclimatised to gunfire."

"Yes, sir!" he looked chastened and I hoped that the lesson had been learned.

I saw that the Chasseurs had been the 15th. I had served in the 17th. It felt as though someone was walking over my grave.

When we reached the British lines, I saw that General Crauford had moved his headquarters so that he was almost sheltering beneath the guns of Almeida. I let Captain Wilson arrange for the burial of his men and I reported to the General. I told him what had happened and what I had discovered. He nodded, "I thought that they might have cavalry out. I have moved us here so that we can have protection from the Portuguese guns."

"Sir Arthur does not wish you to risk your command, sir."

"Major, I know that you are Sir Arthur's lackey but I command here. Do not fret, sir, I will not risk my men nor will I run like a dog with its tail between its legs just because a couple of Frenchmen appear." He pointed to the hilltop close to the Vale da Mula. "I have placed some of the 95th and 52nd there. We will have an early warning. Take a different squadron out tomorrow eh, they all seem a little new to this. You, at least, have experience."

And so, I spent each day riding on patrol with a different squadron. The next two days we were lucky for we saw no one but on the third day, when I was with D Troop, we ran into some Dragoons. Dragoons could fight dismounted and their muskets could cause casualties. I thought discretion was better than foolish valour and we retreated much to the chagrin of the troopers who felt their honour had been impugned.

That night I reported to General Crauford. "With your permission, General, tomorrow I will ride with just Sharp and we will get as close as we can to the French lines around Cuidad. All that we are leaning at the moment is that they have good cavalry and it is just disheartening the men."

"Risky, laddie, very risky!"

The Lines of Torres Vedras

"I don't think so, sir. We have good horses and we can use the hills for cover. I have an excellent telescope and I should be able to see how close they are to breaching the walls."

"Then they will breach them?"

"Nothing is more certain, sir. It is an ancient fortress and the Spanish guns are poor. The Lieutenant-General is a brave man but courage can only go so far when you are being attacked by French siege weapons. They will pound a hole in their walls and then pour through. The Spanish are even worse than the French when it comes to musketry."

He laughed, "Aye, you are right there. Very well then. It will give the horses the chance to rest."

Sharp and I were both relieved not to be nurse-maiding Light Dragoons and we used the hills to ride close to the siege lines knowing that the French would keep to the roads for they feared guerrillas. It was also much easier for the two of us as there was no need for unnecessary words and the silence helped us to see the land for there were no distractions. Approaching from the high ground which overlooked the fortress we were afforded a perfect view of the walls and the siege. We were relatively close but we had managed this because there were just two of us and not a troop of cavalry. We had heard the guns pounding almost as soon as we had travelled ten miles and, as I spied with the glass, I saw that they were having an impact on the walls because cracks had appeared already. The Spanish guns popped while the French boomed and the French attackers were not being hurt.

I dismounted to allow Donna to graze and I walked to the edge of the high ground for I wished to spy out their camp. The siege was interesting but it was the number of men who would attack and invade Portugal which was more relevant to Sir Arthur. I saw a large cavalry contingent but, once again, I only saw green uniforms. It was mainly Chasseurs and Dragoons. I could hear the quality of the artillery and when I looked at the siege lines, I saw the usual balance between light and heavy infantry. There were a few of Bonaparte's German allies.

"Sir, they have seen us!"

I put my telescope back in its leather tube and slung it around my back. Mounting Donna, I saw that a troop of Chasseurs had left the road and were now racing up the trail to reach us. We set off back towards the camp at a steady canter. The French horsemen would tire out their horses climbing the slope and we had seen side trails we could take when we had headed south-east to scout out the fortress. We deliberately rode along the skyline until I spied the little trail which followed the stream. Riding downhill, our horses found the going easier and I was happier for we were soon hidden by the bushes which grew there. The stream eventually found the Côa and we knew from our previous patrols that the sides were not too steep. I heard the Chasseurs' horses but they were not behind us. Instead, they rode the old trail which led along the escarpment. They faded long before we saw the river and the first of the British skirmishers.

"When we reach the camp, Sharp, I will write a report for Sir Arthur. I would have you deliver it tomorrow."

He nodded, "Will not Sir Robert be sending a report, too, sir?"

"He might but I am the one Sir Arthur called his eyes and ears; that means he expects me to report to him. Besides I have written a letter to Mrs de Lacey and you can take it with you."

He gave me a knowing glance. "Is that wise, sir?"

"Manners demands that I do so for the lady wrote to me and I am honour bound to reply." He nodded although I am not certain he understood what I meant.

I had wrestled with the letter for Mrs de Lacey's message had been quite clear and I did not wish to raise her hopes. I knew that my business was one with fine margins between life and death but I confess that I found the memory of her face and voice stirred me.

Sir Robert was concerned and it showed on his frowning forehead as I made my report. "The French, I think, will take Cuidad in the next few days, sir. The walls are fractured already and having been inside them I know it will not take long for the French to reduce them to rubble."

He nodded, "Then I will speak with General Cox in Almeida and write a report to Sir Arthur. By the by I have replaced the 52nd at Vale da Mula with some German horsemen and some of the 14th. Keep your eye on them, eh? We need men there who can move quickly."

I was pleased that Sir Robert appeared to be becoming more cautious. It was what Sir Arthur wanted.

Chapter 6

I rode out without Sharp the next day and I was with Captain Wilson again for there were fewer of the 14th in the main camp now that Sir Robert had sent a squadron to the village. I saw that his men looked more confident than they had and, as we rode, he said, "We have practised firing from the backs of our horses, sir. It is different here to back in England isn't it?"

He was right. In England, the ground where horsemen practised was flat and almost manicured. Here you rarely found flat ground.

We knew, almost as soon as we had passed the ruins of the old Spanish Fort Concepcion, that there was more activity from the French. Hitherto we had been halfway to Cuidad before we had found the French. The horsemen we encountered were within five miles of the Côa. This time, when we spied them, I had the troop dismount as the French would have to negotiate a slight rise before they reached us. I had the Troop spread out and use their horses to aid the accuracy of their carbines and to afford some protection to the troopers. The Paget was a good weapon but its range was little longer than a good pistol. I wanted to create the effect of a shotgun as the French Dragoons rode in column up the road. A Troop's thirty guns would be concentrated on the head of the column and more musket balls would be likely to hit.

The hooves thundered as the medium cavalry headed up the road to the dozen or so horses that they saw in the middle of the road. The undergrowth to the sides hid more than half of the men. There was less nervousness amongst the troopers for they had faced the French before and the French had fled. Of course, Dragoons were a different proposition. I waited until the head of the column was just fifty paces from us and then shouted," Fire!"

The smoke filled the ground between us but I actually heard the crack of lead on flesh and leather. There were screams, shouts and neighs from horses and men who were struck. A French voice shouted, "Ambush! Back!"

I called out, "Reload!"

I did not reload for I had two pistols ready. As the smoke thinned and cleared, I saw two dead Dragoons. They had borne the brunt of the fusillade and the rest of the horsemen were racing back down the road. I walked to the dead men and saw that they were the 25th Dragoons. The men of A Troop were, quite rightly, in ebullient mood.

I turned to the Troop Sergeant, "These were brave men; take their papers from them and then have them buried. I will find the time to let the French know that they are dead."

"Yes, sir." He nodded towards the retreating Dragoons. "These lads will fight better from now on, sir. This has been good for them."

I saw the grey hairs in the sergeant's moustache. He had been soldiering for a long time. "How long have you served, Sergeant?"

"I was with the Duke of York in the Low Countries, sir."

I nodded, "Then we both know that soldiers are like a good sword. Until they have been tempered in fire, they are unpredictable. These will get better but they will need to. We fight a clever enemy and it would be a mistake to underestimate them."

"Aye sir, but with Old Beaky and Black Bob, we'll be alright. Just so long as Boney stays in Paris we can handle the rest."

Good leaders inspired their men and I wondered just how inspired the French were under Masséna. We had just finished burying the Dragoons when one of the scouts drew our attention to a distant column of blue marching down the road. They were sending infantry. Did this mean that Cuidad had fallen?

"Captain Wilson, take the men back to camp and warn the outpost at Vale da Mula that infantrymen are coming."

"Yes, sir. What about you?"

"When you report to General Crauford tell him that I have ridden to Cuidad Rodrigo."

"On your own, sir?"

I smiled, "I am a big boy, Captain!"

To save time I boldly rode down the road. Firstly, it would allow me to see the French and, secondly, I could easily slip up into the hills to evade pursuit. I knew where I was going and all I was trying to do was ascertain if the fortress had fallen. As I neared the French column, I saw that it was a company of light infantry and I mentally cursed myself. We could have threatened them with the Light Dragoons. It was too late now. The French Dragoons had halted further down the road and when I saw them, I headed off up into the hills. Donna was the best horse I had seen thus far and even if the Dragoons pursued me, they would not catch her. I allowed her to open her legs and we soon reached higher ground. The Dragoons gave up the half-hearted pursuit that they had begun and I disappeared below the skyline. I could not see them and they could not see me but the difference was that I had a plan and a map in my head and they did not. Having completed this with Sharp I knew the trail which would take me close and allow me to see the fortress. Ominously, as I closed with the fortress, I could not hear the sound of big guns, just the crack and pop of muskets.

As I neared the viewpoint we had used previously, I walked Donna and took out my telescope. I did not need to expose myself this time and I rested my forearm on Donna's neck as I peered down at the fortress. The reason the guns had ceased became obvious; the French were assaulting the walls. The garrison would have been reduced already and, outnumbered by more than ten to one, it would fall. It explained why Masséna had sent his light infantry towards Almeida. I had no doubt that there were more of them on their way for he would have used his grenadiers and line infantry for the assault. The light infantry would do what the Dragoons could not do. They would go off the road and probe for weakness in the British defences. Turning my horse, I rode back to the camp.

It was dark when I arrived but Black Bob was not dining. He was poring over a map with his senior officers. Captain Wilson's warnings had had the desired effect. They looked up as I entered the tent. "Well, Matthews?"

"By, now, sir, Cuidad Rodrigo will be in French hands."

Colonel Barclay, of the 52nd, asked, "Does that mean we pull back now, sir? Sir Arthur made it quite clear that we were not to be risked."

The irascible Scot shook his head, "Damn your eyes, Barclay, who commands here, you or me? We will withdraw when I say. Major Matthews has seen, what, a battalion of Frenchmen?"

"A company, sir. The rest were still investing the fortress."

"There you have it. No, we wait for their main army and then we slip over the bridge. Well done Matthews, I would have you with the outpost at Vale da Mula for I trust your judgement."

Nodding, I left the meeting and headed to my tent. Sharp would not be back and there was little point in leaving in the dark. General Crauford was confident but I knew how fast the French could move when they chose. I knew that he had horse artillery and Light Dragoons guarding the road closer to Junca but the French cavalry had dash and élan. They would relish the opportunity to capture a whole division and that could be achieved if they took the bridge. Had I been in command I would have had two of the guns actually on the other side of the bridge! Even the six pounders they used would have a devastating effect on charging horsemen!

I decided against packing up everything for Vale da Mula was but a mile or so away and it would be easy enough to return to my tent for anything I had forgotten. I left early the next day and when I reached the outpost I discovered, as I had expected, that I was senior officer. The

German and Light Dragoons were each commanded by a Lieutenant and the 95th by a Captain. When I rode in, early the next morning, I saw the apprehension of the faces of the three officers. Captain Napier of the 95th said, "Sir, are you here to take command?"

I smiled and made light of it, "Good God no! I am General Wellesley's aide and I am here in an advisory role."

Despite my words and the smiles they gave me, they all knew that I was the one who could change any orders which they made. I hoped that my reputation would reassure them that I did not do things that way. I dismounted and after I had taken my saddlebags and Baker from the saddle, a Corporal from the 14th said, "I will take your horse, sir. A fine animal."

"You know your horses, Corporal, aye she is." I pointed towards Cuidad Rodrigo, "Gentlemen, I am here to tell you that the Spanish fortress is about to capitulate. We can expect skirmishers both mounted and on foot soon enough. As I said, I am not here to command but to advise and I advise you to let your men know that we have to be on our toes. When the fortress falls there will be 60,000 men coming down that road. We cannot stop them. We just warn General Crauford and get back to the bridge as quickly as we can!"

"Sir!"

They wasted no time and rushed off. An old Sergeant from the 95th was making a brew of tea and he nodded towards my Baker. "You were with Sir John Moore, as I recall, sir! On the retreat, I mean!"

"I was indeed."

"I remember you being given that gun, sir and, as I recall, you know how to use it."

"The Baker has saved my life more than once."

He nodded and, taking the clay pipe from his mouth, said, "You fancy a brew then, sir?"

"I do indeed."

While the piquets were forewarned I enjoyed a pleasant hour talking to another veteran from the retreat. What I knew was that while we had men like Sergeant Callow, the British Army would never be defeated. We could have as many mad officers like General Erskine who made totally irrational decisions but so long as the rank and file were made up of men such as this, we would emerge victorious; especially in an army led by Sir Arthur Wellesley and under the command of officers like General Crauford.

The officers arrived back an hour later and, nodding, the Sergeant left us. Captain Napier said, "We have less than fifty men, sir. What can we do?"

"We keep their skirmishers from getting too close but as soon as you see their Dragoons and hear the drums giving the *pas de charge* then you run. This is not a good position for you will lose men and you cannot win. If that sounds depressing then I cannot change it. We are the bell which rings when the door opens in the shop. Once the bell has rung then our job is done but know this, gentlemen, I shall be here until we run for our lives. Do not worry about the tents. They can be replaced. The brave men you lead are irreplaceable." I pointed to Sergeant Callow, "I have just had a pleasant chat to another who left with Moore but returned. Trust your men."

Sergeant Sharp arrived after dusk. There was a spare tent which I shared with Sharp although the Lieutenant of the Light Dragoons was surprised that I would bunk with an NCO. I did not bother to explain. Sharp brought good news. Sir Arthur had been reinforced and now had his army just over the border in Portugal. If we had to run there was safety close by. "You delivered my letter?"

"Yes, sir."

For some reason I was relieved. If I was killed at least the lady would have my words and that might at least give her comfort. "This is not a good position, Alan. I fear that the French will not play the game General Crauford expects. I know not when they will come but the French will come and they will come with thunder and lightning."

Sharp nodded, "Aye, sir, I expect you are right. I will fetch some clean clothes for you in the morning. You are a senior officer. You should look the part."

In the end, the French dallied and tarried far longer than I expected. A Spanish officer brought the news that the Spanish Lieutenant General had surrendered and that Cuidad had been invested by the French. In hindsight that was the time when General Crauford should have crossed the river but he did not. Sharp and I rode out each day. Every day brought more skirmishers. Sharp and I impressed Captain Napier with our skill. We joined his riflemen and both managed to bring down tirailleurs. The cavalry duelled with French Chasseurs. Honours were, generally, even but the small detachment did their job and they kept the French from viewing the positions of the Light Division. When the French Army, under Marshal Ney, finally arrived, that lack of intelligence proved vital. I was surprised when twelve days had passed and the French had still failed to launch a major attack. We did not relax our vigilant watch but keeping the men keen and alert was hard.

The attack, when it came, took even me by surprise. During the day, thick black clouds had rolled in and suggested not only rain but also a storm. The three officers had heeded my advice and we had good sentries keeping watch. When the thunder and lightning began it was so violent that it woke me and I rose and dressed. I could not sleep through such a storm with the rain positively bouncing off the canvas. Sharp rose too and, after donning our cloaks we hurried to the horse lines to see that our horses were safe. The Light Dragoon Corporal who had admired Donna was there. I had learned that Corporal Foster was a true horseman. He was singing to the horses. The song was a north country one and had calmed the horses. I did not interrupt him but nodded.

My oiled cloak had a hood and it protected my head. I went, with Sharp, to view the road from the ruins of Fort Concepcion. The thunder had rumbled away and now it was incessant rain which pounded down. The rifleman we saw, smoking his pipe with the bowl upside down to keep it dry, nodded as we neared him, "Well, sir, this will keep Johnny Frenchmen indoors eh?"

Just then I glimpsed a movement and heard hooves. There was no real reason to suspect that the French were here but I could think of no other explanation for hooves. I shouted, "Stand to! Bugler sound call to arms." I did not have my Baker but I had two pistols and I pulled one and aimed at the shadows I saw moving towards us. The Dragoon was just ten paces from me when my ball hit his chest and threw him from his horse. As he fell, he dragged his horse around and brought down another rider. The Rifleman fired his rifle blindly into the dark and another horseman fell.

I turned, "Back to camp! This is a major attack! Captain Napier, pull your men out!" I had spoken each night of what we needed to do and I prayed that my orders were obeyed.

The sounds of our shots were enough to awaken the camp and thanks to my warning the men were ready. The cracks of rifles punctuated the air. I had one unfired pistol and I kept it levelled as we hurried back to the camp. I heard bugles, not only close by but down by the river. Sir Robert had been forewarned and I hoped that there were men already pouring across the river to safety. The horsemen were saddling their horses. Sharp would saddle our two and so I went to our tent to grab our Baker rifles. Emerging I glanced to the east. This was July and soon it would be dawn. That would give us a better picture of what we faced. The sound of the Baker rifles was now augmented by the sound of the French muskets. It was as I had thought, this was a major attack and there were infantrymen with the cavalry.

It was the 95th Rifles which were buying us time for, during the day, there were always mounted horsemen but at night the horses were tied up and now needed to be saddled. Sharp had saddled Donna for me and I attached my Baker to the sling. I mounted my horse and held Sharp's

Baker for him. Some of the Light Dragoons and German Hussars were already mounted and so I shouted, "Form a skirmish line and support the Rifles! The 95th will withdraw!"

When Sharp had saddled his horse, I gave him his Baker and spurred Donna. I found the bugler of the 14th. "Stand by me! When I give the order sound the withdraw."

"Sir."

The French attack was a major one but it was in the dark and there was confusion. That saved lives. I fired my pistol at the Chasseur who charged at the three of us with his sword waving above his head. I had seen it before. It was the thought of a moment of glory but it ended when my ball punched him from his saddle. I was confident that the 95th would be withdrawing down to the main camp. They would do it in pairs of men. One would fire while the other ran and reloaded. It was very effective but such a retreat could only be carried out by the most highly skilled of men. I saw that most of the German Hussars and Light Dragoons were mounted and I shouted to those who were the closest, "Use your carbines."

I holstered my used pistol and picked up the Baker. It was loaded and I quickly primed it and looked for a target. I heard the tramp of feet. There was a French column marching towards us.

Turning to the bugler I said, "Sound the withdraw!"

The command meant that the horsemen would fire and fall back in good order rather than a wild gallop. The night which had been our enemy and allowed the French to get close now came to our aid. Until dawn broke, we could fire at any who came down the road and know that they were an enemy. Carbines cracked in the dark and I heard the clash of steel on steel as horsemen duelled from the backs of horses. I fired at a Dragoon and wounded him. Sharp kept his rifle pointed at the French as I drew a saddle pistol. We began to back down the road. The tramp of feet became more insistent and I saw the dark shadow take form as false dawn came. It was a French column.

"Bugler, sound the retreat!"

By my estimate, we had bought General Crauford some forty-odd minutes. That would have given the Division the opportunity to load our guns and for the General to begin the withdrawal across the narrow bridge and the river. We headed down the road towards Almeida. I had with me Sharp, the bugler and two Light Dragoons. As far as I knew we were the last to leave the camp. The French horsemen had been distracted by the camp and when they had searched it for whatever loot they could find it bought us a valuable few minutes. When I heard the thunder of hooves, I knew that we had lost that lead. I glanced over my shoulder and saw some French Hussars charging down the road. Donna could have outrun the Hussars but I was not sure that the Light Dragoons could.

"Turn and disperse these horsemen!"

I had one saddle pistol left and I drew and fired as I turned. The flash from the muzzle showed me that there were just five Hussars. I holstered the spent pistol and drew my sword. I was barely in time for the officer who led the French was sweeping his sabre at me. My longer blade took him by surprise and he reeled. I had been fighting from the back of a horse for a long time and I used that experience. As the officer reeled, I whipped Donna's head around. She snapped at the smaller horse of the Hussar and I used the hilt of my sword to punch the Frenchman in the face. It was a powerful blow and his eyes rolled back in his head as he slipped from the saddle.

The bugler was struggling to deal with the Hussar he was fighting and it might have gone ill. As Sergeant Sharp's pistol took out one of the Hussars my sword hacked across the arm of the bugler's assailant. His sword fell and I shouted, "Quickly now, to Almeida and its walls!"

General Cox was our only hope for he had men and guns manning the walls. We hurtled along the road to the shelter of Almeida's imposing walls. Glancing behind me I saw that the sun was about to peer above the skyline but even without it, I counted at least three French columns. Ahead of them were the light horsemen and skirmishers. By my estimate, there were already almost as many Frenchmen heading for the small bridge as General Crauford had in his whole division.

We were the last to reach Almeida. I saw that the three officers had all reached safety but the numbers they led was a testament to their losses. The two cavalry regiments were there and their colonels were forming lines. I could leave my detachments. Waving my sword, I shouted, "Well done, the defenders of Vale da Mula. You have done your duty and I shall tell the General so."

There was a ragged cheer from the survivors. They had acquitted themselves well but they had lost tent mates.

I saw that rather than crossing the Côa the infantry battalions were being deployed across the hills. I turned to Sharp, "What is the General thinking? The French will cut them to pieces when they bring up their artillery!"

To my horror, I saw that Captain Stewart and his company of the 95th, as well as the two guns of the Royal Horse Artillery, had been overrun. One-third of our artillery had been lost. When I reined in at the camp, I saw that Black Bob was barking out orders. When he saw me reining in, he said, "What is it, Matthews? How many do we face?"

I pointed behind me, "General, the whole of Marshal Masséna's army is coming down that hill. There are at least five regiments of horse and I have seen light infantry, Chasseurs and line infantry. All that is lacking is his artillery and when they come …"

"Damn! I have been humbugged. It was the storm for who would have thought that the French would attack under such a cover?"

I said nothing but the French were not stupid. British and Portuguese firepower would be negated by rain while the French columns rarely fired their muskets anyway and relied on sheer weight of numbers. I could now see, as dawn broke on a grey and dank day, that the French had done just that.

"How many men do you estimate, Matthews?"

I had the advantage that I was still mounted and had my telescope. I scanned the hillsides and did a quick count. "I estimate thirteen battalions of foot, sir. That would be six thousand men and here look to be two cavalry brigades; that would be almost three thousand cavalrymen. There are close to ten thousand men attacking us."

"Good God man, they outnumber us by three to one! Captain Jameson, get the baggage and cannons across the bridge."

"Sir."

"Major, ride to Brigadier General Anson and ask him if he can stop the French cavalry from disputing the river."

"Sir." His senior aide leapt onto the back of his horse and raced to the brigade of cavalry.

Even as Sharp and I turned our horses I heard the General shout, "Lieutenant Durham, have the 52nd and 43rd begin to pull back to the road!"

This had all the hallmarks of a disaster. Had the General begun to withdraw when the French attacked then most of his army would already be over the Côa and ready to defend an unfordable river. As it was, he was asking eight hundred cavalrymen to hold off almost three times their number, uphill! The guns of Almeida were now firing but, as we neared the cavalry brigade, I realised that they were missing more than they hit and, worse, the French horse artillery had now joined in.

I reined in next to Brigadier General Anson, "General Crauford's compliments, sir, and can you stop the French horse from preventing us crossing the bridge?"

He laughed, "You are a horseman, Matthews, and you know the futility of that." He rubbed his chin. "Still if we form two lines then they might think that we are mad enough to charge them."

"Yes sir, and if I might suggest that we have the men use their carbines."

"Damned useless, aren't they?"

I shrugged, "General Paget found them useful on the retreat under Sir John Moore."

"Worth a try." He turned to his bugler. "Have the brigade form two lines on me!"

The cavalry had been in a compact formation until then but as soon as they spread out, we formed an obstacle which hid the infantry whilst allowing Almeida's guns to continue to fire. The French were four hundred paces from us. The infantry would not attack for they risked us making a charge. I saw the cavalry forming up to charge us. Half of the French were Dragoons and the other half Hussars and Chasseurs. They moved down the hill to be closer to us for they knew the range of our carbines was short. Captain O'Hare and his company of rifles had been badly handled but he brought the survivors to form a skirmish line in front of us. Sharp and I loaded our Bakers.

General Anson asked, "Can you use that thing, Matthews?"

"Yes, sir!" And as if to prove it I aimed at a Hussar who had broken ranks and was galloping towards the skirmish line. The riflemen had already popped off a few shots and wounded a couple of Frenchmen. I fired at the Hussar and my ball managed to hit his boot. He was a good horseman and he wheeled his horse around to return to their lines. The Brigade cheered. It seemed to rouse the French and I heard them order a charge.

"Ready carbines!"

While the Bakers popped away the horses closed with us. When the Brigadier shouted, "Fire!" Eight hundred carbines sent their balls towards the enemy. It stopped them but only because no horseman likes to charge into a fog. The ground, although flattish, still had rocks and hollows which could unhorse a rider or break a charger's leg. I heard them sound the recall. Only eight French horsemen had been hit and all but three crawled and crept back to their lines. I reloaded and looked for a target I could hit. I saw that the French general had moved his men back out of range of the Bakers.

Lieutenant Durham galloped up, "Brigadier, General Crauford says that the cavalry can withdraw across the river now."

"Thank God for that. Captain O'Hare, thank you for your assistance now get across the bridge."

"Yes, sir!"

He turned to me, "And thank you, Major. Will you be crossing with us?"

"I doubt it, sir, the General will need me to liaise with the infantry."

"Good luck then!"

The Lines of Torres Vedras

I took out my telescope and scanned the horizon. All that I could see were columns of blue-coated Frenchmen. There were grenadiers, fusiliers, voltiguers and the Chasseurs de la Siège who were renowned for their skill in assaulting buildings. It did not bode well for the defenders of the bridge.

"Matthews, be a good fellow and tell Colonels Barclay and Beckwith that they can begin to withdraw their brigades towards the bridge."

The General was doing his best to extract as many men across the bridge as he could but it was not the men who would cause the problems, it was the wagons for the bridge was narrow and required a skilled driver to negotiate it.

The two colonels were close together discussing the situation. They saw me gallop up and Lieutenant Colonel Beckwith said, "The General is cutting it fine, Matthews. Does he wish us to withdraw?"

"He does, sir."

While the two colonels, both veterans, gave the orders which would make for an efficient and calm withdrawal I took out my glass again. The four battalions were in a two-deep line with the 95th before them. The French cavalry knew better than to try to charge them. With one end anchored at Almeida and protected by the guns, the other end was close to the river. I heard the drums as whichever general was in command, from a prisoner we later discovered it was Loison, decided to use brute force and send three columns of two thousand men to batter their way through. The 52nd was sent to the right of the line to secure it while the 43rd anchored the left. The 1st and 3rd Caçadores were in the centre.

Colonel Beckwith shouted, "The 1st and 3rd Caçadores will retire by company to the bridge. 95th you will cover the gap in the centre."

The instructions were clear and they were, in the circumstances, the correct ones, however, as is usual in these matters fate intervenes. First of all, the Chasseurs de la Siège and 32nd Light Infantry launched a charge at the centre of our line. The Portuguese had just vacated it and the 95th just had their shorter Baker rifles with the unwieldy sword bayonet to fight off Frenchmen with the longer Charleville musket and deadly bayonet. It was an unequal contest. At the same time, I heard a shout from the bridge and, as I turned, I saw that a wagon had overturned and blocked it. The third factor was that the 3rd Caçadores thought that it was their turn to cross the bridge and they ran. The 52nd and 43rd had left the hill and were walking backwards to safety,

I shouted to Colonel Beckwith, "Colonel, the bridge is blocked!"

"Damn!" Half of the British battalions had vacated the side of the hill and I saw that the French were in danger of turning the 52nd.

"Sharp! Draw your sword and let us see how many of the Rifles we can save."

"Sir!"

I wrapped my reins around my leg and drew a pistol and a sword. I galloped Donna up the hill. She had had a rest and was a good horse. The Chasseurs de la Siège and the Tirailleurs were winning the battle of the hillside, however, thundering horses have a tendency to terrify light infantrymen and the hooves of our horses made a couple of Frenchmen falter so that the riflemen fighting them were able to escape. I fired at point-blank range into the back of a Chasseur about to bayonet a wounded rifleman lying on the ground. His partner picked him up as Sharp skewered the other Frenchman. I slashed down at an officer who tried to swing his sword at Donna's head. Wheeling my mount, I whirled to flail the ground around me with her hooves. The Frenchmen fell back and a Rifle lieutenant shouted, "Fall back! Fall back!"

Sharp and I seemed to bear a charmed life although we were aided by the fact that the Frenchmen had all fired their weapons and they had yet to reload. I rode at one light infantryman and as he raised his musket, I swept my sword at his bayonet. Donna struck him with a hoof and he fell to the ground. It was as we turned to ride down the hill that I saw the red hair which told me that the marshal who commanded this army was Marshal Ney. Now I understood how they had come so close to victory. Ney was a good general! He was reckless but as brave as any and I knew that his men would follow him anywhere.

We had almost reached the bridge and Colonel Beckwith was with his adjutant trying to help organise his companies when Lieutenant Durham galloped up, "Colonel, the General says that the French are about to turn the 52nd. He wants you to retake the hill!"

Colonel Beckwith said, "The hill we have just left!"

"Yes, sir."

The Colonel nodded. There were a dozen or so wounded soldiers patiently waiting their turn to cross the bridge. "Sergeant Bee, watch my horse for me! 43rd Foot, reload and fix bayonets. Centre companies to the fore!"

I dismounted and said to the Sergeant, "If you would watch Donna for me too, eh, Sergeant?"

"Of course, sir."

As much as I wanted to take my Baker, I would not be able to reload it and so I made do with two pistols, primed and loaded in my belt. I drew a pistol. The Colonel smiled, "Damned decent of you, Major."

I saw that Sharp had handed his horse to the wounded men and he shrugged, "I will have to keep my eye on you, I suppose, sir!"

The Lines of Torres Vedras

The Colonel took his place at the right of the line so I went to the left. We would not be taking the colours and Sergeant Bee watched those as well. Ironically the fleeing Portuguese had aided us for the French had thought we were routing and they began to advance down the hillside. In doing so they exposed their flank to us. I think they thought we were beaten and by every military rule, we were. The men we led did not think so and when the Colonel said, "The 43rd will advance!" the men stepped forward as though this advance was expected.

When I had been on Donna my battle had encompassed the whole of the hillside. Now as I walked next to the elite company it was narrowed to the hill before us and the French column. I had my pistol in my right hand and so I swung my left to give me the rhythm. The Colonel knew his business and when we were just eighty paces from the French who seemed oblivious to our presence he shouted, "Halt!" His stentorian tones meant that the French did turn but by then it was too late. "Sergeant Major!"

"Front rank, present! Fire!" I raised my first pistol and fired along with the front rank of the elite company. The French disappeared in a fog of smoke.

"Reload! Second rank, present! Fire!"

I fired my second pistol and then stuck it in my belt. I drew my sword as Colonel Beckwith shouted, "Charge!"

We all roared and screamed and ran as one into the smoke we had just created. I looked down for I knew that there would be bodies before us and there were. I needed fancy footwork to avoid them. I saw a blue uniform and brought my sword down. The Frenchman saw my blade and tried to block it with his Charleville Musket. All it did was to deflect it down the barrel to hack into his shoulder. The 43rd slashed, stabbed and clubbed the Frenchmen. Those with unfired muskets emptied them into the mass of blue bodies and, miraculously, the French ran. They outnumbered us but as with all battles you only saw what was before you and the French saw a wall of red and they fled!

Colonel Beckwith was no fool and he shouted, "The 43rd will retire in good order to the bridge."

I had the luxury of being superfluous and I looked through the fog of war to the bridge. The 52nd were already crossing and that left just us to join them. Had any French officer had the wherewithal then they would have ordered their cavalry to fall upon our flanks but their cavalry had been worn down by ours and were now just watching proceedings. Infantry took bridges, not cavalry. How we managed it I shall never know but we did and we reached the camp and mounted our horses. The Colonel said, "Sergeant Bee, take the wounded over the bridge!"

Grinning he said, "Yes sir!"

The Colonel smiled, "Good man that. Thank you, Major, for your assistance and now, if you don't mind, I shall be the last to leave this field of battle."

"Of course, Colonel and you have earned that honour!"

Chapter 7

I was weary beyond words as I walked Donna into the camp. We later learned that we had lost almost 600 men out of a force of three thousand. They were not all killed, of course. The killed was a relatively low number but some of the wounded would be lost to the regiments and battalions. One armed and one-legged soldiers were of little use. There would be men who were lost, trapped behind the enemy lines. The French artillerymen who had tried to take our horses were a good example of that. The fact that a fifth of the Light Division was not available weakened Sir Arthur's army. We had lost the battle but as Marshal Ney had attacked with 20,000 men that was not a surprise.

I went directly to Sir Arthur's quarters for he had taken over a house in a small village just ten miles from the border. He glanced up from his papers as I walked in and he spoke without looking at me, "You were damned lucky, Matthews! Had we lost the Light Division then it would have been your head on the block." I couldn't say that the decision not to fall back sooner was Black Bob's as Sir Arthur had given me clear instructions. I just took my medicine. "However, all is not lost and I think honours were about even. As for Almeida…"

"You do not think they can hold out, sir?"

"I hope that they can but Cuidad fell within a week or so. Cox is a good man but …," he shrugged, "Who knows? I am just grateful that I have more men arriving and the defences north of Lisbon are almost complete. We shall humbug Masséna, eh?"

"And my orders, sir?"

"You deserve a night's rest but tomorrow see if the French have crossed the Côa. I doubt that they will be that foolish but if they have then we can turn and give them a bloody nose!" I was dismissed.

Sharp had been his usual diligent and efficient self. When I emerged, he was waiting with the good news that he had found us a room in a house. His Portuguese had come on in leaps and bounds. Unlike most British soldiers whose idea of a foreign language was to articulate every English word as slowly and loudly as possible whilst gesticulating like a semaphore, Alan Sharp spoke to them and smiled while he did so. It meant we would sleep in relative comfort.

"Back to the Côa tomorrow, Sharp, although this time we just have to watch."

"Aye, sir. We were lucky at the bridge and no mistake; that was a bad place to be caught." Sharp was an experienced soldier. We had both been fighting long enough to recognise death traps when we saw them.

"I don't think anyone expected Marshal Ney to attack during a thunderstorm."

He laughed as he cut into the bread we had just bought, "Clever move though, sir. The rain and the thunder hid the sound of their hooves and it made our powder wet! I thought Spain and Portugal were supposed to be hot countries!"

"As we are learning, Alan, they are not."

The weather changed again the next day and the grey clouds disappeared to be replaced by fluffier white ones. They were the kind we liked for they afforded some relief from the sun as they sent patches of shade across the Portuguese hills. Sir Arthur had piquets a mile from the village and I stopped to speak to the Lieutenant, "Any signs of the French, Lieutenant?"

"No, sir."

I nodded and pointed towards Valverde, a small hill village to the north, "I intend to scout out that area. Keep an eye out for us when we return just in case we have some green coated friends behind us."

The Lieutenant was young and he asked, "Green coated, sir?"

I saw his sergeant roll his eyes and it was he who answered for me, "Chasseurs, Lieutenant Chadwick, French cavalry! Don't you worry, Major Matthews, we will be primed and ready."

"You know me, Sergeant?"

"Yes, sir, we were at Talavera and saw you and that rifle of yours!" I realised that my usefulness as a spy would be negated if the French began to notice the unusual officer on the battlefield for no other cavalry officer carried a Baker!

We headed towards Valverde which lay just two and a half miles from the river. More importantly, there was a road of sorts which overlooked the bridge and, indeed, joined the road to the bridge. It would be a good place to discover if the French had crossed the river without risking ourselves. We were in Portugal and the Portuguese were fiercely antagonistic towards the French who tended to behave abominably when they occupied a country. We were welcomed by the menfolk in the centre of the huddle of eight houses. These were farmers and they said that they had not seen any French soldiers. That was a good sign and we left the village to take the road which twisted towards the river in a hopeful mood. Two miles after we had left the village, we saw the bridge to the northeast. We dismounted and I took out my glass. There were French soldiers at the bridge and I saw that they also had a couple of small calibre cannon which would be loaded with grapeshot. There were tents on the other side of the bridge and I estimated that the French had a

The Lines of Torres Vedras

company of light infantry and a couple of gun crews. There would be a hundred and fifty men there.

"We need a closer look, Sharp. I want to scout out the road into Portugal. The French can't use this as their guns and wagons would struggle to get up this slope."

I remounted and we made our way towards the road which led to the bridge. It was a stone road but it had been made by using gravel pounded on the rougher stones beneath. The men who used it would have no problem when driving their sheep and cattle but wheeled vehicles could easily become stuck. In addition, it not only twisted and turned, but the gradient was also so steep in places that Sharp and I had to lean back a long way to stay in the saddle. It was still not noon but the white fluffy clouds had all but disappeared and the hot sun was beating down; our relief had evaporated. We stopped where the road twisted to the southwest, away from the river, to take some shelter in the stand of pines. We dismounted and gave our horses some water first before having some ourselves. It was then we heard the altercation. There were raised voices and they were French. As they came from below us, I realised that they were at the river and when the voices became silent, I could hear the river. The twisting road had deceived us and we were closer to the bottom that I had thought. We both grabbed our Baker rifles and cocked them.

Leaving our tethered horses, we headed down the slope, through the trees to the river. The trees ended and we stopped in their shelter. Below us, I saw the road we had taken when we had retreated from Marshal Ney. I glimpsed blue uniforms but also red. There were British soldiers down there as well as French. There was cover between us and the uniforms I could see but it was bushes and long grasses. I took off my cocked hat and jammed it in my frock coat. Sharp wore green and I hoped that we could get closer without being seen. I did not risk my telescope but used my naked eye. I counted six French soldiers and at least two red ones. Had Sir Arthur been there he would have told me to return to our horses and go back to camp, however, that was not my way and I could not leave British soldiers as prisoners.

"Alan, there are British lads down there. What say we go and turn the tables on their captors?"

He nodded, "Good idea sir!"

"Follow my lead."

We had fought together so many times now that my sergeant could almost anticipate me. We slipped from the shade of the hillside and moved, bent double, as we darted from shrub to shrub. We found ourselves in a little hollow and I lost sight of the blue but I could hear the voices for they were much closer now. A French soldier was questioning the redcoats who could not understand a word that was being said. They were too far away to hear every word but the occasional one I did hear gave me the gist. As we climbed from the hollow their voices became clearer. I had fixed their position when we descended but moving from bush to bush and scurrying through grass meant I was not totally certain any more where they were.

Then I heard a shout. The French voice almost screamed, "Tell me where your army has gone or I will shoot you!"

The Welsh voice which answered told me that in all likelihood he was one of the 43rd, the Monmouthshire regiment. "I have told you before that we don't speak your babble! Johnno has a wound, now can you see to him?"

The French voice said, "Prepare your muskets. We will shoot this one and the others will talk."

We had no time to lose and I waved Sharp to the right while I climbed the slope. I saw a large bush above me and I headed to it. As I reached it, I saw that I was behind the Frenchmen and the three British soldiers were on the ground. One was lying on his back while the other two were seated. The French corporal had his five men in a rough firing squad; they were priming their muskets which were aimed at the defiant Welshman. I took in that they were a hundred paces from me and that Sharp was working his way around their flank. The redcoat who had been pleading for his wounded comrade was staring belligerently at the firing squad. He knew he was going to die but he would not show fear. I put on my cocked hat and I began to move from the shelter of the shrub.

Keeping my rifle hidden, I shouted, in French, "Put down your weapons for I wish to question the prisoners."

The French soldiers all turned at the sound of my voice and what they saw, by his sword and cocked hat, was an officer in a blue frock coat. They hesitated and that allowed me to get closer.

The Voltigeur corporal shouted, "Who are you, sir, and where did you come from? We are the most forward unit."

I kept moving, my right hand behind my back holding my rifle and my left hand on the hilt of my sword. Adopting the haughtiest voice I could I said, "You dare to question an officer, Corporal!"

He was a tough soldier and he began to raise his musket, "Sir, if you do not answer me then I will shoot."

Just then one of the other soldiers shouted, "Corporal, I know him! He is an Englishman. He was with those who charged us up the hill!"

The most dangerous of the six was the Corporal for he had his musket almost horizontal. I brought around my Baker and fired at his chest. I was just forty paces from him and I blew a hole in him. Sharp's rifle cracked and the man who had recognised me had his face splattered all over the other four. Dropping the Baker, I drew two pistols and aimed them at the four remaining soldiers who looked shocked.

"My men have their weapons aimed at you and as you can see, I hit that at which I aim. Drop your muskets or you will die!"

They saw Sharp appear with his Baker aimed at them and they obeyed. The Welshman grinned, "Who are you, sir?"

"Major Matthews. Now disarm those chaps, we will have to move quickly. There are more troops at the bridge."

He nodded, "I know sir, that is how they caught us. We had to cross the river. Poor Harry Jenkins was swept downstream and when we crawled out these bastards were waiting for us. The bastard kicked Jones' wounded leg, sir! It was not right!" He kicked the dead French corporal and it was then I saw that the Welshman had had his nose broken. That must have been the shout which first alerted us. I holstered one of my pistols.

I looked at the other two. They were both young and one had a bloody leg. He would have to be carried. I turned to the Frenchmen. "Take the coats off your dead comrades and give them to me." I said, "Sharp, load my Baker eh?"

The Welshman brought over the six muskets. I took the coats from the Frenchman and said, "What is your name, Private?"

"Private Williams sir, 43rd Monmouths sir."

"Use these coats and four of the muskets to make a litter. You and your pal can have the other two muskets and the Frenchmen can carry your wounded friend. There is a village just up the hillside but we have to be quick."

One of the Frenchmen looked back at the river and I lifted my pistol to point it at him. "My friend, I only need two men to carry the wounded redcoat and I will shoot you in a heartbeat!" His shoulders sagged and he nodded.

Private Williams had finished making the litter and said, "How come you speak such good Frog, sir?"

I grinned, "Practice! Now put your wounded man on the stretcher. Sharp, you are the rearguard."

"Sir!" He handed me my Baker and I holstered my pistol.

I said to the four Frenchmen, "Pick up the litter and carry him carefully." I said to Williams, "You and your oppo keep an eye on them. I will lead the way. Jones, just hang on and we will get you looked at."

"Thanks, sir, but don't worry about me! I am just happy that I won't be a prisoner."

"I can't promise you that as there are a hundred and fifty Frenchmen just half a mile along the river."

I could rely on Sharp who knew how to keep a good watch. What I worried about was the four Frenchmen. If they chose to drop the litter and run then the odds were that a couple might escape. As I worked my way back to the pines, I tried to work out what the French would do. They would have heard the firing and sent a patrol to see what was happening. This battalion was the 32nd Light Infantry and they were a good unit. Light infantry could move as quickly over rough ground as horses. They would reach the dead bodies and then search for tracks. By my reckoning, we had half an hour start for they would find our footprints and follow us. We had killed two of their own and they would be out for vengeance.

We had travelled half a mile through the thin trees when two of the Frenchmen stumbled. To be fair to them it was rough ground and they had kept up a good pace. I said, "A short rest and then we move on. Williams watch them!"

I went back to Sharp. He was standing at a spot where he could see the river and the place we had spotted the Frenchmen. He pointed, "There are ten of them sir and they are looking for our footprints."

I looked where he had pointed and saw them. "And they will catch us." I looked at the ground. The recent rain had made the ground muddy and our footprints stood out. "Alan, walk south for a hundred yards and then walk backwards to here. Let us make them think that we have split up. I will do the same to the northeast." Although it wasted three valuable minutes, I thought it might buy us ten, at least. They would see that we had split into three and might fear an ambush. They would have to split up themselves and investigate.

We hurried back to the others. I said, in French, "You have rested enough so no more slips."

One of the Frenchmen said, "We are thirsty!"

I knew that they were buying time. They understood more English than they were letting on. They had canteens on their belts. "Then when we get to the village you can drink! Now move."

I led the way and I kept up a more punishing pace for they had rested. When we emerged from the trees, I saw our horses. The road, rough as it was would be easier going than the slope we had just ascended.

"Lay the stretcher down. Jones, you are going to get a lesson in riding. Williams, hold my horse's head." Sharp had arrived and I said, "Keep an eye on the French!" I put Jones' good leg in the stirrup and then gently raised his leg over Donna's rump. I could see from his face that it had hurt him but he was a British soldier and he said not a word. I handed him the reins. "Donna is a gentle horse and she will not let you fall. Just hold on, eh?"

"Yes, sir."

"Williams put the litter over the saddle of Sergeant Sharp's horse and lead it for we shall need those muskets before too long." When all was done, I said, "Now we run!" I changed to French. "You are French Light Infantry and I have seen you run. Follow this road and know that there are three guns in your backs and I have my sword, it is sharp."

The sound of boots and hooves alerted the villagers and when they saw the four Frenchmen, they grabbed spades and weapons to defend themselves.

I shouted in Portuguese, "Do not fear, these men are our prisoners but we have a wounded man here." I turned to Sharp, "Take the guns from your horse and ride back. I want advance warning of the French."

One of the villagers, he looked like the headman, came over to me, "My wife knows about wounds. She will look after your soldier. Then do we kill these Frenchmen?"

I shuddered for he had a look on his face which suggested that the deaths would not be quick. "We will see. There are four muskets there for you and the other villagers. Load them and keep them pointed at the prisoners."

Williams and I helped Jones from the saddle and we half carried him to the hut where the woman waved to us. "You stay with him, Williams." I turned to the other man, "What is your name?"

He smiled, "Same as my cousin Gareth, I am Private John Williams, sir. They call me 22456."

That was typical of Welsh regiments. "The villagers will keep an eye on the prisoners and I want you to supervise them. Don't let them kill them... not yet anyway!"

"Sir!"

I went to the Frenchmen who had suddenly remembered that they had canteens and they were drinking. I knelt next to them, "I want to know who is at Almeida."

The most belligerent of the men, the one who had said they were thirsty, shook his head, "We will tell you nothing for we are not traitors and you cannot make us."

"Do not let this officer's uniform fool you, my friend." I pulled my stiletto from my boot, "I have slit throats often enough with this so that four dead Frenchmen will not worry me and I will lose no sleep over your deaths but I do not have to do anything." I pointed at the four Portuguese with the muskets aimed at them. "They have already asked me if they can kill you. I said I would let them know. So, you either tell me all that I need to know or I hand you over to them and we will join our army."

He shook his head for he knew that the Portuguese would give him the most painful of deaths and he began to tell me all that he knew. It merely confirmed much of what I already knew. I had the names of at least two of the marshals but he added the names of the other generals and the makeup of the army. It was rough numbers only. However, what I did learn that was valuable, was that the French were short of bullocks, wagons and food. The Portuguese roads would be a nightmare for them as they would have to use men to haul the guns over the roads.

I heard hooves and Sergeant Sharp came galloping in. "They have found our trail, sir, and they are half a mile behind me. There are twelve of them."

"Get your horse out of sight and fetch Williams. He is in the hut over there." I went to the headman, "I am sorry but I have brought trouble to your village. There are twelve Frenchmen coming up the road. I would fight them!"

"Then we will help you."

"Good, 22456, tie these prisoners, hand and foot. Leave them here."

Williams and Sharp emerged, "Find cover. We will use these four for bait." I turned to the four Portuguese, "This is your village, take cover. When I shout fire then you fire but not before! Understand!"

The headman grinned, "Yes Captain! We will obey you and kill Frenchmen!"

I saw that the French were tied up. "One word from any of you and you die first!" More Portuguese had emerged from their huts with fowling pieces and ancient bladed weapons. The Frenchmen nodded.

I shouted to the Portuguese, "Take cover and obey my orders!"

Sharp was behind a wall on the left of the track and I took the wall on the right. I rested my Baker upon it. The rest of my motley crew were spread out and I saw that all were hidden. None of us wore hats. I heard the French light infantrymen as they huffed and puffed up the track. Their boots crunched and slipped on the gravelly track. Sharp and I had range but the Portuguese and the two Williams had the Charleville musket and we would need to wait until they were within fifty paces before we could open fire. It was a sous-lieutenant who led the light infantry and behind him came an old moustache, a veteran. He was the real leader. They came in skirmish order for that was their way. As soon as they saw the four prisoners the sous-lieutenant shouted, "We have them!" and he began to run. "Follow me!"

The old moustache shouted, "No!" but it was too late. The men had obeyed orders and followed the young officer.

I hated to do it but I aimed at the old soldier and when the French officer was fifty paces away, I shouted, "Fire!" The two Baker rifles, six French muskets and the ancient fowling-pieces acted like a huge shotgun. The crack, flames and smoke were concentrated on the narrow path. My ball entered the skull of the veteran. He did not suffer but that was not true of the rest. The Portuguese rose from their hiding places and raced at the dead, dying and wounded Frenchmen. All had been hit but the ones who had died were the lucky ones as the rest were simply butchered. I heard vomiting and when I turned saw two of the French prisoners. It was not simply revulsion, they feared for their lives!

As the smoke cleared the Portuguese tired of their bloody vengeance on the invaders and began to strip the bodies. "You know that if the French find these bodies then you will suffer. You can come with us if you wish."

The headman smiled, "They will find nothing for not even their blood will remain. I wish to thank you, Captain, for you have given us back honour. When last the French came, they sullied and abused our young women. The young men were hanged and we did nothing for we feared for our own lives. We vowed then that we would not bow down again and, thanks to you, we have not done so. We will hide these weapons and when they come, we will plead ignorance but we will be prepared to sell our lives dearly!"

"Then good luck and may God watch over you!"

Sharp let Jones ride his horse and we made our way back to the army and our camp. We passed the camp of the 43rd and there was delight at the return of the three men. Colonel Beckwith shook my hand, "The regiment is indebted to you Major."

"They are good men and I think that Jones should recover."

He nodded, "There were eighty-three men missing from the division. Now there are just seventy-nine. I wonder how many more of my men survive?"

"I would not hold out hope, sir. These were lucky, although the river crossing cost them one man the French will be on the alert now and they will reinforce the bridge."

General Wellesley was delighted with the intelligence and the prisoners. "Good work, Matthews." A new aide had been scribbling down the names and numbers as I gave them. He tapped the sheet, "This gives me a better picture. We have not enough men to face them, not here at any rate." He rubbed his chin and then said, "You may go, Harris." Once alone he said, "Almeida will fall and it is simply a case of when. Honour dictates that I stay here until it does but I have a battlefield in mind which will give Masséna and Ney something to think about."

"The was one thing more, sir, when we were heading back, after the Portuguese had killed the patrol the four Frenchmen became quite chatty. Marshal Masséna has with him his mistress. The French call her La poule à Masséna, Masséna's tart! She is dressed as an officer."

Sir Arthur waved an irritable hand, "And? Many generals like to have their mistresses with them!"

"Yes sir, but few have them on the front line and this one, Henrietta Lebreton, is quite a beauty but the important point is, sir, that she does not like to rough it. She insists on staying in good quarters. I think that Masséna will try to find bigger places where he can be accommodated."

"By Gad, sir, but you are right, this is useful and that fits in perfectly with where I wish to fight him." He grabbed a map and jabbed a finger at it. "Viseu! It is the only large place between the border and Coimbra; when he takes Almeida, he will head for Viseu and that means taking a road which is awful, even by Portuguese standards. You have done well and can stand down for a few days but I want you, when Almeida falls, to be in Viseu. I want a spy in their camp. I believe you are right and we can have you in place before he arrives!"

He told me what he needed me to do and added an extra service I could provide. "Colonel Trant is to the north with a brigade of militia and two squadrons of Portuguese cavalry. If you find a suitable target for him then I pray you let him know. However, your main task is to keep me ahead of the French! I need to know exactly what they are doing while keeping our preparations hidden."

I knew that it made sense but as the meeting in Talavera had proved, each time I was in a French camp increased the likelihood of my capture and my death. I was a soldier and I obeyed orders. I was used to Colonel Selkirk doing this but it seemed that Sir Arthur also regarded me as expendable.

Chapter 8

The end of the siege of Almeida came as a complete shock to us all for its end was dramatic and totally unexpected. We learned what caused it much later but all that we knew at the time was that, in the early evening of August 26th, there was an almighty explosion from the east. We had grown used to the bombardment which rumbled on each day but this was different. The explosion could be heard twenty miles from the fortress. We learned from the messenger who brought us the news of the fall of the fortress that someone had been careless when carrying powder from the arsenal and a rogue flame had set the trail of gunpowder alight. 4,000 prepared charges, 150,000 pounds of black powder and 1,000,000 musket cartridges destroyed the centre of the medieval castle. General Cox bravely tried to hold out but all he managed to do was to send a messenger to the general to tell him that he could not hold on for long.

Sir Arthur was decisive for with Almeida lost, the reason for our presence was gone and he ordered the whole of the army to move west to the village and ridge of Bussaco. Sharp and I would be sent to Viseu. This time we would have to go completely in disguise. We took two old horses and civilian clothes. We left our horses, swords and rifles with the 14th Light Dragoons and all that we took were knives and our pistols.

Our instructions from General Wellesley were quite clear. He wanted as much notice as he could of a French advance towards Coimbra. "But Sir Arthur, what if he does not come to Viseu?"

"He will but do not worry, Major, I have other officers south of the Mondego in case he comes through Fomos. The difference will be that you will be in the town and with your knowledge of the French army and its language you should find out more than they will be observing from a distance. Do not risk yourself for I know that you were almost undone in Talavera. It is what you can bring me which will make the difference for in this war knowledge and intelligence are worth two or three regiments. If I am right then we shall bloody Masséna's nose at Bussaco!"

The horses we rode were the sort a gentleman and his servant might use. They did not look like cavalry horses. I would be Señor Roberto d'Alvarez; I took the name of my dead Portuguese friend in her honour. My clothes had been made in Portugal and looked Portuguese. We had Portuguese coins as well. To confuse my enemies, I wore an eye patch over one eye. Such little disguises were effective in changing a man's appearance and I adopted a stoop such as an older or slightly unfit man might adopt. However, if I saw someone I recognised then we would leave. Although we would not fool the Portuguese, we might fool the

French and so we were playing the part of a merchant from Lisbon looking for new sources of grapes to make his wine. I knew enough from my cousin, Cesar d'Alpini, to know the language of winemaking and I could get by. We had a third horse for our baggage.

As we took the mountain road to Viseu I wondered if Sir Arthur was making a mistake for the roads were so poor that I did not think the French would be able to negotiate them with their artillery. In the end, he was proved correct; Sir Arthur knew war the way my cousin knew wine.

Although Viseu had no garrison it was a prosperous town full of fiercely patriotic people. The news of Almeida's disastrous end had reached them already and as we entered the town, we saw cartloads of people leaving as this was the Portuguese way. The French would simply take what they wanted from the town and those with any sense fled south where they could find shelter with friends and relatives. Sharp and I found an inn and I asked the owner what was going on.

"It is simple, sir, we have endured the French before now. They demand everything and do not like to pay. They commandeer houses with no recompense. We produce grapes and lemons here and that is all. If the French come, they will take all of the food and it will be the people who will starve. If I were you, sir, then I would leave now."

"But you will not be leaving."

He gave me a sly smile, "No sir, you see the officers will come here for they like their comfort and their food. I will not go hungry and we might even profit from them. When they leave the people will return."

I nodded, "We have travelled far but what I shall do when the French do arrive is to send my servant ahead to Coimbra to find accommodation there. Until then we would like a room and stabling for our horses."

"Of course, but you know that when the French come you will lose your room."

I smiled, "Perhaps." I had plans in place.

The first night was quiet in the inn but the next was even quieter as more and more people left. I went with Sharp to negotiate with the grape growers even though it was just a smokescreen to explain our presence in the town. As the innkeeper had said they were all leaving and would not commit to selling me their grapes. They did offer to speak to me again once the French had gone and, playing the part, I appeared happy.

As we rode back, I said to my sergeant, "Remember that Colonel Trant and his Portuguese Militia are close by. If you come across them then let them know that the French are close by. General Wellesley wishes them hurt. The ride to Coimbra is to deceive the French!"

"Yes, sir!"

The French began to arrive from the 18th onwards. The first elements were Chasseurs and the first thing the Major of the 22nd Chasseurs à Cheval did was to inform the innkeeper that Marshal Masséna and his staff wished rooms in the inn. He complained and pointed to me, "But sir, I have guests. I cannot throw them out!"

The Major gave a slight bow and said, in execrable Portuguese, "I am sorry, sir, but if your room is required then you will lose it!"

I shrugged, "I will speak with Marshal Masséna when he arrives. We may be able to come to some arrangement."

The major smiled for it was well known that Masséna, whilst a brilliant and successful general, was also as corrupt as they come. He nodded and pointed to my eye patch, "That alone may allow you to keep the room."

I did not understand, "Why?"

He said, "There is no reason why you should but he was hunting with the Emperor and some other generals when he was accidentally shot and he lost his eye. He may be sympathetic towards a fellow sufferer."

"Was the man who shot him punished?"

Laughing, as he left, the Major said, "No one punishes an Emperor!"

The innkeeper shrugged, "I am sorry, sir, but I did warn you."

"And I thank you for the warning but I shall stay as my business is not yet complete. However, it would be prudent if my servant found us accommodation in Coimbra."

Sharp nodded, "Of course, sir, and if I could have coins for food and lodgings?"

I handed it over making a great show of being unhappy. After he had gone, I said, "I will probably never see either the horse or my money again!"

"He looked trustworthy enough, sir."

I was playing a part and I scowled, "We shall see!"

I took a turn around the town and saw that the only people in the streets were the French. The Portuguese had simply disappeared. Their food and valuables had gone with them and the French would find little other than grapes and lemons. There was a limit to how much of either they could eat!

Marshal Masséna and his entourage galloped into town in the early evening. I had dined and was enjoying a cigar and some wine when they swept into the inn. It was then I saw Masséna's mistress. She was dressed as a Hussar although no one could have mistaken her for a man. She was stunning and very young. I had thought Emily de Lacey beautiful but Henrietta Lebreton made her look dull and dowdy by comparison. I wondered at the disguise which would have fooled no one. I later discovered that she was a dancer and an actress and deduced that, perhaps, she enjoyed playing the role. He and his staff were knocking the dust from their clothes and laughing; I doubted that they had even seen me.

He had a chief of staff who was a major. He saw me and attracted the attention of the Marshal. I affected a disinterested pose even though I knew, from the gesticulations, that they were talking about me. Eventually, the Major came over, "I am sorry, sir, but you will have to vacate your room, the Marshal requires it." He spoke in French but he spoke slowly.

I nodded and when I spoke fluent French, I saw I had taken him aback, "And I have no intention of giving up my room. I would speak with the Marshal. He may be a reasonable man and I am a businessman. I have little to do with war which merely stifles trade and profit."

Both my words and my tone unsettled and unnerved him. Had I been a soldier he would have known what to say but I was a civilian and a confident one at that. He scurried away and went directly to the Marshal. Masséna came over to speak with me. I saw that La poule à Masséna accompanied her lover. I did not see much of her but what I do remember was that she always seemed to have a cheeky smile upon her lips. She reminded me of a sleek cat and, indeed, her movements were very feline. Had she purred I would not have been surprised.

"Señor d'Alvarez, my chief of staff tells me that you refuse to give up your room for the Emperor of France."

I smiled, "I did not say that, Marshal. If Emperor Napoleon was here then I would give him my room but as I have one very small room, I assume it would go to a junior officer. Just have two of them bunk in together."

La poule à Masséna suddenly burst out laughing. The Marshal cast her a slightly irritated glance and then said, "You are a bold fellow, I will give you that. Your French is impeccable. Where did you learn it?"

"I learned my trade in Sicily and southern France. I am fluent in both languages."

He pointed to my eye patch, "And how did you lose your eye? Was it in a war?"

I laughed, "Good God, no! I am no soldier. I abhor violence and I prefer trade and talk to war and musket balls. If you must know it happened when I was younger and we had a snowball fight. One of my opponents must have concealed a stone in his snowball. I lost the eye as well as the fight."

Masséna found that amusing, "You do not seem much discomfited by it."

The Lines of Torres Vedras

"Nor do you, sir. I believe you still make war and this does not prevent me from making wine."

He nodded, apparently satisfied, "Major, let this gentleman have his room. He has wit and that is rare these days. I see you have dined already but if you would care to dine with me tomorrow, I would enjoy the diversion."

I was desperate to know why he was not moving towards Coimbra but I dared not ask and so I adopted a bored expression, "Until my servant returns then I am stuck here. Of course, I shall dine with you but I shall pay the bill. It is the least I can do."

It was his turn to laugh as did his officers, "You do not think that the French army pays for quarters and food, do you? But it is a kind offer and shows that you are a gentleman." He turned to his officers. "Come let us change and, hopefully, there will be a bath in this hovel of an inn!"

As he turned, I saw his mistress wink at me and then her fingers played with Masséna's. She was a bold one. I remembered the Black Widow. This time I would not become embroiled.

I retired but there was no chance of sleep as Masséna's staff were both loud and raucous. However, once the Marshal retired then silence descended. I suppose I could have left the next day but as Sharp had not returned, I stayed in the town. During the day his army rolled in and Marshal Ney arrived. Where Masséna was cunning and suave, like a fox, Ney was like a red-haired bear. He filled a room with both his body and his personality. It was lunchtime and I was dining for I wanted to be in the inn to observe the army as they arrived. The innkeeper had been impressed that I had kept my room and I was treated like an honoured guest. I think he saw it as a Portuguese victory! The two marshals conducted their conversation in the dining room and as Ney was loud, I heard every word.

"What fool chose this road, André?"

Masséna shrugged, "The Portuguese officers, loyal to the Emperor, whose advice I followed, Michel, did not know the area but they did know that there was a town here."

Ney laughed, "It is a pity they did not know that the only food here is grapes and lemons! We should push on and get to Coimbra before Wellington is reinforced."

"The artillery train is still on the other side of Sotojal and Montbrun's cavalry is even further back. Whether we like it or not we are stuck here. We have little to fear. We drove away their Light Division at Almeida and their cavalry at Guarda and Freixedas. Wellington is running and I hope to trap him on the Mondego at Coimbra but, if we give him enough time, then he will flee to Lisbon and then we shall have him for the sea will be at his back and all that he will be able to do is sail away and Portugal will be ours!"

"Do not underestimate him, André. So far, he is the master of Spain and Portugal. His cavalry isn't worth a damn but his redcoats are the match for anyone and, although I hate to say it, he has put some steel into the Portuguese. Put your sword into his back!"

"As soon as the artillery arrives then we shall push on and I will do just that!"

I spent the afternoon visiting the few merchants who were left in the town. I negotiated a price for grapes I had no intention of purchasing but I needed my story to be believable. I knew I had been lucky. Apart from Masséna's staff, there was no one below the rank of Brigadier General in the town. The rest were camped outside and that suited me for it meant I was unlikely to run into one of the officers who had seen me in Talavera.

That evening I made sure that I looked as smart as I could. I would not fall for the charms of the mistress of the marshal but as she appeared to find me attractive, I might be able to use that to my advantage. To my surprise, she came into the dining room dressed as a woman and I wondered at that. It became obvious to me that it was an open secret amongst the marshal's staff but, perhaps, the illusion was for the benefit of the men. If so, it was wasted as I had been told about the affair by a light infantryman. What it did do was give me some information which I could use to my advantage.

"This is the wife of Captain Lebreton and as he is still in Almeida I am acting as her escort. I hope you do not mind me bringing her here."

"Of course not, for she brightens the room like a walking work of art."

She giggled coquettishly and Masséna smiled at the compliment. He waved the owner over, "We will have the best food that you have and the best wine!

"Yes, sir!"

"I doubt that it will be worth eating but one must try. Now tell me Señor d'Alvarez..." The Marshal leaned forward.

"Call me Roberto."

"Of course, Roberto, tell me what it is that you do."

I had practised this story on the way north and felt confident with my choice of words and manner. "It is simple enough, I make money. I was brought up in the wine trade, buying and selling from vineyards and it occurred to me that there were many producers of wine grapes who did not produce enough grapes to make bottling wine viable. I began to buy up their surplus produce. As I did not need a vineyard, I bought a place in Lisbon where I make wine. I have the advantage that I can send it quicker by sea and do not have to risk the Portuguese roads. I can make red, white and rose. I can make a port; in short, I can do that which would take many vineyards to do."

"Fascinating. I confess that until you explained what you did, I was suspicious of you for I could see no reason for you to be here but the Viseu area is known to produce good grapes. Of course, the wine will not be as good as that from a single vineyard."

"Probably not but, by the same token, it is better than many wines from some vineyards. The mixing of the different grapes makes for a more robust wine which travels well. It is also cheaper to produce than single-vineyard wines. However, the blockade did hurt me."

"I apologise but since the French Fleet was destroyed then it is us who are blockaded."

"And that is why I am in need of grapes for I can send my bottles out of Lisbon and they are not stopped by the British Fleet!"

He clapped his hands and laughed, "Bravo! Bravo! I can see that Fate sent you here to me. We will talk a little more but first, let us eat!"

The food had arrived and we spoke about food and wine. His mistress became bored and she spoke of the theatre and Paris. I knew most of the places she mentioned but I had to keep to my story that I was Portuguese. When the food was finished and it proved better than the Frenchman expected, we lit cigars and had a brandy.

His mistress said, "I will retire for I am tired." I stood and kissed the back of her hand. She squeezed mine as I did so. "Are all Portuguese gentleman as well-mannered as you?"

"In your presence, my lady, they would be."

Masséna nodded and kissed her cheeks. "I shall not be long Mme Lebreton. I shall finish my cigar first."

I knew he had something on his mind for he leaned forward, "Tell me, Roberto, are you a patriot?"

"I told you, Marshal, I am a businessman, why do you ask?"

He took a drink of the brandy and said, "France will win this war or we shall, at least, conquer Portugal. As for Britain, they are an island stuck on the edge of the world that is Europe. Bonaparte is the master of Europe and eventually, Britain will come cap in hand to beg to be part of it. If you were a friend of France life would be so much easier for you."

"Friend of France?"

"Let me be blunt. From what you have told me, you travel through Portugal and the British soldiers with consummate ease. If you were to pass information about their numbers and dispositions to me then I would make it worth your while. When we conquer Portugal, I could give you the concession for all of the surplus grapes in Portugal."

"And Spain?"

He laughed, "I knew I had your measure. Of course!"

"You wish me to be a spy."

"Spy is such an ugly word. You would be saving lives for if I knew what the British were doing, I could win the battles with fewer losses."

"And how would I get the information to you?"

"A good point." He stubbed his cigar out and waved for more brandy. "I would not wish written communication for that could compromise us both. Face to face is better."

His reputation for cunning and avarice was well deserved. "And yet if I meet with you regularly then does that not give the game away?"

"You are a clever fellow; I can see that." The brandy arrived and the Marshal turned and shouted, "Lebrun, a map!"

The aide brought a map and then was waved away. Masséna studied it. "From Lisbon, the easiest way in and out of Spain is through Badajoz."

"Which is held against you."

"True and we will be taking Coimbra soon. From Coimbra to Lisbon is, what, eighty miles?"

"Near a hundred and thirty."

"Too far." He jabbed a finger at the map. "Then here, Golega, it is on the Tagus and there must be vines there."

"There are."

"And it is close enough to Lisbon for you to reach it easily."

"And what if you are stopped at Coimbra?"

He frowned and then smiled, "I like your caution but, trust me, we will drive the British back over the Mondego and then there is nothing to stop us save winter. By November we will have reached the Tagus. However, I like your caution. You will know where I am to be found. If you come seeking grapes then stay at the best hotel that there is in the town and I will find you. I will send an aide for you so that we can, if it is necessary, meet in secret."

I nodded, "That sounds good. And the payment?" I knew that Masséna was corrupt and did not like to part with money. I was not bothered about payment but I was interested to see how he would find the money.

He took, from his pocket, a gold Louis. "Let us call this a down payment and we will pay according to the value of the information you bring. Remember, however, that the rewards when we win will be far greater." He pushed his chair away and rolled up the map, "Thank you, this has been a most instructive meeting."

And with that, he left. I had become a French spy over dinner!

The Lines of Torres Vedras

I breakfasted alone but when the Marshal came with his officers I saw him pointing to me and speaking to two of his aides. I lifted my cup in acknowledgement and he nodded. He was identifying me for future reference. That was both a good and a bad thing. I reflected on my disguise. My choice of eye patch had been inspired but had been both instinctive and lucky. My back story and the character I had created had also been perfect. I am not sure it would have worked with some of the other officers who led Bonaparte's army for few of them were as corrupt as Masséna. I had a long and leisurely breakfast for, in truth, I had no more to do and dared not risk riding through the French army yet. Until Sharp returned then I would have to stay.

The Marshal left and more of his officers came in to take their table. They had obviously been waiting for him to finish. Sharp arrived as I was leaving my table. He was dusty and dirty. The French officers looked up until I spoke in Portuguese to him. "Is everything arranged?"

Alan was quick thinking and he nodded, his eyes flicking to the French officers, "Yes, Señor."

I put my arm around him, "Let us get you out of these dirty clothes." The innkeeper was fetching a tray of food for the Frenchmen and I said, as he passed, "If we could have some food and drink in the room. My friend is tired and hungry."

"Of course."

We said nothing more until we were safely in the room and even then, we spoke in whispers for we were speaking English. Clarity was all!

"Sir, I found Colonel Trant," he shook his head, "at first I thought that they were bandits for they are a wild bunch. I gave him the news and went with him. I don't think he really trusted me."

"Understandable. He didn't know you."

"Anyway, we attacked the French baggage and artillery train and we cut them up pretty badly. The French with the guns were about to surrender when the next regiment arrived. They were the Irish Brigade; now they were a wild bunch of mercenaries fighting for the French. We left but we have slowed them up. I have a better idea of the numbers of men in the French army now, sir."

"Good."

"Just then there was a knock upon the door and the serving girl had a tray of food. I gave her a copper coin and Sharp had already begun to eat before she had left. "Sorry sir, but I could eat a horse, with the skin on!"

"That is alright, Sharp, because I have news for you, too," I told him all and I saw his eyes widen at two points. He was hard to surprise but the Marshal's offer took him aback. "And we will need to leave today. If the baggage train arrives then you might be recognised besides which we have the news that Sir Arthur needs. You pack and I will go and pay our bill." He had his mouth full of bread and ham and his eyes pleaded with me. I laughed, "Of course, finish the food first!"

By the time I reached the desk, which was used by the innkeeper, the dining room had almost emptied. "It is time for us to go. Could I have the bill please?"

He smiled, "The Marshal has said that the French will pay the bill for you, Señor."

I nodded, "Nonetheless, you have done me a great service and I will pay, anyway." I took out a handful of silver coins and pushed them across the wood.

He smiled as he slipped them into his hands and they disappeared. He smiled and lowered his voice, "I always prefer the English, for they are true gentlemen and you should know that I am a patriot and your secret is safe with me."

I did not know how he knew but it was obvious he did and there was little point in denying it. Had he wished to turn me over then he would have done so. I was about to speak when his eyes flashed a warning and he said, "Thank you for your kind comments, sir, about my establishment and I hope to see you again in more peaceful times."

"Of course."

As I turned, I saw a staff officer. He had a document in his hand, "Sir, Marshal Masséna said to give you this. It is a safe-conduct through our lines."

It was only then that I noticed the hurried movements of officers up and down the stairs. "Is something amiss?"

The fact that I had the safe conduct loosened the officer's tongue, "Yes, sir, the baggage train has been attacked and Marshal Ney leads our advance units towards the British. You will need this for the roads will be busy!"

"Thank you!"

I raced up the stairs and saw that not only had Sharp finished but he had packed, "I heard a noise outside, sir."

I nodded, "Colonel Trant's attack has, indeed, set the cat amongst the pigeons. Luckily we have a pass but we shall need to move swiftly for the French are marching on Sir Arthur."

The roads from Viseu were congested for the narrow streets made movement difficult but once we hit the road to Tondela we made better progress. We did not need the pass until we neared Marshal Ney and his staff. Ahead of him were Brigadier Lamotte and the vanguard, the 3rd Hussars. The French were walking and we were cantering. One of

Marshal Ney's staff stopped us, "Where are you going? This road belongs to the French army and none may pass."

I saw Marshal Ney turn and frown. He must have remembered me from the inn. My eye patch was distinctive. I flourished the pass, "Marshal Masséna has given me this!"

He read it and then rode to Marshal Ney who read it and waved me over. He spoke in French which told me that he had not only seen me with Masséna but heard me too. "It seems you are a friend of the Marshal. A word of advice, friend," the word 'friend' was laden with sarcasm. Ney was sharp. "I would not stop at Coimbra but keep going until you reach Lisbon for war is coming and with it great hardship!" He handed me back my pass and I nodded as I spurred my horse.

The Hussars had halted while the interchange had taken place and they parted to allow us through but I saw suspicion on their faces. Why had we been allowed through? I waited until we were a mile clear of the closest Frenchman before I spoke to Sharp. "We have another thirty-six miles to go and I will do it in one ride. Sir Arthur needs as much warning as he can get and Marshal Ney is just three days from Bussaco! Are you up to it?"

"I am, sir, but I fear it will be the end of this horse for it has ridden far."

"It cannot be helped. We knew they were expendable when we set off. Soon we will ride our own horses and we will wear our own uniforms again!"

Chapter 9

It was the middle of the night when we finally reached the British outpost. I had shed my disguise but, even so, it took some persuasion to get past the detachment of the 31st Foot. Once through we had to repeat our story for the sentries at the various camps knew that the French were coming. We were directed to the convent on the ridge at Bussaco where Sir Arthur had his headquarters and we reached it shortly after dawn. I did not know how Sir Arthur managed to survive on so little sleep for he was already up and poring over maps with his senior officers. I was, of course, ushered in directly.

"Well?"

"Marshal Ney and the 2nd Corps are approaching Mortagua and will be there sometime later today."

Sir George Murray said, "That is just a day or so away, Sir Arthur!"

Sir Arthur said, irritably, "Then let Major Matthews finish his report, General, and we will see if we need to pick up our skirts and run for Lisbon, eh?" Sir George looked suitably abashed. "Carry on, Matthews."

"General Loison, who led the attack on the bridge is the vanguard. There are over 60,000 men in four Corps. Your saving grace, my lord, is that Masséna likes his night in comfort for his mistress is still with him and he is tardy, in addition, there is conflict between Ney and Masséna and that does not make for good bedfellows. His cavalry is at the rear of the column and Colonel Trant has destroyed some of the wagons which were bringing his artillery. Even if Marshal Ney reaches us within the next two days his guns could take another week to arrive here."

Sir Arthur nodded, "Matthews, you have done well and I will need a more detailed account of your activities however, I must alter my plans slightly. Go and get changed. Eat something then meet me back here at noon!"

With that, I was dismissed. Sharp and I sought out the 14th Light Dragoons for they had our war gear and horses. Sadly, for us, they were not close to the convent and we had to travel almost to the Mondego river to get our belongings. It made sense to me for the ridge at Bussaco was no place for cavalry. It was light infantry country. Leaving the three horses to be used by the Light Dragoons we changed into our uniforms, ate a hearty breakfast with our friends and then headed back to the convent. We found a deserted house at Sula which was close to the convent. It was almost derelict but it had a roof and, more importantly, grazing for our horses close by.

"Sharp, make it more homely eh, and see if you can get some food for us. I daresay I will be some time with the General."

I was taken directly in for I arrived promptly at noon. Lieutenant Mountshaft said, as we made our way through the cloisters to the cell the General was using, "He is just speaking with Sir Robert but he said to take you in."

"Good."

"How was it, sir, behind the lines I mean?"

"Interesting, Lieutenant, and not for the faint of heart."

As I entered, I saw a map on the wall and while I listened to Sir Arthur briefing Sir Robert, I analysed it. I could see that the whole of the ridge was occupied by British and Portuguese battalions. I could see 66 guns but only one cavalry regiment marked on the map.

Sir Arthur said, "We do not know where he will come, Sir Robert, which is why we have to occupy the ridge between Moura and Luzo. If Major Matthews is correct then it will be an infantry attack. For that reason, I want just skirmishers and rifles on the forward slopes. The Light Division will act as line infantry for this battle. Let our guns and skirmishers do our work. From what I know of both Ney and Masséna they will use the normal French formation of column of battalions which they will try to deploy into line when they meet solid opposition. I think that your rascals can give them a surprise. However, I want you as our eyes and ears. Take your division and position yourself between Mortagua and Moura. I do not want you to defend against the French, just stop their scouts getting close to our lines. I want to surprise them when we rise like wraiths from the ridge. You were nearly caught with your breeches down at Almeida, Sir Robert, I hope that you have learned your lesson!"

"Aye, sir." He turned and saw me, "Colonel Beckwith was asking after you, Matthews. You made quite an impression on my lads. We would be honoured if you would fight alongside us."

I saw Sir Arthur roll his eyes but I said, "If that is at all possible then my sergeant and I will be there, General Crauford!"

He nodded and left. Sir Arthur sat back in his seat, "Romantic nonsense! You will be where I need you. You have proved time and time again that you are a sensible fellow who makes wise decisions. Now, a full report, for my ears only and leave nothing out!" He gestured towards a seat and I sat.

I began with what I had seen in Viseu and ended with my meeting with Ney on the road. The fact that I had surprised the General was obvious for he did not speak straight away. He stared at me and then the map.

"You have been busy and resourceful although I can see that Colonel Selkirk has had an influence on you. I had worried that there might have been a whisper amongst the French of my defensive lines but, from what you say, Marshal Masséna is blissfully unaware of the trap which I have set."

"Are the lines of defence finished then, sir?"

"The first one, the one we showed to those politicians, is and the second will be finished in the next month or so. It seems that the land of Portugal is proving to be our best ally. What is your best estimate for the arrival of their army? I ask you because you saw them on the line of march and you seem to have a natural affinity with all things French."

"I think that today or tomorrow we will see their scouts and it will take another day to bring up all of their battalions."

He nodded, "That is my assessment too. Despite what General Crauford wishes, you will be at my side during the actual battle but for now I would have you attach yourself to the Light Division. This time you return to me as soon as you recognise their advance guards rather than their scouts!"

"Yes, sir!"

I chose to spend a night in our run-down shack before we left to join the General. We had had a hard ride and I wanted a night of sleep. Sharp had managed to acquire a dixie of stew and some day-old bread from some nearby soldiers. It was heaven-sent. I told Sharp of our mission as we ate and then I wrapped myself in my cloak and fell asleep. Old habits die hard and Sharp and I were up and dressed by 3 a.m. We rode towards the Light Division even as reveille sounded. We reached their camp as dawn was breaking and we could smell the food that was being cooked. The six miles journey did not take us long and that showed what a tight defensive position Sir Arthur had chosen. I saw that General Pack's two Portuguese brigades were there also and there was artillery. It boded well, just so long as General Crauford obeyed his orders.

The 43rd saw us and called us to their camp for breakfast. I waved Sharp towards them, "I must report to General Crauford but I promise that I shall join you."

The two generals were in conference when I arrived, Black Bob pointed towards the village of Mortagua a mile or so away. "Looks like blue uniforms, Matthews, what do you think?" He proffered his telescope and I peered through it.

"Looks like the 32nd Light Infantry, Sir, Loison's Division. They were the ones who captured those chaps from the 43rd."

"Ah, you have good eyes. Then this means that Ney will not be far behind." He suddenly looked around at me, "You are here as my nursemaid, aren't you? Make certain I don't make a hash of it again?"

He was right, of course, but it would not do to confirm it, "I think that you will obey the General's orders and I am here to take the news to Sir Arthur for, as you know, General, once you pull back to your position then General Wellesley can put his whole plan into action. We passed the right flank and they are all dug in with artillery, Sir Arthur needs you on the left flank!"

"You may be right but it does not sit well with me to run before these Froggies! Damnit we almost beat them at the bridge."

He was wrong but Black Bob was not the man to question. "Quite, sir. I will go and see to my horse and then join you shortly."

One reason that Black Bob was so highly rated by his men was that he knew when they needed food. They would not be called to arms until they were needed and Sharp and I enjoyed a camp breakfast made with a whole variety of foods which had been foraged. It did not do to ask whence it had all come.

When the trumpet sounded Sharp and I grabbed our weapons and raced to the road where the two generals were surrounded by their staff officers. I heard Black Bob shout, "Gunners, you know your range best; keep their heads down. Rifles go for the officers, eh?" Both orders were unnecessary but they needed to be given. "Stand to!"

We were not in a standard line formation. There were spaces between the light infantrymen. Indeed, the undulating ground was studded with obstacles which would have prevented such a formation. The rifles began to crack as blue uniforms appeared. As I had expected there were no cavalrymen for this ground did not suit them but I caught a glimpse of green on the road behind the advancing light infantry. If General Crauford made a mistake then they would be upon him in a flash.

The French skirmishers fought in the same manner as we did. They worked in pairs and used whatever cover was available. When our horse artillery fired, I almost jumped they were so close to me. The smoke began to envelop the 95th Rifles before us and that would encourage the French to advance. The sergeants were walking amongst their men chivvying them and ensuring that they were ready. Light infantrymen could think quickly and react even quicker. Suddenly there was a rattle of musket fire from our left which added to the smoke and confusion.

"Come along, Sergeant, let us see if we are needed, eh?"

As luck would have it the French had tried a sudden attack on the 43rd. As we arrived some of their skirmishers were using their bayonets and it was a close fight which we witnessed. I fired my Baker into the side of a French Sergeant's head and then dropped my rifle. I drew my sword and one of my pistols. A musket with a bayonet was a longer weapon than my sword but it was far more unwieldy. I fired my pistol at an officer and hit him in the leg. I holstered my gun and was just in time to push away the Charleville musket with my hand. The barrel was hot but I ignored the pain as I brought my sword down above the tirailleur's stock and my razor-sharp sword bit the flesh of his neck splattering blood over those who were close to him. I had observed the effect before. It made the men around slow as they were uncertain if they had been the one struck! Sharp's pistol sounded and I deftly parried away the bayonet which was aimed at my middle with my sword. I punched the tirailleur on the nose and rendered him unconscious with the hilt of my sword. Our sudden attack had allowed the Rifles and the light infantry to reload and as soon as they began to fire the French fell back. It would be different once their line battalions arrived but for the moment it was just skirmishing.

Leaving the 43rd to take their prisoners and recover their wounded I picked up my rifle and made my way to the two generals. There were bodies which I could see before them and I also saw a larger block of infantry gathering along the road. "General Crauford, I believe that we have delayed the enemy long enough. Your division is too valuable to lose and men are dying."

"They are soldiers and that is what soldiers do!"

"If you wish I can ride back to General Wellesley and have the orders put in writing. I always think that having orders in writing is handy, especially in the aftermath of a battle."

The threat was clear. It was one thing to delay obeying an oral order but quite another to disobey one which was written down. Court martials could follow.

He nodded, "Very well, Major White begin to withdraw down the road to Bussaco. Have the Rifles and the Caçadores cover our withdrawal." He turned to me and gave me a steely stare, "Satisfied, Major?"

I smiled, "Indeed I am and with your permission, sir, I will stay with the rearguard for the General is keen to know the mettle of the men he faces."

I turned to Sharp as the generals and their staff turned their horses to head towards the ridge. "We will stay with these men, Sergeant. I know we will be targets on our horses but I need to see who is leading this army. If it is Ney then we can expect action sooner rather than later."

"Right sir." He went to fetch the horses.

I had met Reynier, Heudelet, Mormet and Solignac or seen them, at least, in the inn in Viseu. Thankfully Junot had still been on the road for there was a chance he would have recognised me. I was confident that without my patch and wearing a cocked hat, fore and aft, I would be unrecognisable. I knew that Reynier would obey Marshal Masséna to the letter of his orders while Ney would ignore those he did not like.

I mounted Donna and immediately saw far more of the enemy. The skirmishers were using cover but the line infantrymen were marched along in a half company. They were sixty men wide and could move quickly when they needed to. They were the danger. I observed that the Royal Horse Artillery had their horses ready to make a quick getaway. I had seen them wait until an enemy was in canister range, fire and then have their guns hitched and gallop away before the survivors could reach them. They would judge the moment to turn well. While we waited, I reloaded my pistol and Baker and then hung the rifle from the sling.

I heard the French drums begin and knew what it portended. They were going to attack. I shouted to the horse artillery, "Be ready to pull out! I think they are bringing the big battalions!"

"Yes, sir. Load canister!"

It was Captain Stewart in command of the 95th Rifles detachment and I nudged Donna close to him. My horse ignored the musket balls which zipped around her. We would be unlucky to be hit. The Charleville was not an accurate musket and explained why the British normally won the skirmishing duels. The French won when they used weight of numbers to duel with bayonets. "Captain, when the artillery fires pull your men out. There is nothing you can do against a column of four battalions."

"Right sir. Are you staying?"

"It would be rude not to!"

I raised my Baker as I heard the drums change to the *pas de charge*. The gunners had heard it too and when the head of the column was a hundred and fifty paces from us, they fired. I raised my Baker and fired along with the other rifles. I heard Captain Stewart shout, "Right, lads, sharply does it."

One French light infantryman had been playing dead and he rose like a wraith and raised his musket to fire at Captain Stewart. My pistol was faster and at twenty paces I could not miss.

"Thank you, sir!"

I wheeled Donna and Sharp and I followed the riflemen as they scurried across the open ground. They left the road for the horse artillery which careered along it. Horse gunners were famously known to be mad as fish! We soon outdistanced the line infantry which jeered when we fled. General Craufurd had set up another position two miles down the road. It was early afternoon by the time we stopped a mile beyond that point. The Light Division was executing a withdrawal in the same manner as the riflemen. We prepared our position and waited for the next group to fall back. In this way, we edged back towards the convent at Bussaco and by the time darkness fell we were within the British defences. The withdrawal should have been the one the general employed at the bridge but he did not. I do not think we lost above thirty men wounded and a handful only were killed. More importantly, I had identified General Loison as the man leading the French. It was not Marshal Ney!

While the Light Division prepared their own line of defence, I went to Sir Arthur with my news. "Well, we have prepared well thus far." He turned to his aide. "Mountshaft, I want no fires lit tonight! The men will have to make do with water and dry rations. I do not want the French to know either our positions or our numbers!"

"Sir!" he hurried out to have the clerks write out the orders.

"Matthews, before you retire for the night be so good as to count their fires. I do not doubt the veracity of your report but it will be confirmed by their fires, eh?"

"And when we win sir, what then?"

"If we can we hold them here but I suspect Marshal Masséna will try to outflank us. I am surprised he has not done so already. If and when he does, we will fall back through Coimbra where I will instruct the Portuguese to leave as the people of Viseu did. The Portuguese soldiers did a fine job of stripping the land of all food on their way here and we will continue to do so. Let us see if the French can find food where there is none for I have no doubt that Sir Richard's defences will prove too strong for these Frenchmen! And then, Matthews, when winter begins to bite you shall return to your new master and give him information."

"What information, sir?"

"That I have not decided yet but you have given me a golden opportunity and I shall not spurn it."

That meant Sharp and I would have to risk discovery again and enter the den of the wolf. I ate and then went to the mount above the convent. It was the highest point on the whole ridge and afforded a fine view of the villages the French had occupied: Moura, Cerqueda, Pendurada, San Antonio do Cantaro and Carvalho. I began to count the fires. I had picked up a stick to help me as I climbed and I used my knife to mark every fifty. There were more than one thousand fires. As there would be officers in commandeered houses then this was a much bigger army than the one which Sir Arthur had deployed along the ridge. Only part of the army would be seen when the French attacked as more than four-fifths of the army were on the reverse slope.

It was late by the time I reached Sir Arthur and he nodded when I told him what I had seen. "Then we will be well outnumbered and it will be down to who has the better plan and the better men. Let us hope that it is us, eh? Tomorrow, I want you and your fellow up early. The French will attack but it could be anywhere along the line. When you find out where then send your sergeant to me and you get to the sector they are attacking. We must be quick-witted on the morrow. One slip and Marshal Masséna will steal my victory from me! Can't have that, can we Matthews? Now cut along and get some rest!"

Chapter 10

I did not sleep well that night for, although I had confidence in Sir Arthur, the fact that Black Bob had made errors in the two recent actions made me worry about the rest of his leaders for Black Bob was one of the best! Consequently, I was awake before Sharp and I slipped out to make water and have a quick wash. By the time I was dressed he was awake and giving me dark looks. I washed my mouth out with water for there would be no hot tea! I went to saddle Donna. Most officers would wait for their servants to do so but I did not mind the task as I had been saddling horses almost since the time I had learned to walk. We had loaded and sharpened our weapons the previous evening before retiring and when Sharp was ready, we rode along the ridge.

"Hellfire sir, but it is foggy!"

My sergeant was right. I could not see the fires of the French and there was a thick fog covering the lower slopes. The British skirmishers who had spent a cold and damp night there would have had neither hot food nor tea. The French might not have had much food but they would have been warm before their fires. If the French were sneaky then they would be advancing even as we rode along the ridge. They would not use drums and they would just appear from the fog. Reveille was sounding but the French could be marching from their camps towards us and we would not know. There was no way that Sir Arthur could have foreseen this fog. It was just bad luck but it might cost him the battle.

Suddenly I heard the pop of muskets from up ahead. I guessed it was from the village of San Antonio where we had an outpost but I could not be certain. As I neared General Picton and his staff I heard the crack of some Portuguese cannons. "Sharp, ride back to Sir Arthur. Tell him the attack has begun on the slopes beneath the 3rd Division."

"Sir." He whipped the head of his horse around and sped back to the convent.

I rode close to Sir Thomas but he was busy organising his men and I heard him giving his orders out in his usual, calm and unflustered manner, "Send a couple of companies from the 45th and the 8th Portuguese to support the 88th. Have the rest of the Division stand to. Johnny Frenchman is attacking and in the fog, too! Damned unsporting!"

Suddenly we saw that some of the light infantry companies who had been our skirmish line had been driven back and were now running to kneel before their mother regiment. I peered down the slope, "I believe that the fog is thinning, Sir Thomas. I can see the head of the column."

The Lines of Torres Vedras

Just then I heard hooves and Sir Arthur and Sergeant Sharp along with half a dozen aides galloped up. "Morning, Picton, I see the French have chosen you to attack! Must be your appalling sense of dress eh?"

That Sir Arthur was making a joke put everyone at their ease. We could all see the French now as the fog, despite the smoke which was being added, thinned.

"Colonel Wallace, be so good as to take some men and fire on the flank of that column, what?"

"Yes, sir."

"Go with him, Matthews, I believe you fought alongside the 88th at Oporto, they might appreciate a friendly and familiar face."

"Yes, sir!" I spurred Donna and followed Colonel Wallace who took command of the 45th Nottinghamshire Regiment and the three closest companies of the 88th Connaught Rangers.

"Right you fellows, form a line perpendicular to the General and present your muskets."

It was a masterful display of discipline and precision. The 700 men were under fire from skirmishers yet they managed the manoeuvre as though they were on a parade ground. I heard Sharp's Baker bark and a French skirmisher fell dead.

"Present!"

"Fire!" A wall of flame, musket balls and smoke filled the ground between us and the French column. The screams told me that the French had been hurt. We could not see the full effect of the volley because of the fog and the smoke. At the same time, the 8th Portuguese Cazadores opened fire at the head of the column. The column was still trying to move up the slope propelled by the sheer weight of men behind. It had been slowed but not stopped.

I aimed my Baker through the smoke as I heard Sir Thomas Picton shout, "The 88th and 45th will form line." Drawing my sword, I spurred Donna to follow the line companies as Picton shouted, "Present!"

I aimed Donna at a gap between two of the files of the infantry as they formed up.

"Fire!" The companies made up of the two regiments were only 60 paces from the French and they could not miss.

Colonel Wallace shouted, "At them, boys! Give them the bayonet!"

Then the red-coated warriors were amongst the French column and attacking their flanks. Bayonets plunged into men already demoralised and shocked by fire on their flanks and at the head of their column. There were just three companies of Connaught Rangers but they were fearsome men with a bayonet. As the Rangers hit their flank, clambering over their dead and dying, the four battalions, which had begun 2000 strong, began

The Lines of Torres Vedras

to run back down the slope. Many stood no chance of making it as there were three companies of wild Irishmen who loved nothing better than a bayonet charge. I spurred Donna, not to get at the French but to prevent the 88th from running into the rest of the French Corps. The French backs were to us and I used the flat of my sword to render those in my path unconscious. When I saw that I was ahead of the 88th I turned my horse and shouted, "The 88th will retire to their original positions!" I saw a sergeant I recognised from Oporto, "You lads have done well now back up the hill. Good fellows, eh, let us not incur the wrath of General Picton!" After Talavera, he had famously called them blackguards and they had been offended.

The sergeant grinned. His face and uniform were bloody. "Right you are sir, come on lads, back up the hill! There will be plenty of Froggies for us!"

As the men began to move, I saw him pick up a French officer's sword. It was finely made and richly decorated. He offered it to me, "Do you want this, sir?"

"No, sergeant, you have earned it!"

"You are a good man and that's no error!" The sergeant would make a nice profit from another soldier or one of those ancillary troops who never saw battle. The keepsake might persuade someone at home that they had actually fought in a battle.

By the time I reached Sir Thomas the fog had cleared and we could see the blue and red uniforms littering the hillside. There were far more blue ones than red. Sir Thomas said, "Nicely done, Matthews. Sir Arthur said for you to rejoin him at the convent. Things are warming up, eh?"

"Yes, sir."

Sir Thomas was eccentric and irascible but I felt a lot safer knowing that he had the right flank of the army.

I did not reach the convent for General Wellesley had stopped close to General Leith and as Sharp and I rode up I heard the tail end of the conversation. "I don't like that, General Leith. There are seven battalions advancing against the 45th. They are good fellows but they will be driven off the ridge and I do not need that. Send in some of your chaps and drive them back eh?"

"Yes, sir!"

Seeing me Sir Arthur said, "I shall be closer to the convent, Matthews. There are two more Corps just waiting to advance and I shall need to be on hand. You stay with the general and let me know the outcome although, in truth, I do not doubt that these fine fellows will prevail!"

With that, he and his aides rode off. I did not know General Leith and he did not know me. He ignored me as he shouted his orders. I saw that it was the 9th East Norfolk Regiment which was the closest to the general and they, along with a Portuguese battalion were told to advance towards General Picton's beleaguered 45th regiment which was now enduring the fire of a fresh division of Frenchmen. I joined them. Colonel Cameron was marching at their head as I rode up. "Good of you to join us, Matthews!"

I doffed my hat in salute, "I should warn you, Colonel, that there are seven battalions advancing to take the ridge and the 45th have been badly handled already!"

"Thank you, Major. The battalion will fix bayonets!"

It was a sensible move. Although it would render the volley slightly less effective it would give the regiment a better weapon to drive the French from the ridge. As we advanced at a slight angle to the enemy I saw that the French were winning. Even the volleys from the red-coated defenders could do little to hurt the almost three and a half thousand Frenchmen who were resolutely marching up the slope. The ground was littered with bodies and that slowed the French slightly. Colonel Cameron kept a steady pace but he would not reach the ridge in time. Sure enough, the 45th had suffered too many casualties and they began to fall back. I saw a French officer stand and raise his hat to signal that they had taken the ridge. Even as the Colonel halted the 9th, I raised my Baker and shot the French officer. My ball struck his arm and his hat fell.

"9th Present!"

I heard the same order in Portuguese as the six hundred English men and almost eleven hundred Portuguese levelled their muskets. Even as I reloaded my Baker, I saw the ridge filling with Frenchmen as they deployed from column to line.

"Fire!"

Seventeen hundred muskets make a lot of smoke and the noise almost deafened me. It was as though the fog had descended again. Both the 9th and the Cazadores were well trained and they were already reloading as the smoke began to clear and I heard the order to present repeated. The sheer weight of numbers had sent more Frenchmen over the ridge despite the casualties that they had suffered and when I heard, "Fire!" the leading Frenchmen were just sixty paces from the muskets. It was carnage.

I saw General Leith wave his hat over his head and Colonel Cameron shouted the order to advance. It sounds ridiculous for the French battalions, despite their losses, still outnumbered the two battalions which advanced towards them, but they were facing red coats with bayonets and they turned and fled. What was remarkable about the advance that day was that the 9th had learned the lessons of Talavera and they did not run but advanced steadily down the slope driving the survivors of the attack before them. I dropped my Baker to hang from its sling and drew my sword. I saw two French generals, I recognised one as General Foy, being helped from the battlefield for they had been wounded and as we passed over the bodies, I saw another general whom I did not recognise, face down on the ground. He was dead. The fog had not totally cleared from the valley bottom and, indeed, still clung in places to the valley sides. We did not know into what we were marching.

I was about to shout for Colonel Cameron to halt for I saw cannons being unlimbered when I heard the order, "Well done, 9th, now let us retire!"

Raising my sword in salute I waved to the Colonel and turned Donna to head back to the convent. As I did so I saw that there was still a heavy patch of fog. The musket fire had created a fog on the ridge and as I turned to look back to generals Picton and Leith I saw that it was difficult to discern who held the ridge. I now understood why General Wellesley wanted verbal confirmation of the situation and I urged Donna on. With Sharp close behind me, we reached the convent quickly. Sir Arthur had not dismounted but he was peering through his telescope. He turned and just looked at me.

"The enemy attack has been repulsed, sir. The 9th drove them back and Colonel Cameron now has them back in position on the ridge."

"Good for it looks like our fiery friend Ney is about to attack!" I saw two columns, each of about six battalions, marching from Moura, through the fog. There were six and a half thousand men advancing on our position! He pointed to Sula, "Have General Crauford prepare his men for an attack. I want him to hit those chaps in the flank!"

"Sir!"

Once again Sharp and I rode to join the Light Division. As we neared them, they were seated on the ground and resting, I saw that the slope close to them was very steep. For regular infantry, it would have been impossible to move but this was the Light Division and they were like mountain goats. I turned to my sergeant, "Sharp this is not the place for horses and besides it will alert the French to our position. Let us tie our mounts up here and proceed on foot."

I saw that there was a small windmill and General Crauford was using it as an observation post. Handing my Baker to Sharp, who would reload it, I made my way up the interior to join the general. "General Crauford, Sir Arthur wishes you to attack these columns in the flank."

The Lines of Torres Vedras

He was grinning as he turned, "By Gad, sir but we have them! We have them! Look!" He pointed to the column which was oblivious to the presence of the Light Division. He turned to his aide, "Have the battalions fall in but keep them below the ridge." I looked to see what the general had seen. The 3rd Cazadores and about 300 of the 95th were in skirmish order and as their 1300 hundred musket balls slammed into the French the guns of Ross's battery added to the slaughter but the French columns kept advancing. I recognised General Loison. He had led the attack at Almeida too. "Come along, Matthews, you and your rifle may have some target practice today!"

As we emerged from the windmill, I saw that the French would have no idea that we were waiting for them with almost 4,000 men! General Crauford positioned himself where both Colonel Barclay and Colonel Beckwith could see him. I joined the 43rd for they felt like old friends. Major Gromm waved his sword as I stood to the left of the line. Below me I watched the battle unfold. The French columns had driven the 95th Rifles and the Cazadores up the slope and they were now sheltering around the guns of Ross' Battery. The musket fire had almost ceased but the six pounders continued to fire and that made the French columns advance towards them to end the torture. The path up which they laboured was so steep that the remains of the twelve battalions were struggling to keep any sort of order and I could hear, in the gaps between cannon and musket fire, French sergeants, as they chivvied their men back into formation.

Sharp pointed and I looked beyond Loison's columns. The fog had cleared and another 13,000 men were forming up. Marshal Ney had reinforcements at the ready. I wondered if Sir Robert had mistimed his attack when he stood and, waving his hat, shouted, "Now 52nd, avenge the death of Sir John Moore!"

I levelled my Baker and aimed at the Brigadier General leading the first column. He disappeared, as did the rest of the column, in a cloud of smoke as I fired. I laid down my Baker and drew my sword as the order was given to fire again. There were three volleys and I saw, as the smoke cleared, carnage. Six companies of the Light Division had been moved so that we had a crossfire at the head of the column. Miraculously, the French Brigadier I had hit was still alive although I could see that he had lost his lower jaw. Raising his sword, he tried to urge his men on.

Colonel Beckwith shouted, "43rd Charge!"

Colonel Barclay and the Portuguese colonels shouted the same. The 95th, the Caçadores and the 3rd Cazadores emerged from around the guns and they joined in the charge. Over 6000 men scrambled down the hill. The weight of the musket balls had broken the spirit of the French attack and the sight of the bayonets coming from the fog and the smoke was too much. They broke and ran. Some even surrendered while there were others who were wounded and could not fight on. I saw Private Williams take prisoner the wounded general while other Frenchmen surrendered. I joined the charge down the hill. For the first part of the charge the French were surrendering but as we neared the untouched columns there was more resistance and French batteries began to fire. The measure of the progress made by the Portuguese was shown when the 19th Cazadores came under fire from a French battery. They charged it and slew the gunners before retiring in good order.

General Crauford, mindful of Sir Arthur's wrath, ordered a halt when we began to take casualties. This time it was the Light Division and not wild Irishmen. They obeyed and, firing as they went, they made their way back up the hill to the ridge. The battle did not end there but it was, to all intents and purposes, over. Marshal Ney might have had 13,000 fresh men but Sir Arthur's line still held firm and another attack would yield the same result, failure. As we tramped back up the slope, I marvelled that the French had kept their formation for as long as they had. The British wounded had been taken up to the doctors and the French would be taken later although the French whom I passed were the dead. As I glanced to my left, I saw that Reynier's men were still attacking General Picton and Leith but I could see that it was not being reinforced. Once the word reached General Reynier that the other half of the attack had failed then they would withdraw. The losses on this side of the battle had been far greater and it had been the Light Division and the Portuguese who had won the battle. The French still held the villages from which they had begun their advance and there was little likelihood of Sir Arthur wishing to waste men attacking them. We held the ridge and if the French came again then they would be repulsed, again. By the time we had recovered our horses and rejoined Sir Arthur we saw that he had used General Hill's untouched and unused division to reinforce those units which had suffered losses.

He was in a good mood when he greeted me, "A good day, thus far, Matthews and everyone did well. It was good to see General Crauford obey my orders for once!"

"Sir!"

Lieutenant Mountshaft rode in, "Sir, I have the casualty figures." Sir Arthur nodded. "We lost 200 dead and there are about 1000 men with the doctors."

Sir Arthur looked relieved. Despite his reputation, he did not enjoy men dying on the battlefield. I knew from personal experience that Bonaparte would not even have asked for the returns.

"And by my estimate, sir, there are 4,000 dead Frenchmen there." In the event, he underestimated for the French lost almost 6,000.

"I believe it is over for today but we will stand to until dark. I doubt that my opposite number will attempt an attack in the dark. Let us see if they will try to winkle us from our rocks. Tomorrow, Matthews, I want you to take a troop of the 14th Light Dragoons and see if the French army is to the north of us. I was surprised when Marshal Masséna did not try to outflank us. I cannot believe that he will not try to do so tomorrow. He has all of his cavalry as yet unused."

"Yes, sir. I shall just go and see how the 43rd fared."

"Of course."

I turned to Sharp, "Take Donna back to our hut. We will have an early start tomorrow." I handed him my Baker, also.

"Sir."

I picked my way back down the slope to where I had seen some of the wounded being tended. Private Williams was there and he had with him a woman who was carrying a musket and smoking a clay pipe. He looked relieved to see me, "Sir, I have found this Frog woman and she won't give me her musket. I don't understand a word of what she says. Could you help?"

I recognised her for what she was, a vivandière or cantinière. They were the women who accompanied the French army and sold them food. They had been known to fight and were as tough as the women who had followed Sir John Moore's army through the snow of Northern Portugal in 1808.

"Madame, the soldier requires your gun for you are an enemy."

She was totally unfazed by my uniform and my tone. I had met this type of soldier when I had served under Napoleon and they were formidable women. "I am from the 26th Line Regiment and I seek General Simon for I heard that he was wounded and I wish to tend to him. I will keep my gun for I know what English soldiers are like and they will wish to interfere with me." She glowered at Williams and fingered the bayonet she wore in her belt. "I will castrate any man who comes near to me!" I almost smiled for she was one of the most frightening looking women I had ever seen and Williams looked terrified.

Williams said, "What did she say, sir?"

"Better that you do not know, Williams. Leave her with me. I know what she wants." Turning to her I said, "Follow me but keep your hands from your weapons."

She nodded, "You speak good French."

I smiled and said, simply, "I know!"

The French wounded were being tended by our doctors. We had had fewer wounded than was expected and so they were receiving attention quicker than they might have anticipated. I found the French general who was having his face bandaged. "Doctor, this is a cantinière. She wishes to tend to the General."

The doctor was amused at the woman's appearance. "I have heard of these women. Can we trust her?"

"She came through our lines to tend to him and he does not look as though he can run anytime soon. It will mean your staff have less to do and I daresay there might be a prisoner exchange."

"Very well."

"She does not speak English!"

He laughed, "Thankfully I can get by with French. Thank you, Major."

By the time I reached Sharp, the battle had totally ended. The wounded had all been recovered and now the bodies were being recovered. The French dead would have all of their valuables taken and as neither British nor Portuguese had fallen on the French side then the British won the battle of the looters also. This time we did have hot food. Sir Arthur was pleased and fires were lit and food distributed. The army had tea which meant that, once again, they could take on the world! While Sharp prepared our food, I walked a mile or so to the rear to the camp of the 14th. After speaking with Brigadier General Slade, I sought out Captain Wilson. "Tomorrow your troop will see some action. I have been asked to patrol to the north and west. We are looking for French cavalry."

"Thank God for that, sir. My men and I were chafing at the bit today. All you chaps were engaged and fighting gallantly and we sat on our arses, sir! Sorry, sir!"

"I am not offended, Captain, and do not worry, the 14th will see action soon enough. I wish to be moving before dawn."

"Don't worry, sir, we will be ready!"

I knew that Brigadier General Fane had the bulk of his cavalry south of the river and that they would discover if Marshal Masséna was foolish enough to try to outflank us there for we had the advantage of the ground and our cavalry. The north side was more likely as there was a local track which the French could use if they could discover it.

The troopers I led now had the experience of the battle along the river as well as the patrols with me and they were not the same soldiers. They rode with their carbines across their saddles and I knew that they were loaded. They all watched ahead and to the sides. I was looking not for French blue but the green of their horsemen for that would be what they would use to scout out the route. The track eventually led to the small town of Sardao Agueda and there the road ran south to Coimbra. If the French could reach Coimbra then the war would be over as we would be trapped at Bussaco, north of the river.

Troop Sergeant Harry Hale was the oldest man in the troop and should have had the worst eyes but he had something the younger ones did not have, ten years of experience.

"Major Matthews, up ahead, through the trees, Dragoons!"

I saw where he pointed. Our small track was heading towards the larger one which led to Sardao Agueda and they were about to converge. I looked ahead and saw that the tracks met just five hundred paces from us. We had done our job and discovered that Marshal Masséna was, indeed, seeking a way to outflank us to the north. I was about to order the troop to turn when one of the Dragoons spied us. We were just two hundred paces apart. The French trooper shouted and foolishly fired his musket. It was a wasted ball. Sharp's Baker, however, had the range and he dropped the Dragoon. I wanted confusion and the best way to do that was to use the carbines.

"Troop, aim! Fire!" I doubted that we would hit much but the thirty carbines and my Baker made enough smoke to hide our position as well as making the Dragoons raise their own weapons. "Bugler, sound retreat!"

I knew that Captain Wilson would find it ignominious to retreat before the Dragoons but the French would now know that they could get around us. A combination of the smoke, our musket balls and the fact that they needed to find a way to get around us meant that we were not pursued. As we neared the convent, I heard the sound of muskets. There were skirmishers approaching. Was Sir Arthur wrong and were the French going to attack again?

"Thank you, Captain Wilson, rejoin the regiment." I rode to the general whom I could see in conference with his aides, "Sir Arthur!"

He turned and gave me the ghost of a smile, "You have come to tell me that you have discovered the French are trying to outflank us."

I smiled, "Are you clairvoyant, General Wellesley? Yes, we found Dragoons and they have discovered the trail which heads north and west."

"You were back too soon to have discovered nothing. This skirmishing is merely to delay us! Gentlemen, the Light Division will cover our withdrawal and the army will retire to Coimbra."

Only once had I met such a confident and quick-thinking man and that was Napoleon Bonaparte. Sir Arthur had surrounded himself with, largely, competent and like-minded officers and there was neither fuss nor panic.

Sir Arthur turned to me, "It goes without saying, Matthews, that you will be with the Light Division."

"Of course, sir."

"We will only pause at Coimbra for the French Army is damned quick but I will see you at Torres Vedras. I now know what it is I wish you to tell Marshal Masséna!"

The 14th Light Dragoons were to be the rearguard and we waited at the convent as the rest of the army pulled out. General Crauford and his men were in their element. They had high ground and cover, more, they knew that as soon as the main column was on the road to Coimbra they could disengage. I had confided in Sir Robert that this attack was meant to deceive us and that when we pulled out the enemy attack would peter out but it did not matter to the general. He wanted to prove that his Light Division was superior to every other light unit. In that, I knew he was right. I had little to do but to watch and admire as the Rifles picked off sergeants and officers. When the French skirmishers approached the 43rd and 52nd came into action and their muskets proved to be superior to the French. I noticed that there were just the blue uniforms of the dead and wounded on the hillside; the Light Division had not lost a man.

Captain Wilson turned to me and pointed to the light infantry, "Sir, how do they get this good?"

"Practice and the belief that the man next to them will be as good as they are and will not leave them behind. I marched with these men behind Sir John Moore in 1808. I do not believe that any other division could have done what they did. Do not worry, Captain, your men are good and they are getting better. The French will chase us and harry us. I will help you to learn when the time is right to turn and show your teeth and when it is better to put your tail between your legs. At the end of the day, success and failure will be measured by who holds Portugal. I believe that it will be us." I looked up at the sky and saw that it was filling with clouds, "Sir Robert, I believe that the army will be well on the road to Coimbra."

He nodded, "Aye, laddie, you may well be right and there is little pleasure in shooting boys instead of men! Colonel Beckwith, withdraw your brigade by companies and set off down the road to Coimbra. Light Infantry speed, if you please, we will double time!"

"Yes, sir! The Brigade will disengage by company!"

Once again it was a masterful display of discipline as the companies left the line and formed up on the road. With their packs now upon their backs, they began to march and then to run down the road. It was the way the Light Division covered such large distances!

By the time Colonel Barclay brought away the last of his men darkness had fallen. I drew the troop up before the convent and ordered them to draw carbines. I knew that the French skirmishers would be approaching cautiously for they would be expecting an ambush. I was listening and when I heard feet on rocks I shouted, "Troop A, open fire!" I fired my Baker too. The darkening gloom was illuminated by thirty-four guns and I saw in their light, the four of five Frenchmen who had reached the top of the ridge. Only one was hit but the other faces disappeared. "The troop will retire!"

They all turned and formed, in turn, pairs as they followed the 52nd companies as they quick marched down the road. Sharp and I were the last. I was confident that the French would wait until they could no longer hear hooves before they followed. They would not pursue us down the road for their army was already heading north for the better road there. I knew that the bulk of our army would already be in Coimbra and the Light Division would be there by midnight. We had seventeen miles to go and it would take us but five hours to reach it. We would have some sleep before we marched the one hundred miles to the lines of defence so carefully prepared by the Viscount and Sir Richard Fletcher.

Chapter 11

When I awoke, a little later than normal, the army had already headed south. I decided that I must be getting old for I ached as I mounted Donna. I know not what Sir Arthur had told the masters of Coimbra but the roads were filled with wagons and refugees heading south. The city was like Viseu although as it was a bigger city more people remained.

The wagons and the refugees meant that we became detached from the 52nd and the Rifles. I did not mind for we had horses and could move away from danger quickly. The civilians could not. If we were between them and the French then some might escape. We made barely thirty miles that first day and I knew that French Dragoons would be thundering down the road to try to find out where we were. As I sat with Captain Wilson and the NCOs in a nameless village south of Pombal, I explained to them what I thought would happen. "The French will waste time in Coimbra because it is a large place and I was in Viseu and saw that they dallied there longer than they ought. Marshal Ney is impatient and fiery. He will demand that Marshal Masséna lets him pursue Sir Arthur. His army is fast but not as fast as the Light Division. His Dragoons are heavier than we are. They may well catch us but not until we are close to the Lines of Torres Vedras. Sir Arthur does not want them to know of the defences until Marshal Masséna arrives. We will need to make the Dragoons turn and tell the marshal that they have reached our lines before they actually have. We have to make them think that our troop is a regiment."

Troop Sergeant Hale tapped out his pipe carefully. Clay pipes were hard to come by. "A neat trick if you can pull it off, sir."

"Luckily Sergeant Sharp and I travelled these roads before Talavera. There is, ten miles north of Torres Vedras, a pass through which the road crosses. It twists and turns. Not only that, there are places where it climbs steeply. You all know that when cavalry ride uphill, they lean forward and tend to look down. They will have chased us for more than eighty miles and will not be expecting an ambush. We will line the road and take cover in the woods. Sergeant Sharp will lead half of the troop and I the other half. We will ambush them with our carbines and then set about them with our sabres. It will be a brief fight and they will flee. Then we will ride to meet with the General."

I saw Harry Hale nod but Captain Wilson shook his head and said, "You make it sound easy, sir."

"Like all plans, the planning is easy. It is the execution where work is needed but I have confidence in you and your men."

When we reached the ambush spot and I was waiting with a cocked and primed Baker, I was not so certain about my words. It seemed to me that there was much which could go wrong. I would be the first man that the French would pass. We had been keenly aware of the Dragoons for the last twenty miles. We had heard their hooves in the distance for they were riding hard to close with us. It was late in the afternoon and while that gave us the chance to slip away in the dark it also gave the French the opportunity to evade.

I had the youngest two troopers at my side and I turned to them. I saw that Trooper Ashcroft was chewing his lip; it showed his innermost fears. "When they come, Trooper, I shall fire at the man just ahead of me and you will shoot the next. Aim at your man's horse for your carbine will buck and you will probably hit him in the chest. Just drop your carbine and draw your sabre. The neck is the best place to aim your blade for there is little protection there. We have the easier side for the Dragoon's sabres and muskets will be to their right. All that they have to block your strike is their arm and they hold their reins. They will pull their horse's head around and that will expose more flesh. Pull down hard as you strike and it will tear open the neck. There will be blood but be grateful that it is your enemy's and not yours!"

"Yes, sir." I saw Trooper Cowell nodding too for my words were intended for both of them. They had fired their carbines and fought the French but they had, as yet, not fought a man blade to blade.

Dusk was falling and I wondered if the Dragoons might have camped already and then I heard their hooves. "Stand to!"

We were just ten paces from the centre of the road but we were hidden by the trees and the darkness was more intense because of the foliage. I was confident that the Dragoons would not see us. That feeling was confirmed when I heard the two leading Dragoons laughing and joking as they rode along. Talking of the pursuit as though it was a victory and anticipating being the first in the next town showed that they were not alert and that lack of vigilance might well cost them their lives. There were forty Dragoons and I allowed the first fourteen pairs to pass before I shouted, "Fire!"

I had told every trooper to aim down the road to minimise the risk of hitting our own men. That meant that the last few pairs of Dragoons also suffered injury for my ball and that of Sharp not only hit one man but carried on through. The lead ball might not kill a second man but it would wound and that might make the difference.

"Charge!" We had to use every element we could and dropping my Baker, I drew my sword and galloped, screaming, at the Dragoons. I heard the clash of steel as the Light Dragoons sparred with the few

Dragoons who had not been hit. There were four dead men close to me and as I turned to ride up the road the last unwounded Dragoons turned and fled. I saw some Dragoons leaning in their saddles and that told me that they were wounded. I heard hooves behind me and I turned and blocked the sword from the Dragoon sergeant. As he passed me, I lunged with the tip; you could not do that with a sabre and my longer heavier cavalry sword found flesh as I thrust through the back of his tunic. The sergeant kept his saddle. As the Dragoon's horses receded in the distance I looked and saw that we had accounted for nine Dragoons; there would be others who were wounded. Eight horses milled around.

"Captain Wilson, have the horses secured. Well done A Troop. If the dead have anything of value then it is yours. We leave for camp in ten minutes."

Sergeants Sharp and Hale joined me. Alan said, "Well done sir, but we were lucky! They were useless cavalrymen!"

"You may be right Sergeant but you can only defeat that which is before you and the lads did well."

Troop Sergeant Hale nodded and took out his pipe, "Aye you are right, sir, but that was smartly done and the young lads will be better for it. I think the Captain learned too."

"As you know, Sergeant Hale, you either learn quickly or you die. I am just glad that, thus far, they have survived and this winter there will not be much need for cavalry. Your lads will see another summer."

"And we will put the winter to good use too, sir. The Captain is aware of the deficiencies of the troop. They will be remedied."

It was late when we rode through the provosts and sentries at the lines of Torres Vedras and the beginning of the awesome defence which the Portuguese had built. My Portuguese came in very handy for, in the dark, it would be easy to become lost and I asked help from the militia who manned the defences. We rode directly to the town of Torres Vedras. There was a corporal from the 14th waiting for us. "Captain Wilson, the Colonel has our camp just three miles south."

"Right Corporal." The captain rode over to me and saluted, "Thank you, sir. The lesson was learned and I shall be a better soldier from now on. Troop, salute!"

I have no idea when they had practised but all thirty-two swords came out as one and I was given a salute. I was honoured. I nodded, "Well done A Troop, enjoy your winter!"

The look Troop Sergeant Hale gave me told me that he knew that I would not have an enjoyable winter. We headed for Sir Arthur's headquarters. A weary-looking Lieutenant Mountshaft awaited us, "Sir, Sir Arthur will see you first thing in the morning. He is meeting with his

The Lines of Torres Vedras

senior commanders and the Portuguese. These are your quarters." He led us to the hotel we had first stayed in before Talavera.

"Sharp, see to the horses." I looked at the Lieutenant, "You look exhausted, Lieutenant."

"A ride to Lisbon and back will do that to you, sir. If I never see the back of another horse's head again then I shall be a happy man!"

I wondered why he had been sent to Lisbon and then put the thought from my mind for my stomach thought that my throat had been cut. As I walked into the hotel I said, "Any food?"

The man shrugged and I took out a silver coin I had taken from a dead officer at Bussaco. I placed it on the counter. He beamed, "Of course sir!"

The ham and stale bread, not to mention the overripe cheese, were not worth the coin I had given but the wine was and Sharp and I enjoyed a restful sleep. We rose well after dawn. If Sir Arthur wished to see me then it would be at my convenience. We were eating breakfast when Lieutenant Mountshaft found us, "Sir, Sir Arthur is waiting and he grows impatient! He blames me for he said it was to be at first light!"

"And we shall be there as soon as we have breakfasted!"

Sir Arthur had a glowering face when I arrived, "You have taken your time, Matthews! Did that fool Mountshaft fail to give you the message?" I saw the Lieutenant colour.

"He told me, Sir Arthur, but we have had rough rations and open fields for the past few nights. We have sent packing a troop of Dragoons. I thought that the Sergeant and I were entitled to a good night's sleep and a decent breakfast!"

I wondered if I had gone too far when I saw a smile play upon his lips. He nodded, "You may be right. Dragoons you say?"

"Yes, Sir Arthur. We ambushed them north of the lines, Marshal Masséna does not know, yet, of their existence!"

"Well done then all is forgiven! But do not try my patience again!" He gestured to the seat, "Now sit. I have much to tell you." As I sat, he said, "I have done with you for a while Mountshaft. See that we are not disturbed." He leaned back in his seat, "You are to go to Masséna and play the spy again." He shook his head. "I do not like to play these deceptions. That is the work of the likes of Colonel Selkirk but I can see that sometimes it is necessary. Had not Marshal Masséna begun the game by coercing you then it would not have entered my head but if I sup with the Devil then I must play his game sometimes. I have a Royal Navy ship waiting for you in Lisbon. It will drop you as close to Coimbra as it can manage. You will find Marshal Masséna and give him some intelligence. You are to tell him that there are a large number of empty transports in

Lisbon harbour and the rumour is that they are there to remove the British Army to Madeira. Tell him that we suffered large numbers of casualties at Bussaco."

"Will he believe that, sir?"

"From the prisoner we took, we discovered that the French newspaper Le Moniteur reported that Sir Robert Crauford lost almost half his men in the battle of the River Côa. We know that the newspaper similarly reported a French victory at Talavera. I think that the French marshals are sending exaggerated reports but, who knows, they may well believe them. I believe they will similarly exaggerate our losses at Bussaco. You, of course, can confirm this when you speak with the Marshal."

I was puzzled for I could not see how this would change anything. "Sir, I do not mind heading behind the lines but what will this achieve?"

"I need Marshal Masséna to be eager to get to Lisbon. When he reaches my defences he will not, at first, realise how formidable they are and when he sees that they are manned by Portuguese militia he will be eager to finish the war before winter. If you raise a man's expectations then his fall when they are not realised is greater. I wish to demoralise Marshal Masséna and his French army. I want Marshal Ney and him to have words and for Marshal Ney to be his normal, fiery self. In short, I wish to blunt this French knife over the winter so that in the spring we can drive him back into Spain. The Lines of Torres Vedras will defeat Marshal Masséna and, I hope, save Portugal."

That made sense. "And how do I get back to Lisbon, sir?"

"Your ship will await you in the estuary. You will have to make your way there yourself." His dismissive tone told me that he had not thought out an escape for me. I was serving him and that was all that mattered.

That would be hard for if I was followed and seen to be boarding anything other than a Portuguese ship then my disguise would be ruined. On reflection that might not be a bad thing. I did not like the duplicitous nature of my work.

"Well, Matthews, you had better be off! You have far to travel!" He smiled, "And do not forget your eye patch, eh?"

Leaving our horses with the 14th, for we knew they would be well looked after, we borrowed two of the horses used by Sir Arthur's aides. We took only civilian clothes although I did take a short sword I had acquired over the years. This time we might run across someone who knew me and I wanted to be able to defend myself. I also took one of my French pistols. All that I had been told was that I was to report to the quay in Lisbon which was used by the Royal Navy. I was confident that Masséna would not have any other spies in Lisbon. Joseph Fouché might but they would have to send the news that I was seen boarding a Royal Navy vessel to Paris first and by that time I would be back in Lisbon.

We were stopped by the sentries at the entrance to the quay. Luckily for me, it was commanded by a Lieutenant and Sir Arthur had given me a pass. "I wish you, Lieutenant, to watch these horses until we return. I dare say there are officer's horses stabled nearby and we shall need them when we return to Sir Arthur!"

The familiar use of the Viscount's name worked and he nodded his agreement. "Private Wilkinson, carry the officer's bags to the sloop!"

As we headed to the riverfront and the quay, I looked at the masts of the ships in the harbour. Most were the smaller vessels which serviced the battleships blockading the European coastline. Since Trafalgar the seas were British. Even the Mediterranean was ruled by the Royal Navy. The Navy could not win the war, for that we needed Sir Arthur but I for one knew that without it then we would not even have a toehold in Europe. We owed much to Admiral Nelson. I had met him once, in Naples, and I liked him. As a leader, he was more likeable than Sir Arthur but both of them would go down in history as the saviours of Europe. Of that, I had no doubt!

As we neared the ship my spirits soared for I recognised her. She was the *'Black Prince'* and I had sailed in her before. Her commander, Jonathan Teer, was a throwback to the privateers like Drake. He stood, grinning, at the tumblehome. I saw the blue frock coat and white waistcoat and the epaulettes which told me he had been promoted to Lieutenant Commander.

"Wilkinson, you can leave our bags here and return to the gatehouse."

"Thank you, sir, and good luck!" That he would speculate with his fellows was obvious. There was too much mystery about an officer who travelled incognito with a pass signed by Sir Arthur. What he would have made of the pass signed by Marshal Masséna might have kept him in ale for a week!

He saluted, "Major Matthews! We meet again!"

I did not salute back for I wore neither uniform nor had a hat upon my head. Instead, I said, "And I thought that you would be an admiral, at the very least!"

He laughed, "I would be bored to death! They tried to give me a frigate but they are just the escorts for the larger ladies of the line. This is better for we still get to grips with the enemy and catching blockade runners is more profitable! Come aboard, the tide is on the turn. You have made good time and it means we can leave earlier than I thought."

He turned, "Middy, take the two gentlemen to my cabin, I shall get us underway!"

"Sir!" As the young midshipman, whom I took to be about fifteen, led us to the cabin by the stern, I recognised some of the hands I had known before. They grinned and knuckled their foreheads. We had shared adventures and risked death together. That made messmates of us. The Midshipman spoke as we headed for the cabin which was on the next deck down. "I have heard much about you, sir, from Lieutenant Commander Teer. You have an exciting life!"

"As will you, Midshipman, if you stay with Mr Teer. He is a superb captain!"

"That I know, sir. My people were delighted when he agreed to take me on his ship. It is just a pity that the French are beaten, sir!"

We reached the stern of the ship and Sharp took the satchels down to the cabin. He knew his way around the sloop of war.

"I had better stay on deck, sir. The Captain will have plenty for me to do, I expect." I followed Sharp down the steep ladder to the captain's quarters. We stayed in the cabin while the ship, first of all, prepared for sea and then edged her way out of the busy anchorage. I was just being careful for I did not want to be seen by any potential spy and, besides, I knew that Jonathan would appreciate being able to sail his ship without a visitor peering over his shoulder. As soon as the motion of the ship became more pronounced, I knew that we had left the port and we were heading into the estuary. Sure enough, a short while later the Midshipman opened the door, "Captain's compliments, Major, and you can come up on deck. We are clear of the port."

I donned my cloak and stepped out. The weather was far from cold but we were heading into the Atlantic and it was early October. It was, as the crew might have said, a little fresh! Jonathan was, as usual, hatless. He ran his ship his way and I think that was why he had avoided promotion to a larger ship. He was a free spirit and this suited him. He gestured for me to come to the leeward side of the steering position. Sharp stayed to talk to the bosun whom he knew well.

"Well, Robbie, from your lack of military dress I am guessing that this is a clandestine rather than a diplomatic mission?"

"Yes, Jonathan. How close can you get me to Coimbra?"

"If you wish I could land you in the centre of the city but I fear that would rather ruin your disguise eh? The best I can do is to land you a mile or so from the centre. I have acquired some charts from a local. He thinks I can turn far upstream from Coimbra and our draught is no problem. He said there are woods a mile or so west of the city and there are riding trails the lords use."

"What does he think you intend to do?"

He laughed, "I told him I had a lover there and I was going to save her from the French. He thought that was romantic."

"It will take us at least a day, maybe a little longer to conduct our business. What will you do?"

"Our blockade is working, Robbie, but there are still blockade runners. I intend to take down our flag and pretend to be a blockade runner. The fact that the French have only just taken Coimbra helps us. My French might get us by. What I will do is to return every twelve hours to the place I drop you. If you mistime it then you will have a long time to wait." He shrugged, "It is the best I can do."

"And that is good enough. I have a pass from Marshal Masséna and if you bear no flag, we might be able to fool any who follow us."

He nodded and said, "It is a pity there will be no profit in this!"

"You never know, Jonathan, you never know!"

By dawn, we were halfway up the coast. I saw that there were a pair of two deckers and three frigates moored off the mouth of the Zizandre river. That estuary marked the end of the line of defences built by the Portuguese. If the French tried to turn it, they would have to brave the firepower of the Royal Navy. I wondered what the crews of the blockading squadron thought was the purpose of our voyage for we sailed close to the coast. '***Black Prince***' was a lively vessel and in the hands of her captain could be made to move like a thoroughbred horse and he was showing off as we sailed perilously close to the rocks along the shore.

He saw my look and shrugged, "They think I am mad as it is. I like to confirm that now and again just so that they do not think to promote me. It is one thing to wreck a sloop but quite another to wreck a ship of the line!"

As we neared the Mondego River, he shortened sail to allow us to negotiate the river in the dark. I knew little about sailing but even I knew that what he attempted was dangerous. It was still light when we entered the estuary. Fortunately, the wind was from the north and west and we did not need to tack as much as we might have expected. Sharp and I were on deck with our bags. I had my patch on and the crew found it funny making comments about my piratical look. We just had a small leather satchel each with what little we would need for a brief stay in the city. The fact that the river was quiet helped. The empty river was understandable for the French had just taken Coimbra and would be imposing their will upon its populace. We passed not a ship, not even a fishing boat and when I saw Jonathan give the signal to lower the sail then I knew that we had reached our destination. By some miracle or more likely skill, he had found a small landing stage. We later learned that it had been used by a Portuguese lord who had lived fifty years earlier and had had a fleet of ships. The wooden dock was a little weatherworn but it meant we did not have to row ashore. While Sharp carried our small satchels ashore, I spoke with Jonathan. I had a timepiece as did Jonathan. Sailors were even more reliant on time than soldiers.

"Twelve hours from now, give or take thirty minutes we shall be here. I will turn the sloop around ready for a rapid escape should we need one. You will see our mast easier than we can see you. The password will be Prince Edward."

I nodded, that was the name of the Black Prince. "If we are not here after three visits then we are lost and you should save yourself."

"I pray that it will not come to that!" That was the extent of our goodbyes for we were both warriors.

I clambered over the tumblehome and lowered myself to the dock. The sloop slipped slowly downstream on the current. I joined Sharp and slipped my satchel across my back. The well-worn path led to the trees ahead. We spoke in Portuguese. I knew that it was hard for Sharp but he was getting better at it. "Sir, if this was used fifty years ago why is it so well worn?"

"I am guessing that smugglers will use this. Don't forget that the Portuguese tax goods too and there are always people who do not wish to pay taxes."

The river to our right was a good guide and by keeping it to our right we could keep taking paths which would, inevitably, bring us into Coimbra. Dawn would be in a couple of hours and I guessed that there would be a curfew. I had the magic pass in my hand and I hoped that would get us through any French patrols we might meet. In the event, it proved to be a lifesaver, quite literally. Even before we reached the outskirts of the city, we could hear squeals and screams. It should have been silent for it was the middle of the night. What we could not know, but soon discovered, was that the French army was out of control. They had lost a battle and found a city which had drink, food and women. The Marshal could not control his men. That became obvious when we passed a house with the door beaten down and, as we passed, we saw four drunken French soldiers raping a woman. The fact that the woman was past middle age did not seem to bother them. I was suddenly glad that most people had left the city but for the ones who remained, it was a nightmare. There were butchered dogs lying in the street and from other houses we heard shouts, screams and cries which told us that the rape was not an isolated incident.

We were two men and as such of little interest to most of the gangs of soldiers we saw roaming the streets looking for drink or women. We almost made it to the Cathedral before five young soldiers chanced upon us. One, a little larger than the rest shouted, "I bet these have money! Hand over your money, your clothes and your boots and we will not harm you." His laughter told me that he was lying.

I proffered the pass and spoke in French, "My friend, we have a pass from Marshal Masséna. If you hurt us then it will not go well with you!"

I saw that my French, the pass and my lack of fear worked with two of the five but the loutish looking one was not intimidated. He pulled a wicked-looking knife from his boot, "I spit on Masséna! If he had done his work then ten of my comrades would not lie dead in Bussaco! If you are a friend of his then that guarantees your death!"

I put the pass back in my frock coat pocket and took out my pistol. I knew that Sharp would be ready for whatever I did. The lout looked at the pistol and laughed, "I am a soldier of the 1st Line and your pissy little pistol does not frighten me!"

He launched himself at me as did one of his companions. The third ran at Sharp. The lout tried to swing his knife into my side but all he hit was my leather satchel. I had had no intention of firing my pistol but, instead, I brought it around to smack so hard into the side of his head that I heard a crack. He fell in a heap at my feet. I had the pistol in the mouth of the other one before he knew it. His eyes widened. "So, putón!" I used the Spanish curse for it had the same meaning in French! "The tables are turned." Sharp had laid out his assailant. I shouted, "You two, come here!" The two fearful ones were cowering but they approached. "Take the weapons and put them in the hat of this one and do it fast or you lose this friend." I cocked the pistol and I heard the Frenchman as he pissed himself. He tried to speak but the barrel of the pistol prevented it. "The time for talking has passed. So when I see my friend, Marshal Masséna, I shall tell him that there are three of his soldiers from the 1st Line who need to be broken on the wheel." The two frightened soldiers handed me the hat filled with weapons. "You two run back to your unit and tell your sergeant what happened. You may escape with just a whipping!" The two men fled. "As for you," I took the gun from his mouth and holstered it. The look of relief on his face soon disappeared as I rammed my fist into his solar plexus and the half-drunk man fell, gasping for breath. "I suggest that you and your companion desert unless he is dead already!"

We left. Sharp said as we moved off, "Sir, that was a bit harsh. They were drunk!"

I nodded, "Aye Sharp, and what would they have done if they had found a woman?" His eyes widened as he took in the implications.

By the time we reached the Cathedral, dawn was breaking and I heard the tramp of feet as soldiers marched, albeit a little late, to reimpose order. I waited until one such patrol of line soldiers approached us and they levelled their weapons at us.

"What is your business and why are you out after curfew?"

In answer, I handed him the pass. He stiffened and saluted. I handed him the hat of weapons, "We were attacked by three members of the 1st Line not far from here. We left them to the west somewhere. I do not think that the Marshal will be happy with our treatment."

"No, sir!" He turned to two of his men, "Leforge and Ludon, escort these two gentlemen to the hotel the Marshal is using."

I nodded, "I will tell the Marshal of your assistance and diligence to duty!"

When we reached the hotel, I saw that there were Dragoons on guard and they were the elite troop. The presence of the two soldiers accompanying us meant we were not stopped and we walked straight into the hotel. We had done what the Marshal had asked but we had not used the method he had suggested. The foyer of the grand hotel was empty and we slumped in two chairs for we were playing a part. I waved over one of the hotel staff and said, in Portuguese, "Coffee for two and some pastries!" I think he was going to question me but there is something about looking at a one-eyed man which seems intimidating. It is as though the one remaining eye becomes fiercer somehow. He scurried away.

By the time the General Staff were up, we had breakfasted and I was enjoying a cigar which had been given to me by the hotel manager. It was La poule à Masséna who spotted us. She was wearing a Hussar's uniform once more and she squealed when she saw me. Masséna smiled and said, "You are resourceful, my friend, but this is a little public." He turned and saw a private dining room with a curtain. "Come and join me there." He turned to his mistress. "Keep Señor d'Alvarez's servant company!"

Once inside the small room, he wasted no time and spoke French for it was obvious that he was surprised at my arrival. "What has happened? I did not expect you so soon!" He frowned, "What is amiss?"

I spoke calmly, "I discovered news which I thought would be of interest to you and financially rewarding for me. When I heard you were in Coimbra, I thought to come here to speak with you."

"How did you get here?"

"I told you in Viseu, I am a dealer in wines and I have ships which I charter. I chartered a small one and it dropped me along the river. It is now collecting wine I bought when I passed through Coimbra."

The Lines of Torres Vedras

He looked relieved, "You are resourceful! What is your news?"

"Lisbon harbour is full of empty British transports!"

His eyes lit up for he was a clever man and understood the import of my words, "They are preparing to leave." I nodded. He rubbed his chin, "But they hurt us at Bussaco!"

I shrugged, "I know nothing about that but when I left there were ambulances fetching large numbers of wounded and a source of mine says that camps are being built in Madeira. I thought you would want this news sooner rather than later although the behaviour of your men in Coimbra makes me think that you are unprepared for a war!"

He frowned, "What do you mean?" I told him what I had seen and he shook his head, "Animals! I will have them flogged. My apologies."

"Marshal, the British might be leaving but treating the civilians this way will only encourage them to fight you. If we are both to make money then you need the Portuguese on your side!"

"You are a clever man and I am grateful that you are an ally of France and of me. How long will you stay?"

"We will leave after lunch; I have a little business to conduct and then I will return to Lisbon. If the British knew I was here then I would become a prisoner as they do not tolerate spies!"

"Then I will have your first instalment brought before lunch. The food here is adequate." He stood and held out his hand, "Thank you, my friend, and I have heeded your words. Please, use this room as your office. I will inform the hotel and my men that it is to be so!"

"Thank you, Marshal. That is most kind of you."

Sharp joined me, carrying our satchels. He cocked his head to one side and I spoke in Portuguese. "The Marshal is pleased with our efforts and we have this room to use while we are here."

He grinned, "That is most kind of the Marshal."

"Ask the hotel manager for a menu. We will eat lunch and then head back to the river!"

The lunch was excellent and I think that the Portuguese hotel manager was keen to stay on the good side of the French. I do not know what he would have thought if he had known that we were spies! We had just finished the meal and I was enjoying a cigar when there was a cough from beyond the curtain and a voice said, "I come from Marshal Masséna."

"Enter!"

An aide came in with a small wooden box. "The Marshal said I was to give you this."

I nodded, "Place it on the table and then you may go." I could see that he was desperate to know the contents but I would not give him the satisfaction. If Masséna had wished him to know then he would have told him. With the curtain closed, I opened it and saw that it was filled with coins. Some were gold but most were silver. They were all Portuguese. I said, quietly, "It seems it is not just the rank and file who have been robbing Coimbra. Come it is time we left." We emptied the coins into our satchels and I carried the small chest.

I waved cheerily to the hotel manager. He did not wave back but raced out of the back. I was suspicious. The streets were now patrolled by soldiers and as we left a Dragoon Lieutenant approached and spoke in halting Portuguese, "Señor, we are to escort you to… out of the city."

I nodded.

The eight Dragoons flanked us as we walked. I knew not what the populace thought but it kept us safe. When we reached the house which had been the scene of the rape we had witnessed I saw that the door had been boarded up. It marked the edge of the city.

I turned and waved to the Lieutenant, "Thank you, Lieutenant."

He turned and left. As he did so I caught sight of a movement behind him. Walking towards the woods I said, in French, "We are being followed. Make certain that your pistol is loaded."

Sharp nodded and we walked with our hands on our pistol's butts. The men who followed us were good but we were better for our lives had depended upon our skill for many years. This was not the French who followed us it was the Portuguese and they were after the chest. Not all the Portuguese were loyal. They had a criminal class too and I had no doubt that the hotel manager was part of it. We still had an hour or so for the rendezvous and I was confident that we could make it but I did not wish these criminals to see the sloop. I took a decision, "Let us run and when I shout, we stop and face them!"

"Right sir. By the way, sir, there are four of them!"

Sharp was good and I was lucky to have him at my side. As we ran, I heard footsteps pounding behind us. We were fit and I doubted that they would be as fit as we were. I headed for the quay. As soon as I saw where the path left the main track and headed south, I shouted, "Now!" I said it in French.

As we turned, I was already preparing to hurl the chest. I saw that they were just twenty paces from us and were armed with swords and clubs. They had the scarred and weathered faces of fighters. I hurled the box at the man next to the leader who was not sure whether to catch the box he thought contained treasure or to bat it to the side. In the event, he did neither and the box hit him on the forehead and he fell to the ground. I drew my pistol and aimed it at them. They were not fazed by that. I daresay the pistols that they had seen used were poor quality but mine

The Lines of Torres Vedras

was the best and my ball took the leader in the chest. Sharp was even more ruthless and his ball hit his target between the eyes. The one I had struck rose unsteadily to his feet and seeing his two dead and dying companions joined his last companion and ran. I went to pick up the box. It would not do to leave it.

I ran to the quay and placed it on the wooden deck. Running back, I helped Sharp to carry the bodies, one by one, and dump them in the river. We were just throwing in the one who had been killed first when I saw **'Black Prince'** edge around the bend. She was early.

As she turned, I heard Jonathan shout, "We heard firing and thought you might need help!"

We clambered aboard and I said, "There were brigands trying to take us."

He nodded, "Let slip! Well, there is more bad news I am afraid. The French have a sloop too and she is heading up the river. We will have to fight our way out! I hope you have more balls for your pistols!"

As we headed downstream, I said, "But I did not know the French had any ships left in the Atlantic."

"They still have some smaller ships at Royan and La Rochelle which are small enough to evade the big boys. My guess this is nothing to do with us and the French are just using it to send messages to Masséna. The irony is she is British built!"

"British built?"

"Aye, she was HMS Speedy until the French captured her. We captured her and then the French got her again in 01. She is now the **'Saint Paul'**. Don't worry, we can handle her."

We hurried to the cabin and dumped our satchels. The coins we had gained seemed unimportant somehow. I began to reload my pistol as we raced down the river. Jonathan knew his business and he had the minimum sail set to make the smallest profile. His guns were loaded and run out. I joined the captain at the helm. The bosun had the wheel.

"She has four pounders unless the French have uprated her. We have six pounders and my crew can outgun any Frenchman!"

"Do they know you are here?"

He grinned, "I doubt it as it was my topman who spied her masts. My lads are good and he knew her straightaway. We turned around and headed back to pick you up. We knew that we could beat her but if we had any damage then we might have missed you. It worked out well in the end!" He looked up to the lookout perched precariously on the cross trees. "Any sign of her?"

"Not yet sir!"

Jonathan pointed to the starboard, "That is the side we will take her if you fancy a pop!"

Sharp and I went to the starboard side. Darkness had fallen and this was not like a land battle for a ship was silent. It had neither hooves nor boots to clatter on stone. The only sounds which could be heard were the crack of a rope or the sail and that was all. By shortening sail Jonathan had minimised the risk from them seeing the shadow of a sail. A stone hit the deck and we looked up. The lookout pointed ahead. He had seen the other sloop. I found it quite remarkable that Jonathan's crew did not need verbal commands. He made a signal with his arm and I saw the gun captains prepare to lower their linstocks. I peered into the dark, desperate to see the enemy but I saw nought. How did you fight a battle when you could not see the enemy? Suddenly, as we turned a bend the French sloop hove into view. Jonathan's gun captains must have had total confidence for the guns fired in pairs as they came to bear. The first two balls took out the bowsprit and the mast and, as the rigging fell into the sea, the enemy sloop slowed. The next two guns took out a section of the gunwale and one of the guns. The next gun took another gun out and the last two guns managed to topple the mainmast. As it crashed down across the wheel the crew of Jonathan's ship all cheered. They had won.

I heard Jonathan laughing, "If we did not have to return the Major to Lisbon then *'HMS Speedy'* would be British once more! Major Matthews, you have cost me money! Drinks are on you when we reach Lisbon!"

I laughed, "Do not worry, my friend, you will not lose out!"

"We will have to take a diversion and give this information to the frigates at the mouth of the river. I suspect the Admiral will be less than happy!"

By the time we reached the mouth of the river, it was dark and Jonathan headed for the dark shape of the nearest frigate. He had the Midshipman use the ship's lamp to give the recognition signal. When we received the correct response, we closed up and hove to. As we bobbed up and down Jonathan shouted our news across. I heard the ship's captain growl, "Heads will roll for this! Thank you, Lieutenant Commander, I commend your zeal and prompt action. I shall inform the Admiral but he will need a written report."

"Yes, sir, I expected that."

As we headed south, he grumbled, "I can manage to avoid the writing of reports on most days but not this one. It means we will have to, albeit briefly, rejoin the fleet."

"I meant to ask what were you doing in Lisbon harbour?"

"Viscount Wellesley asked for us to be there. We take messages to Cadiz and back. It is quite profitable for there are Arab pirates as well as blockade runners. We normally manage to take one every other voyage."

We reached Lisbon in daylight and that meant that Sharp and I could enjoy an evening in Lisbon. As we were tying up, I gave Jonathan half of the coins we had received from the Marshal. His eyes widened, "I cannot take this!"

"Sharp and I have as much and I feel you did your share of the work. Use it to compensate your crew for the loss of the revenue from the French sloop." I smiled, "And I expect no written report!"

He took the coins and clasped my forearm, "You are a good fellow and the eye patch you wore while aboard seemed appropriate. Until the next time!"

Chapter 12

We reached Torres Vedras the next day. The General was still at the defences and so, leaving Sharp to see to our war gear, I rode Donna to speak with him. If Sir Arthur could do two things at once then he was a happy man. I found him at the large fort at Sobral; this was the lynchpin of the defences for it guarded a major crossroads. He glanced down when Lieutenant Mountshaft announced me, "Ah, Matthews, I take it you have had a successful trip?" He waved a hand, "We will speak shortly but I spy the first of our blue-coated opponents discovering that we have been busy!" The Great Redoubt afforded a fine view of the French approach. I saw skirmishers in the distance. Sir Arthur used his telescope and had a better view but the flea like movements of the blue soldiers told me that they were skirmishers. I heard the pop of muskets and knew that they would be the Portuguese in the smaller forts and emplacements around the Sobral complex. The French would not fire until they found a place to hide and the defences were such that it would be hard to do so. I saw a couple of soldiers fall and, after a short while a trumpet sounded and the French fell back. This was not an assault, it was the first of their advance units scouting.

The Viscount turned, "Now we can talk. Come, we will ride back to Torres Vedras and you shall tell me all on the way."

I gave him the bare facts without any embellishment for that was the way he liked his reports: terse and to the point. He did not react when I told him of the abominations committed by the French Troops. When I finished, he nodded, seemingly satisfied. "I thought that you had succeeded for the French sent their scouts south yesterday to the west of us. They sent Hussars first and then received a bloody nose for their troubles. Today was more cautious and I think that Marshal Masséna will be devising a way to take Sobral. He will find that a hard nut to crack for there are almost two thousand men at Sobral alone." He looked up at the sky. "In England, October means the start of harsh weather with falling leaves and icy, frost-filled nights. You were here in 08 with Sir John Moore, what is it like in winter?"

"Despite the fact that we are further south, because Portugal is such a mountainous country, winters are worse than in England. Add to that the fact that there is little food and it will be miserable for all. I think, Sir Arthur, that even our men will find life difficult. For the French? I cannot conceive!"

"I hope so! The penny pinching and self-serving politicians in Parliament have tried to starve me of funds. I am grateful that Sir

Godfrey is such an advocate of our endeavours and he has managed to persuade his colleagues to support us. If we can survive this winter, and I believe that we can, then, with more reinforcements in spring and a depleted Marshal Masséna and his army of Portugal, then we may be able to venture back into Spain."

I did not mention that we would have to take both Almeida and Cuidad Rodrigo to do so.

"Tomorrow you will accompany me to Sobral again. We will make my headquarters there for a week or so. If Marshal Masséna believes your report then he will try to get to Lisbon as soon as he can. Sobral is just 21 miles from Lisbon and has the best road; I believe he will see this as his quick route to Lisbon. He may think that we have defended the crossroads only. I cannot believe that he will, as yet, have discovered the extent of our defences." He smiled, "You see, Matthews, I have learned a little from Colonel Selkirk. By making Marshal Masséna attack prematurely we delay his exploration of the defences and the longer he delays then the worse the weather will be when he finally decides to see their extent. The time he spends probing our lines will be time he should spend making shelters for his men. Your little trip might well spell disaster for the French." I nodded, "Of course none shall ever know of it. Who knows I may need to use you again!"

"Surely my story is blown apart, sir. The Marshal will not trust me again!"

"Who knows. If he believes that you are a businessman looking to line his own purse then he might think that you would not recognise the formidable defences we have constructed. However, that is for the future. For the present you are once again, Major Matthews, attached to my staff, and we will go to war again, soon!"

The next day Sharp and I joined Sir Arthur Wellesley as General Spencer marched the 1st Division and General Cole marched the 4th Division towards Sobral. That Masséna and the French would attack there was now obvious for the Portuguese sentries had reported large numbers of French arriving. The General joined the Portuguese in the Great Redoubt and then the light companies from the two divisions were spread out amongst the forts which lay before Sobral. This time it was not the 95th Rifles, it was the 60th. They, too, were a good regiment but here they were used in penny packets across the front. They would give the defenders better range.

As darkness fell, we were all in position and I was with the General in his new, temporary headquarters. Although he was confident that the defences would hold, I sensed nervousness from Sir Arthur for the concept was his. Success could only be measured in complete victory. If

The Lines of Torres Vedras

the French made any gains then the idea was flawed and he would have failed.

I knew that I was correct when he took me aside as most of the others prepared for bed. "Matthews, I want you to join Spencer's forward position in fort 120. That will be the first one they will strike. You are a calm and measured fellow and do not make hasty decisions. Join them and be my eyes and ears. If you have to pull back then I shall know that it is a serious attack and will act accordingly."

"Yes, sir."

This time we would not need our horses. Grabbing a blanket and our guns Sharp and I made our way along the path which had been constructed to link the forts with the redoubt. The paths were cunningly built so that we could not be seen by an attacker. We could reinforce any fort which came under attack. The earth had been piled up to give a sort of barrier so that if we were under fire we could crouch below its top. The path also zigged and zagged to throw off any gunners. Sir Richard had done a good job and he would save many lives. We passed other forts for each fort protected two others. 120 was the closest to the north and was the most isolated. While the bulk of the regiments were in trenches and behind small parapets, the fort was manned by the light company of the 71st, 61 Riflemen from the 60th and a couple of companies of two Portuguese Battalions. The Portuguese gunners had a single eight pounder gun. I saw that they had canister close by. Captain Jamieson of the 71st, the Glasgow Highland Light Infantry, was the senior officer and I saw his face fall when he realised that he had a senior officer to contend with.

I pre-empted any questions, "Captain, I am here as an observer. The General believes that the French will attack and you are likely to bear the brunt of the attack. I am here to observe and to advise."

"We have only seen skirmishers, sir, are you sure?"

"Captain, there are 65,000 Frenchmen within a few miles of here. There is no food for the Portuguese have taken it all. Do you think that they will just sit there and wait for winter to descend?"

The 71st had been in Portugal since Vimiero. They were down to just 490 men on roll and Captain Jamieson was no fool. He looked north and nodded, "Then any help you can give would be appreciated." He turned to his sergeant, "Find a space for the Major and his sergeant."

"Yes, sir."

I handed my gun and blanket to Sharp and went to the front of the fort. All the forts were slightly different but they all had some things in common. One common feature was a ditch with a berm and a parapet. I took out my telescope and, in the fading light, scanned the horizon. The

French were there, I could see their shakoes and their blue uniforms, but they were not close enough to launch an attack. In the ditch were *chevaux-de-fries* and *crows' feet*. These obstacles could be avoided in daylight but a night attack would be disastrous. They were not going to attack before dark and if they attacked in the morning, they would wait for the sun to rise.

"Did you get some grenades from your grenadier company, Captain?"

His face fell, "We don't normally use them."

"A pity for if the French get into the ditch, we could make it a killing ground. Still, we shall have to make do with what we have. Is there enough room for all of the men on the firing steps?"

"Yes, sir." His face showed questions and the resentment about my arrival had been replaced by concern that he was not as secure as he thought he might be.

I looked around and saw that the defenders of the fort looked vigilant. "Then I shall retire as I am sure we will be busy come the morning."

Sharp and the sergeant had found us a sheltered corner at the rear of the fort. Half of the men were in tents just behind the fort; in winter they would be cheerless and cold. Sharp had rigged his oiled cloak above the corner to afford some shelter.

"The sergeant offered to get us a tent, sir, but I thought you would want to be here."

"Quite right, Sharp. Tomorrow will be a busy one for us. The rest of the division is spread out on either side of this position and if the French attack is as forceful as I believe it will be then they will struggle to hold them." Sir Arthur liked ridges and dead ground but the very nature of these defences meant that we had to use the opposite. The French had to ascend and that, in turn, dictated the places the Division would defend.

After we had eaten, I rolled in my blanket and slept. I saw the surprise on the faces of the other officers when I curled up in the corner with my sergeant. They were still hidebound by the conventions of their regiments where officers and their sergeants led separate lives. The work Sharp and I did had resulted in a different way of life and I was quite comfortable with it.

I woke well before dawn and, before I even made water, I went to the Sergeant in command of the section of fort closest to me. He started as I ghosted next to him. I could be as silent as any when I chose. "You fair gave me a turn there, sir."

"Sorry sergeant. Any movement out there?"

"Funny you should say that, sir. One reason you gave me such a shock was that I was looking out there and I think I saw a movement but I could not be certain."

"Where?"

He pointed down the slope which was all black. As my eyes adjusted then the darkness changed a little and some parts became lighter. I just focussed on one patch as moving your eyes could miss movement. I saw a shadow move and knew that the sergeant was right. "I will go and speak with your officer. Have your men wake, silently, their messmates."

"Sir."

Sharp was already awake, "I will get the rifles, sir."

The duty officer was Lieutenant Bushnell of the Rifles. He saw my approach and turned, "Sir?"

"I believe that the French are out there. I am unsure if it is just a reconnaissance or an attack but let us assume that it is the latter and wake the men but do so quietly so that if they do attack at dawn then they will get a rude surprise."

"But sir, when they hear reveille from the rest of the Division sounded, they will know that we are awake!"

"And that may well be the moment when they attack for reveille means that the enemy will know that most of our defenders are awake. Were you at the Côa?"

"No, sir."

"There they were already attacking when it was the middle of the night and during a thunderstorm. At Bussaco, Loison and his mean came before dawn. It is how this French Marshal fights."

"Sir." He padded off.

After making water I donned my jacket and put my sword belt and holsters around my waist. Sharp handed me the Baker and we went to the firing step. The men were not silent for they had been woken and could see no reason for it. There were mumblings and grumblings. They might carry to the French but as they only came from one section of the front, I did not think that they would read too much into it. Captain Jamieson came over to me. "Are you sure about this, sir?"

Just then the sergeant who had seen the French first brought me a mug of tea, "Here y'are sir. The first brew of the day. I daresay the fires will be out soon enough!"

"Thank you, sergeant." I took the cup and he went to rejoin his men. "Your sergeant there saw movement, Captain, and I confirmed it. It might well just be scouts but losing an hour of sleep is better than losing men, eh?"

He nodded, "I suppose you are right."

By the time reveille sounded in the camps of the rest of the division the fort's parapet was lined with muskets and rifles and the eight-pound gun was loaded and the linstocks readied. The last notes were fading when the muskets began to pop all along the line. A company of Portuguese were below us and I saw the flash of muskets in the twilight as they were attacked by the French skirmishers. Then there was a French command and a long, loud, rolling volley was fired followed by a cheer as a French line suddenly attacked. The length and nature of the volley told me that this was a major attack by a number of battalions. We could not return fire for we could see nothing and there was little point in wasting ball. Suddenly one of our men shouted, "Sir, the Portuguese lads are running!" He pointed to the trenches before us.

The Cazadores were brave but they had been attacked whilst just waking. Attacking as an army is waking is a clever move and the French had already broken our first line of defence. I risked peering over the top and saw that the rest of the 71st and the 60th were also falling back. The fort was a bastion and they were running to take shelter behind it. I looked at Captain Jamieson and nodded. This was his command and I was just advising.

"Prepare muskets! Artillery await my command!"

I rested my Baker on the parapet. The fort had been well designed and there was just enough room for the men to all fire at the same time. Should any of those who had fled wish to enter the fort then there would be replacements for any who were incapacitated. The firing was intensifying as the French prosecuted their attack. This would be the first test of the lines of Torres Vedras.

I heard Lieutenant Bushnell give the command, "60th, choose your targets and fire at will." Baker rifles did not volley. They chose their targets carefully and the riflemen took pride in hitting exactly where they aimed. I peered through the smoke and the gloom of dawn. I saw the French Light infantry as they scrambled up the rock slope and through the scrubby undergrowth. I tracked a sergeant who kept urging his men on. I heard other Baker rifles as they opened fire and saw men falling. I waited until my target turned to head up the slope and when I fired, I hit him in the shoulder and he spun around.

"Fire!"

The ground before us disappeared in a fog of smoke as the three companies opened fire with their muskets. I saw the flash of muskets as the French fired in reply. They were ragged. The line infantry who followed would be the ones who would give us a volley. The fact that I could hear little firing around us told me that the bulk of the division had retired behind the fortification. That was not a defeat for it was how the forts were designed to be used. The men behind us would now be formed up into the disciplined lines which would tear apart any column which tried to outflank the fort.

I heard the drums in the distance and that told me that columns were coming. I peered over the top as I reloaded my Baker and saw the French skirmishers, for the sun had risen and illuminated the scene. Captain Jamieson saw them too and he shouted, "Artillery! Fire!"

The cannon belched its deadly canister and it acted like a giant shotgun. It tore through the skirmishers and into the head of the column which I could not see but which I knew was there. The French tried to force their way around us and I heard the distinctive sound of a battalion volley as they met the men they had driven from their position. The attack ended and we saw the remains of the French making their way back to their original defences.

We had suffered no casualties and Captain Jamieson saluted me as he approached me, "Well sir, the defences worked."

"I never had a doubt, Captain."

"Will they come again, do you think?"

"Perhaps but we have some time before they do so. I would have the men fed but let them eat on the firing step. Vigilance eh?"

The morning passed and we saw the French three hundred paces from us. They were beyond the range of muskets and rifles. Our solitary cannon now had just ball loaded and that would not be wasted.

It was noon when Sharp said, "Sir, there is a movement! Horses!"

I took my telescope and saw Marshal Masséna and his staff approach. He stopped on a hillside which afforded him a good view of the fort. I recognised most of the officers with him from Viseu and Coimbra. He took out his telescope and began to scan our lines. I went to the artillerymen and spoke in Portuguese to the Lieutenant there. "Do you think that you can hit that group of officers?"

He grinned, "I could try, sir! The ball we loaded was the best that we had and should fly true."

Obligingly the French officers did not move and so the Lieutenant had the time to aim. When he shouted, "Fire!" I watched the ball as it flew through the air. It was aimed well and the gunner knew his business. He had aimed at the ground before the officers so that the ball would bounce up and tear through the group. Fate intervened and the ball hit not earth but a rock in the ground. It deflected the ball which flew to the right of the Marshal and, showering stones from the rock, struck some engineers who were assessing our defences.

That we had almost struck the officers made the whole fort cheer and Marshal Masséna took off his hat and swept it in an exaggerated salute before leading off his officers. We did not know it then but that was the end of the only conflict that the Lines of Torres Vedras had to endure. After seven days of desultory skirmishing, I rode back to Sir Arthur to report that the French attacks on Sobral had ceased. As I travelled back the weather became even more autumnal and rain began to fall. If nothing else that would help us for it would dampen powder and make the ground even more treacherous.

"You were at the front line, Matthews, tell me how the defences did."

"They worked, my lord, although had they attacked at multiple points, I am not so sure."

"You have a point and I will not relax my vigilance but the fact that Masséna did not use a large number of men fills me with hope. From what you say it was just a division."

I nodded for we had taken prisoners and they told us that it was General Clausel's Division of General Junot's Corps which had attacked. He had just committed 2,500 men and showed his caution. Had Ney commanded then all 6,500 men of the Corps would have attacked. It was a reconnaissance in force and had been beaten back. I had seen, as I rode back, the problems the French would have. The two forts which supported fort 120 each had two guns and attacking French columns would have been blown apart with shot and shell from the front and the sides.

"You shall stay here at Headquarters for now. Let us see what the French do."

For the next month, French skirmishers and patrols probed all along the front line of the defences. When they ceased the General sent for me. "The frontline troops report that the French are no longer probing. Take a patrol from the 14th Light Dragoons and investigate for me, would you?"

He made it sound easy but it was far from that. I rode immediately to Captain Wilson and his troopers, who, bored with life in camp leapt at the chance to be riding forth once more. I found a place to cross into French territory which had been reported as being quiet for two weeks. As we left the last British outpost, I had the men load and carry their carbines. It was Sharp who spotted the French. I spied them on the skyline and, leaving the troopers to guard our back the two of us dismounted and headed through the undergrowth. I wished to listen to the French sentries. From my experience, you learned much from such eavesdropping. What surprised me, as I walked closer was the silence. The sentries were not speaking. We approached a little closer and I sniffed the air. What I could not smell was woodsmoke nor could I smell pipes. That was unusual. It was November and as cold as the middle of winter. I took a risk and approached the sentries. I was wearing a frock coat and I just shouted, in French, "Officer approaching the camp!" My hand was on my pistol. As we stepped through the undergrowth, I saw that what I had taken to be sentries were straw-stuffed dummies. Masséna had gone.

I turned and shouted, "Captain Wilson, our horses!"

The troop galloped up fearing, no doubt, that there was danger. When they saw the dummies the Captain said, "Humbugged!"

"Let us ride along their defences first and then we can make a judgement!"

He was right, of course, and the French had gone. When I told the General, he was livid. It was with himself more than anything. Roused, he summoned his leaders and the army was mobilised. The 14th was attached to Fane's Brigade and Sir Arthur sent me with them to see if we could catch the French. I doubted that we would for who knew how many days had elapsed since they had abandoned their defences. We found them just 40 miles north of Sobral at Santarém on the River Tagus. Their well-constructed position told me that they had been there for more than two days and we returned to Sir Arthur with the news that Lisbon was no longer under threat but the French were still in Portugal.

Chapter 13

If the winter was hard for us then it was impossible for the French. The Portuguese had taken everything of value as well as every animal and grain of food. It was winter and there was little fodder for their cavalry. Brigadier Fane's cavalry patrols prevented the French from venturing either west or south. He was guarding the road to the besieged Spanish fortress of Badajoz.

Sir Arthur allowed me to spend the winter in Lisbon. He even intimated that if I wished to take a leave in England then it would be acceptable. Despite my letter from Mrs de Lacey, I was not confident enough to call upon her unannounced and so we stayed in Portugal. Sharp and I lived in Donna Alvarez's home which was familiar and I found the house reminded me of the fine lady and was comforting rather than maudlin. It was January when I received the reply to my letter to Emily. She was far less guarded in this missive and almost blunt. She asked me why I had not called upon her as she had read that the army did not fight in winter. I felt a fool when I read that for it was now too late to return. I wrote a long letter in reply and assured her that as soon as Sir Arthur released me then I would take ship for England and I would visit with her. When I handed the letter over in the middle of February to the Packet Captain, I suddenly felt much better.

Neither Sharp nor I had been idle. Our Portuguese was now fluent and we had been able to speak with the knowledgeable businessmen of Lisbon. We learned of the stranglehold which Napoleon had on the whole of Europe. His laws were now making the countries he had conquered into part of France; they no longer had their own laws; they were subject to the laws of France. He had even created a country, Belgium. Before Napoleon, it had been part of the Spanish Empire but now it had its own king! In terms of the British and Portuguese, it was disastrous news for it meant he had more money now to finance his armies. I wondered why he did not bring his armies south to finally rid himself of the Spanish ulcer the annoying British who refused to bow down before him as the rest of Europe had done. As good as Sir Arthur undoubtedly was, Napoleon Bonaparte with the full might of France and Europe would have been unbeatable. I think Sir Arthur was also mindful of the position he found himself in for I was summoned back to Torres Vedras at the end of February.

Our horses had been grain-fed over the winter and were in good condition. We took with us those supplies we knew we might need in a land plundered by the French. As we neared Torres Vedras, we saw that the British and Portuguese who were camped there appeared to be in good spirits. Sir Arthur's presence did that for the morale of the troops. There were many senior staff at the Headquarters for Sir Arthur was planning his offensive. Lieutenant Mountshaft met us and showed Sharp our quarters while I went directly in to the headquarters where the generals and Sir Arthur's aides were studying maps. He did not acknowledge my presence and I just stood to examine new faces.

One that stood out was Major General Sir William Erskine. I had heard of him from Sir Robert Crauford. That Sir Robert did not like him spoke volumes for Black Bob was a good judge of character. Sir William proved to be the strangest man I would ever meet in King George's service. Not only was he extremely short-sighted and refused to wear eyeglasses, but he also appeared to be even more unstable than many of the generals I had met. I had learned not to judge a man before I got to know him, however, the fact that none of the senior officers were standing by him seemed to confirm Black Bob's opinion.

Sir Robert was in England on leave and Lieutenant Colonel Beckwith who was in temporary command waved me over, "Matthews, good to see you. This is Sir Stapleton Cotton. He will command the cavalry. I just told him that you two will get on famously. You transformed the young bucks in the 14th."

I had seen Sir Stapleton for he had commanded the cavalry at Bussaco but as they had not been involved in any action I had yet to speak with him. I knew that he had a good reputation and was well respected by all cavalrymen, light and heavy.

"Pleased to meet you, my lord."

"I have heard good things about you. Sir Edward Paget said that you should have been given the command of a regiment for what you did with Sir John Moore."

"Very kind, I am certain, but I am content with my lot."

Lieutenant Colonel Beckwith laughed, "I told you, my lord, the man is rare. I cannot think of another officer who will happily serve under those less competent than he."

Sir Stapleton pointed over to Sir William Erskine who appeared to be talking to himself, "Then you have never served under Sir William."

"No, sir, this is the first time I have met him."

Sir Stapleton said, "He has taken over Leith's Division, more's the pity. Still, he is just one bad apple. Let us hope he does not ruin the barrel!" He shook his head, "Just so long as Sir Arthur does not give him the Light Division then I shall be happy."

One of the Viscount's aides came in with a document. Sir Arthur read it and then, shaking his head, said, "Gentlemen, could I have your attention?" Sir Arthur had presence and everyone, including Sir William, fell silent. "Badajoz has but days left. The French will take that fortress and, I dare say, Elvas will follow soon after. Marshal Soult has another Corps and he will reduce both fortresses. Once he has taken the last fortress then there is nothing to stop him from coming to the aid of Marshal Masséna. Although we believe he has lost upwards of 15,000 men the reinforcements which Soult could bring would increase his force by more than 10,000. We must drive Marshal Masséna from Santarém and force him north before he can join with Soult. I intend to order Marshal Beresford to bring his Portuguese army to help us at this time. Until the Spanish can recover, we have only the Portuguese upon whom we can rely." He put his palms flat on the table, "So let us put our minds together and work out how to drive the French hence." To those who did not know him, it would sound as though he was inviting suggestions. That was not Sir Arthur's way. He had decided upon his strategy and we would follow his plan, to the letter.

There were already 25,000 troops close to Santarém and so we just marched the rest of our army east to join them. Perhaps Marshal Masséna had already decided to leave or it may have been pure luck but as we headed towards the French the scouts from around the town sent the message that the French were pulling out and heading for the Mondego. That changed our plans. Sir Arthur sent out flying columns of horsemen and light troops to find the French. We entered the Portuguese town but what we found both sickened and disgusted me.

Santarém had been a beautiful place before the wars had begun. Even before this most recent invasion, it had been a quiet and happy place. Now it was like Coimbra and a shell of its former self. Although most of the people had left and fled the French, some had been unable to do so and the first elements into the town discovered houses filled with the dead. Fine furniture had been burned as firewood and the butchered corpses of all sorts of animals littered the town as well as the corpses of murdered Portuguese. The French had left because there was neither grazing for their animals nor food for their men. The mood of our Anglo-Portuguese army was one of anger and we hurried along the road after them. I was still with Sir Arthur for he had not yet decided how best to use me. The slaughter of the animals had backfired on the French for they had no draught animals to pull their guns and they had had to abandon most of their artillery. The Portuguese and our artillery were the beneficiaries. We did not know at the time that they had split up and we found ourselves following Marshal Ney. He was courageous and the men who were in his Corps were equally resolute. On the 11th of March, three days after the pursuit had begun, we had our first losses. Some

Caçadores, a brigade of them, no doubt still angered by the treatment of their town, closed too quickly with Ney's rearguard and his men turned and trounced the Portuguese. It was a defeat but at least we knew that we were close.

Sir Arthur took personal charge and our vanguard was led by him personally with the Royal Dragoons, 4th Dragoons and the Light Division supported by the 3rd and 4th Divisions and Pack's Portuguese. It was a formidable force and would not be dismissed as easily but Ney's rearguard proved a doughty enemy. We caught up with them at Redinha. Although we outnumbered them, they had unlimbered the six guns from a horse artillery battery and were prepared. This time it was Sir Arthur who commanded and he prepared his attack carefully. He sent in the Light Division first and had his cavalry on the flanks. I think it might have gone ill for us had not the Rifles been with us. The 95th began to pick off the gunners while the 43rd and 52nd duelled with the French Light Infantry. The French Chasseurs looked eager to engage with the Royal Dragoons but the Chasseurs realised that they would come off worse against heavy cavalry. When two of the officers from the horse artillery were killed and one crew was incapacitated then Ney decided to withdraw. Our own Dragoons were keen to chase after them but Sir Arthur, wisely in my opinion, made them hold their position.

I thought all was going well until the next day when one of our columns, led by Major General Erskine, marched through a valley in thick fog without skirmishers and when the fog suddenly lifted found themselves under the French guns. Sir Arthur had made the mistake of allowing Major General Erskine to command the Light Division and it almost proved disastrous. The Portuguese bore the brunt of the casualties and the French lost none. I was with Sir Arthur when the news reached him and he was incandescent with rage although he kept that side hidden until the messengers had gone. It was the face he showed his aides for he trusted us.

He turned to me, "Tomorrow I will lead Sir William's men and the Light Division together. I shall have to show him how it is done!"

We raced after Ney's rearguard. I knew from conversations with the Viscount that he did not want Ney or his commander to head north of the Mondego. He wanted them headed for the mountains. We faced, at Foz de Arouce, the same men we had routed at Redinha. They were not prepared for, even though Erskine had made a mess of his attack, at least he had kept them moving and they were hungry and tired. Tired men make mistakes. This time Sir Arthur used General Picton to lead the attack behind the skirmishers and that gallant General was so successful that the French 39th Regiment panicked as it tried to cross the river. Its eagle fell into the river. I was not certain if the rest of the army knew the importance of that but I did. The eagles had been presented to each regiment personally by Bonaparte and to lose one was the greatest disgrace. It did not matter that it had fallen, almost by accident, for the regiment would have to suffer the ignominy and shame until it could regain it. When next they fought, they would have little heart and the general in command would not be confident of them in line. Not only did we capture the eagle but the commanding officer, and they also lost 250 men. In contrast, we had just seven men killed.

The French were now retreating faster than we could keep up. I was close to the General and I could almost see his thought processes. The French had taken everything from the land and there was neither food nor grazing to be had. On the retreat to the Lines after Bussaco a few English regiments had behaved badly and he had had to hang a few men. He was determined to keep the morale of this army high and so wagons plied the tortuous roads from the south to fetch us food. We could have pursued the French closer but that might have cost us dear.

We received constant reports from the rest of the country. Sir Arthur could never have too many reports; he seemed to consume them. A column commanded by Marshal Beresford was heading for Badajoz and the fortress of Campo Mayor. Brigadier Long was scouting with the 13th and two Portuguese cavalry regiments. With just 700 men he surprised General Latour-Maubourg with over 2,400 men. That he made them flee was one thing but the Colonel of the 13th could not control his men and instead of capturing the heavy guns which were being escorted to Campo Mayor they charged after the French cavalry. The guns were recovered by some resourceful Frenchmen. When the messenger brought the report, I was there and heard Sir Arthur's angry comment, "British Cavalry are good for nothing but galloping!" He turned to me, "From now on Matthews, you will accompany the cavalry and I want to know who is responsible for these reckless actions."

"Sir!" I would not relish that task. I understood why the troopers behaved the way that they did. The officers who led them, in the main, were from the nobility and saw battle like some glorified fox hunt.

It was obvious by now that Marshal Masséna was heading for the Côa and then the relative safety of Cuidad Rodrigo. Black Bob was still in England on leave and I could not see why Sir Arthur had given command of the Light Division to Major General Erskine. He had shown in his first action that he was unstable. Along with General Picton's division, we were heading for Sabugal on the Côa. As directed by Sir Arthur I accompanied the cavalry, the 16th Light Dragoons and the King's German Legion Hussars. Sir Arthur's instructions were quite clear. The Light Division was to cross the river and get behind Reynier and his rearguard. General Picton was then to advance and trap Reynier between the two forces. It was a good plan but Erskine was not the man to command.

From the moment we set off there were problems. Erskine did not like me and refused to allow me to ride with his staff. "You, sir, will ride with the infantry for you carry a rifle and are clearly not a gentleman!"

The only reason I could see for him to dislike me was that I was known to be close to Black Bob and Erskine was determined to show Sir Arthur that he was a better general. I did not mind being with Colonel Beckwith and the 43rd Monmouths. They were like old friends but it meant that I was unable to do that which I had been ordered. When we reached the river there was a thick fog. Erskine sent for Lieutenant Colonel Beckwith and Lieutenant Colonel Drummond who commanded the other half of the light infantry brigades. Erskine pointed to the river, "Beckwith, take your brigade across the river and outflank the French!"

In many ways that made sense, despite the fog. However, Erskine's next command took us all by surprise.

"Colonel Drummond, you will wait here for General Picton and under no circumstances will you support Colonel Beckwith."

"But…"

"No buts, Colonel Drummond, those are my orders. I shall take the cavalry and we will support the attack."

I felt honour bound to speak, "General Erskine, Sir Arthur asked me to ride with the cavalry!"

He snapped, "It is Major General Erskine to you, Major, and it is I who command here. Obey your orders, Major and accompany the 43rd or I shall have you charged with disobeying orders and that means a court-martial and firing squad. Do I make myself clear?"

"Yes, sir."

Putting spurs to his horse he led the cavalry brigade down the river to look for a crossing point. I dismounted and said to Lieutenant Colonel Drummond, "If we could leave our horses here, sir."

"Matthews, this is ridiculous. You do not have to go with the 43rd."

"Sir, I have never disobeyed an order in my life and I will not begin now. My sergeant and I will join the brigade."

"And we shall watch your horses. Good luck Beckwith!"

Lieutenant Colonel Beckwith nodded, "Aye well, let us hope that the French are not alert or this will go badly for us!"

With our Baker rifles slung over our shoulders, Sharp and I headed upstream to find the crossing point. We could not see the other bank and

I hoped that the fog might just be our salvation. I was wrong for it was nearly our doom!

When we found the ford and began to cross, I looked at the ground and said, "Lieutenant Colonel Beckwith, have you noticed, there are no hoofprints. The cavalry regiments were supposed to cross before us and secure our flank."

"You are right, Major. We had better proceed with caution. Skirmish order."

"I will join the Rifles, sir." I had a Baker and this would mean I would be out in front. I hoped that my knowledge of French and the French army might just help us.

There were four companies of the 95th and they would be the eyes and ears of the brigade. There were almost 1500 of us but we were advancing on a position held by more than 8000! The fog was more like an English one and was wet; I guessed the fog would soon turn to rain. It meant powder would be damp. I had my powder horn beneath my oiled cloak. There were some of the 43rd with the Rifles and Caçadores; it was they who fired the first shots with their muskets. They made a different sound to the Baker rifle. The skirmishers were on the left flank and that meant they had found the French. I quickly primed my rifle with fresh powder and knelt. Resting my forearm on my knee, I scanned the ground ahead for a target. Some of the 95th were in a better position than I was and they began to fire. I saw blue uniforms and as four of the Frenchmen stood to fire I sent my ball in their direction. I quickly, or as quickly as I could manage it, reloaded. The browned muskets of the 43rd and the Caçadores were quicker to reload and they kept the attention of the French on them. It was the Baker rifles which were causing the damage but the slow rate of fire hindered us.

I heard Lieutenant Colonel Beckwith as he shouted, "43rd, up and at 'em!"

He must have had a better sight of the enemy than I did. I slung my Baker and took out my sword. The 95th had a sword bayonet but, to me, it was unwieldy and hard to use. I preferred to wield my heavy sword. I knew that Sharp would be guarding my left as we raced up the hill towards the waiting French. Suddenly I saw why the Colonel had ordered the charge. A French Regiment, the 4th Light, was forming up and we hit them whilst they were in the process of doing so. I found myself amongst six of the 95th and their sword bayonets caused terrible wounds to the French, however, they were outnumbered. I drew my pistol and fired at a French sergeant who had parried a rifleman's weapon away. The pistol misfired but I was close enough to bring down my sword and it caught his right shoulder. The rifleman whipped his sword bayonet around and caught the light infantryman under the chin. This was not the time to stand and we hurried on through the Frenchmen who were now beginning to flee.

An officer, seeing my sword and hat, recognised me as a senior officer and he ran at me. He sought glory. Sadly, for him, I had been taught to fence by the best and it was something in which I excelled. I doubted if the young sous-lieutenant had used his sword since he had trained. I parried his clumsy strike and as I flicked away the blade using the tip of my sword to lunge at him over his stock. My sword entered his throat and, attempting to stem the flow of the blossoming blood he gasped and slid to the floor. None had seen him die and there was no glory. The hill was to our left and we carried on following the French who were trying to fall back in good order.

Some of the Rifles had reloaded and were now kneeling, in their pairs, and systematically targeting officers and sergeants. It worked and soon the French had fled the hillside. Lieutenant Colonel Beckwith, his bugler and Sergeant Major Jennings appeared at my side. The Colonel shook his head, "Have you any idea where we are, Major Matthews?"

I shook my head, "I am not sure that we crossed the river at the right place, sir and the cavalry are certainly not where they ought to be. With the 52nd on the other side of the river, my advice would be to consolidate here."

He nodded, "You may be right. We have been lucky up to now but we could stumble into guns at any moment." The Lieutenant Colonel turned to his bugler and said, "Sound the recall!"

It was as the men returned to the sound of the bugle that a Rifleman and his comrade ran up and said, "Sir, there are seven battalions forming up!" They pointed down the slope.

That could be as many as 8,000 men. Lieutenant Colonel Beckwith said, "We cannot hold those here. We will reform on the hill and hold them there. Matthews, take some of the 95th and clear it for us."

"Sir!" I turned to one of the rifle companies which was reforming, "Captain Hathaway, have your men form a skirmish line and follow me."

"Yes, sir!"

I sheathed my sword and reloaded my Baker as the men formed up behind Sharp, the Captain and myself. The Rifles, and that included their officers, fought in pairs. Sharp and I would do the same. We started to run up the hill. The fog was patchy so that in places you could see almost forty paces and in others, you suddenly found yourself blind. In many ways, I would have been better off leading men from the 43rd as our Baker rifles were long-distance weapons which were slow to load. As it turned out luck was on our side and, as we neared the top, we suddenly saw a French howitzer and its crew with a company of light infantry. That they had not seen us was the luck but it was the skill of the Rifles which won the battle.

"Fire!"

We were more than a hundred paces from them. The howitzer could not fire at us and it was left to the light infantry with their outranged muskets to try to stop us. Half the gun's crew fell and the rest fled. The French officer commanding the light infantry and his sergeant, as well as the bugler, were also hit so that the leaderless light infantry fled over the top of the hill. We reached the howitzer and I could see that the fog was clearing but it had turned to rain. Visibility would still be poor but I saw the seven French battalions as they marched after Beckwith's Brigade.

As the 43rd and the Caçadores arrived the Colonel formed them up in lines with the Rifles before them. We would not fight as light infantry but as regular infantry. We watched the French as they marched in six columns. If they remained in that formation then we had a chance for over a thousand muskets could do some serious harm to them and they were advancing up a hill. We discovered later that it was General Reynier who led them and he was not a fool. He had two of the battalions deploy into line while the other four kept in column. It meant that the four columns would reach us first.

"Brigade, prepare!" I was with the Rifles and we kept up a withering fire on the men leading the columns. My barrel became hotter and hotter as I fired and reloaded as fast as I could manage. I was desperate for a drink as my mouth tasted of black powder. Their skirmishers were cut down and then the sharpshooters of the 95th began to pick off the officers who were encouraging their men on. I hit a skirmisher in the shoulder and the heavy ball spun him around. We were all kneeling or lying down but, even so, we knew we could not stay there when the brigade opened fire.

The Colonel shouted, "Rifles, retire!"

We turned and ran up the slope to throw ourselves down on the ground before the 43rd and the Caçadores. I took out my pistols and primed them both with fresh powder.

"Fire!"

Behind us, the 1000 muskets barked and the fog returned in the form of musket smoke. Some of the 95th had reloaded and they fired too. I raised my pistols as the second volley fired from behind us rippled. In the smoke, I saw the flash of muskets as the three French battalions deployed in line opened fire. Behind us, one or two men were hit. I saw blue uniforms and that meant they were close enough to hit. As the third volley rang out, I fired my two pistols. I dropped them and waited for the next order.

"Bayonets!"

I was on my feet and, drawing my sword, joined the Rifles to charge the French. The last volley had cut holes in the enemy lines so that we were more or less solid and they were not. We had the advantage of height and here the Rifle's sword bayonet was deadly. I used my left hand to grab the Charleville musket which was thrust at me while I swept my sword across the three closest Frenchmen. My hand was burned by the barrel of the musket but not enough to incapacitate me. My sword slashed through the throat of one man and into the cheek of another.

Just then we heard a volley from our right and then a second. We heard a British trumpet sound the charge. The fog had cleared a little and we had swept away the French before us. I was able to see Lieutenant Colonel Drummond bringing the 52nd to our aid. He had disobeyed Erskine and I thanked God for that. Attacked in the flank the French began to fall back and Lieutenant Colonel Beckwith's brigade began to cheer.

Lieutenant Colonel Drummond grinned as he approached Lieutenant Colonel Beckwith and me. "Heard the firing and thought we cannot let you have all the fun!" He pointed his sword at the French, "You must have got lost in the fog, Beckwith. You attacked their flank and not their rear."

The Colonel nodded, "But where is the cavalry?"

Drummond said, quietly, "They are with Erskine so they could be anywhere."

One of the officers of the 52nd, Captain Napier said, "Sir, the French are reforming! There are more infantrymen and they have cavalry, too!" I turned and saw that there were almost 9000 men preparing to attack. Even with the reinforcements, we were outnumbered by more than three to one.

Lieutenant Colonel Beckwith said, calmly, "Right, gentlemen, form line. Rifles, you will have to be the skirmishers today!"

Picking up my rifle I joined the other four companies and headed down the slope. This time we could position ourselves further away and when we had fired, fall back up the hill. Sharp pointed to the French cavalry. "If General Erskine had kept the cavalry close then they would not be a problem."

"But he did not and we have to deal with the enemies who lie before us." Sharp was just voicing what everyone else thought but such speculation did us no good. We had to fight the enemy before us with the men we had.

The Lines of Torres Vedras

The Rifles were the better judges of range. In comparison to them, I was just an amateur. When they knelt Sharp and I joined them. I knew that the range of the Baker was 300 paces but I had been told that some of the marksmen had hit targets at more than 500 paces. The marksmen began to fire when the French were still 500 paces from us. When I saw men were hit, I aimed, not at an individual but at the horsemen who were marching at the same pace as the infantry. A horse is a big target and a horseman on a horse an even bigger one. I managed to hit a German Chasseur and, as he fell his hand retained hold on the reins of his horse. Suddenly there was a hole in their line as his horse made others step to the side.

We kept loading and firing until the French were two hundred paces from us. Their horses could catch us and so when I heard the command to fall back, I said, "Right, Sharp, off you go." I still had a ball in my Baker and I aimed at the French. I had seen the Rifles do this and knew that they aimed at the nearest threat and then ran back. Seeing half of our number run back up the hill one or two of the German horsemen spurred their horses up the hill. I aimed at one and when he was a hundred paces from me hit him in the chest. I turned and ran. I knew that Sharp would have his rifle loaded but would not fire until I was threatened.

I heard him shout, "Down!" when I was thirty paces from him and I obeyed. His rifle barked and, looking around, I saw another German Chasseur fall from his horse.

I reached him and we both reloaded. I kept watching the French and suddenly they stopped. I wondered why for we had done little enough to hurt them. Sharp pointed. The fog had cleared a little more and we could see the Côa. General Picton had arrived and was leading his 3,500 men to come to our aid. General Reynier was not a fool. We had seen evidence of that already and the French began to pull back. Had General Erskine and the cavalry been close then this could have been a great victory but no one knew where he was and although we had won the French still had more than 8000 men who should have been either dead or prisoners. I knew that Sir Arthur would not be happy!

Chapter 14

"What happened, Major Matthews?"

The army had reached the Portuguese border and Sir Arthur had Portuguese troops surrounding Almeida. We were at the Côa close to the bridge which had almost cost us dear just over a year earlier.

I knew that the General had asked for a private meeting so that I could speak openly. I told him all that Sir William had said and done. I then went into detail about the action. He nodded when I had finished.

"Thank God that Sir Robert is now heading back to join his division. I am disappointed in Sir William and, rest assured, I will ensure that he can no longer hurt my plans. The Light Division did well then?"

"Yes, Sir Arthur. I could not see how they could have done any better for we were outnumbered by three to one."

"I am sorry to say that it looks like that will become the position of the whole army. Marshal Soult has now taken Badajoz and marches to aid the Army of Portugal. I also heard that Ney has been dismissed." He smiled at my expression. "The resourceful Colonel Selkirk has not been idle. In addition, Marshal Bessières is on his way with reinforcements including the Imperial Cavalry!"

I knew Jean-Baptiste Bessières, 1st Duc d' Istria and had served with him in Italy and Egypt. He was a close friend of Bonaparte and while I did not fear him as a leader, the Imperial cavalry were a different matter. The Army of the North was a small one, just 1500 men but as 800 of those were the finest cavalry in Europe, including Polish Lancers, Mamelukes, Chasseurs à Cheval, my old regiment, and the fearsome Grenadiers à Cheval then they were the most experienced cavalry in Europe. The other half was also specially selected. They could defeat any other horsemen on the battlefield. My heart sank.

Sir Arthur smiled, "I see you know the threat this presents. Fear not. We have Almeida surrounded and I intend to make a line with Fuentes de Oñoro as our lynchpin. I will not risk an assault on Badajoz for we have too few men but I will starve them out and then force Marshal Masséna to do battle before Soult can reach him. I want you to take the Light Division to Fort Concepcion and await Sir Robert there. You know the place from your last encounter with the French and the men know you. Picton will be there, too, with his 5th Division."

"Yes, sir."

"Meanwhile, I will have to have words with Sir William. This will not do! We have few enough men without Sir William risking them. But for Lieutenant Colonel Drummond and Sir Thomas…"

I wondered what difference it would make to the unique William Erskine for he seemed to operate in his own little world. The orders had already been sent to the two divisions and they were preparing to march north. Logically the Light Division should cross the bridge first as they were quicker and they knew it but for the sake of diplomacy and while the two divisions took down their tents, I sought out Sir Thomas. He was a reasonable man and if all generals were like him then going to war would be simpler. He smiled at me and said, "Of course, Matthews, makes perfect sense to me. Just make sure that there is a decent house for me and my staff, eh?"

"Of course, Sir Thomas."

The last time we had been across the river it had been summer and we had not needed shelter. Now it was springtime and the weather was more unpredictable. Sir Thomas was an old campaigner and I did not blame him for seeking to be comfortable.

The presence of the French meant that most of the inhabitants of the small town nestled in the hills astride the east-west road had fled. There were empty houses although, as I looked around them, I realised that none was either large enough or grand enough for a Major General. I was there as a liaison really and the two colonels began to set up the perimeter and the defences. That there were no cavalrymen with us I felt was a weakness but Sir Arthur knew his business. I resolved that as soon as Sir Robert arrived then I would go with Sharp and scout. I fretted as I allocated defensive lines for this was not a comfortable area for me. When Sir Thomas arrived then I felt happier for it meant that there was a senior general who was reliable.

Sir Robert arrived fresh from Lisbon the next day. He had emulated the feat of his Light Division when they marched in record time to Talavera. He brought intelligence too. "The guerrillas have brought us news, Matthews. Their General, Don Julian Sanchez has also brought mounted men. We have some irregular cavalry! However, the bad news is that the French are coming from Cuidad Rodrigo and they will outnumber us when the two armies conjoin. We are to move to Aldea do Obispo. It is just east of Vale da Mula."

That suited me for I saw that Spencer was bringing the 1st Division to the village of Fuentes de Oñoro. Accommodation would become tight! "Sir, would it be all right if Sharp and I reconnoitred to the east, towards Cuidad? We have no cavalry out and we do not want to get caught out again, eh sir?"

"Quite right. Yes, of course. We shall see you by dark in Aldea.".

We had last been on this road a year ago when Cuidad was still in Spanish hands. The French knew it well and so we rode with loaded weapons and an eye and ear set for danger. As we descended from the plateau, I saw that Sir Arthur had chosen Fuentes de Oñoro well. The slope was not steep but an attacking army would have to climb up to the village and the ground behind was dead ground where our army could shelter from French artillery. It also meant that we had a good view ahead of us. The main road from Cuidad Rodrigo to the river was to the south of us and our road was a small country road which twisted and turned as it passed through small clumps of trees and rose and fell over the smallest of undulations. The result of the peregrinations of the road was that we almost stumbled into a French patrol. Donna's reactions warned us for, as we passed a deserted and half-ruined farmhouse and turned a corner, her ears pricked. I knew my horse well enough to know that meant trouble and I reined her in. Sharp was a heartbeat slower but his horse stopped too. I cocked my Baker and I listened.

The smell of pipe smoke identified Frenchmen. When I had left French service to join the 11th Light Dragoons, one of the first things I had noticed was the difference in pipe tobacco. The French preferred a more aromatic one than the British and I smelled aromatic tobacco. The words they spoke confirmed that they were French.

"We could go back now, Corporal. We have seen the smoke from their fires and observed the movements in the village. They are in Fuentes."

"And do you remember last year when we came? We thought we had the Roast Beefs then but they slipped away. General Loison will not be happy if we do not give him accurate numbers. We now have Marshal Bessières and the cavalry of the Imperial Guard! Every general and colonel will be desperate to show that their regiment is better than the vaunted Guards. We have to be better than the best."

"Corporal, there are less than one hundred and fifty of us left! The winter in Portugal and the battles we have had mean that we should not even be here. The 3rd Hussars is finished until we get replacements."

Just then one of the French horses neighed. The voice I now recognised as the corporal snapped, "Stand to! My horse does not neigh unless she senses strange horses. There may be guerrillas close by!"

I heard them as they moved their horses and slipped pistols from holsters. We were in a predicament. If we moved then we would alert them and I was not yet sure how many men there were. I took a risk and shouted, in French, "Stand to! Guerrillas coming down the road. Form a skirmish line!"

I turned Donna and nodded to Sharp. We spurred our horses. I was buying time with my confusing words and it worked. We had fought these Hussars before and knew that they did not use carbines. Their pistols had a limited range and all we needed was a forty-pace start. I glanced over my shoulder and saw that we had that, almost. The six Hussars burst from behind the deserted farmhouse and I saw a pistol flash. That was a mistake as the trooper would not be able to reload. We had good, well-fed horses and we knew that the French horses had suffered during the winter. It became obvious that we were extending our lead. Then disaster struck. The road was not a well-made one and Sharp's horse managed to find a small hole which had been made deeper in the winter. With few people using the road it had not been filled. Sharp was a good horseman and as his horse's head dipped, although he flew from the saddle, he still managed to keep hold of the reins.

I reined in and levelled my Baker. I took a breath and aimed at the leading rider. I guessed it was the Corporal. When he was 150 paces from me and while Sharp was still attending to his horse I fired. The Corporal was hit but, like Sharp, he was a good horseman. He did not fall but the horse veered off.

"Sharp, your gun!" I dropped mine as Sharp threw me his Baker. I levelled it and fired at the second trooper who was just 80 paces from me and did not expect a second shot. This time I hit him squarely in the chest and he was thrown from the back of the horse. As Sharp mounted his horse, I drew one of my saddle pistols and fired. I did not expect to hit anyone and I did not but the four who had yet to be hit reined in. Sharp and I rode west. I kept glancing behind me but they did not follow. They had a dead trooper to recover and a wounded Corporal to tend to.

"Sorry, sir."

"It couldn't be helped and we learned much that Sir Arthur will need to know. Let's get to the new quarters and report to Sir Robert. I think I may well have to visit with Sir Arthur in the morning."

We did not reach the village until dusk but I made a point of speaking with Sir Robert. He appreciated it and he doubled the sentries. Before I left for some much-needed food he said, "Oh, Matthews, Sir Arthur has placed General Erskine's division to the south of us!" He saw my face and laughed, "Aye Colonel Beckwith told me what he did. Don't worry; I can handle him! I just thought you should know!"

The next morning Sharp and I went to the Viscount's headquarters. I could see his dispositions. He had the whole of the army spread out along the plateau. The Light Division anchored one end and, in the distance, I could see the Spanish guerrillas. He was busy but he had given me a job to do and so he took the time to speak with me.

I told him what I had both seen and heard. He nodded, "That confirms what Don Julian Sanchez told me. Don't worry about the cavalry. I have sent two brigades of Portuguese Cavalry to guard the flank of the Light Division." He smiled, "By the way, Don Julian knows of you. One of his lieutenants mentioned that he knew you. You gave him horses and weapons." That would be Juan. "He also told me that the French have 8000 more infantrymen than we do and more than 4000 more cavalrymen. We have a few more guns but that is all! When we hold them, it will show those penny-pinching politicians in Parliament that their money is well spent. We have the best soldiers in the world and we have trained our allies to be as good!"

"Quite right, sir."

"I need you here now. The French are coming but I have to play my cards carefully. The Light Division is to the north to stop us being outflanked but I would rather have them closer if I can manage it. Go into the village for me. We have placed twenty light companies, five rifle companies and the 83rd Foot there. Colonel Williams is commanding. Go and have a chat with him. Some of his chaps have been talking about you and he is keen to meet someone who was with Moore and can fire a Baker!"

When I reached the village of Fuentes de Oñoro I was impressed both with the defences and with Colonel Williams. He was my kind of soldier for he knew his business. He beamed as he shook my hand. He had a grip like a wrestler. "I had to meet you, Matthews, as my riflemen have been talking about this cavalry officer who rides to war with a Baker! Thought it was damned odd." I told him how I came to use it and he nodded approvingly. "The other reason I wanted to speak to you is that my chaps seem to think you understand the French mind. You speak French, don't you?"

That was not unusual. Many officers had been to schools which taught French. The difference was that I could speak it fluently!

"Yes sir, I speak French and I think I do understand the French mind. They believe that they are better than any other soldier in Europe and, with the exception of us, they may well be right. That is why they will follow the orders of their marshals and attack in column, they will endure great numbers of casualties because they believe that they will win. For Marshal Masséna this is his Rubicon. Bonaparte wants victory here and if Marshal Masséna does not deliver then he will be replaced. Sir Arthur has beaten him too many times for him to survive another defeat."

"Then that makes our task even more important. Thank you for that, Major Matthews. I hope to see you in the battle but if not, then God speed."

"And you, sir!"

Sharp had sorted us out a tent and he had found the officer's mess by the time I returned. Sir Arthur was never particularly bothered by food

The Lines of Torres Vedras

but I enjoyed eating and eating socially. As the illegitimate child of a French Marquis, I had eaten either alone or just with my mother. It was good to meet other officers. I do not say that I liked all that I met but it was good to hear their opinions. The mess was filled with the various aides and the senior officers. I left Sharp at the sergeant's mess and he was quite happy to be there. I sat with Lieutenant Mountshaft who looked suitably haunted; after all, he was Sir Arthur's aide. I was lucky as I did not have to be at Sir Arthur's side every minute of the day.

"You are a lucky boy, Lieutenant. You have escaped Sir Arthur."

"Do not joke about it, sir. I wake up, in the short times he lets me sleep, fearful that I have missed a summons! You were his aide before, sir. How did you cope?"

"I was not an aide such as you Lieutenant. I came as an officer whom the general knew had seen action and," I lowered my voice, "as you know only too well, he uses me for dangerous missions."

"Which I would crave, sir! Can you not ask him if I can come with you on one of them?"

I nodded and his eyes lit up, "Your name is Jamie, is it not?"

"Yes, sir."

"Well, Jamie, how many languages can you speak?" He looked at me blankly. I smiled, "Let us begin with something which is less challenging. How many weapons do you possess, here in Portugal?"

He smiled, "My sword and my pistol!"

"Good. And do you have a mould to make your own balls?"

His face fell, "No, sir, for I have a good supply."

"And if you ran out? Sergeant Sharp and I can run out but we can take enemy ammunition and make it fit our guns for we have two moulds. However, as we have both French and English pistols, it does not matter overmuch but we are prepared." I leaned forward as though I was going to reveal some magical way for him to become a spy but all that I was doing was drawing my stiletto from my boot. I tapped his leg with the tip. He looked down and his eyes widened. "And I have knives. This is one which an Italian brigand tried to use to kill me. He is dead and I am not." I replaced the knife.

He looked shocked, "And you have used that to kill men?"

"I have used a wide variety of weapons with which to kill men. Do you really wish to enter that world?"

"No, sir, and I am sorry for I thought that what you did was exciting. I did not see the danger nor the risk that you take. I do not mind dying for my country but I would that it was in battle and not…"

"Not in some grubby little room where no one will mourn your passing." He nodded. "Lieutenant, instead of thinking about dying for your country think about living for it. England will need fine young men like you. This war cannot last forever. Learn from it but survive. Sir Arthur will allow you to be a soldier but be in no rush."

He then told me about his family. His father had been wounded in the American Revolution and the Lieutenant was determined to be as honoured as his father. I decided I would ask Sir Arthur if he would allow the Lieutenant the opportunity to be a soldier. I did not doubt that it would earn me a reprimand but I liked the young Lieutenant and admired his diligence.

My plans were thrown into disarray by the arrival of the French army. Scouts and guerrillas rode in to tell us that the French were coming down the road from Cuidad Rodrigo and they were coming in three columns. Aides were sent to warn the various commanders and I went with Lieutenant Mountshaft and Sir Arthur to a high point on the plateau where we could see the approach. He seemed satisfied. "I believe, gentlemen, that it is as I predicted. Our foe will make for this village. We will give him a little while to change his mind but if he continues to do as I expect then I will bring the Light Division here. I am sure that General Erskine can cope with the threat of a cavalry brigade for he has Portuguese cavalry close by. I do not see the Imperial Guard yet!"

We watched the approach of the enemy and this time, as the ground suited horses, the cavalry would be a much more serious threat and already I could see three brigades of cavalry. I estimated that there were almost 4000 men and we had yet to see the 1500 of the Imperial Guard with Marshal Bessières. It became obvious, within a very short time, that the main attack was to be down the road to Fuentes de Oñoro.

"Matthews, fetch the Light Division and have them place themselves closer to the village. Mountshaft asked Sir Brent to bring the 1st Division ready to support the village."

"Sir!"

Sharp and I had the furthest to travel but the Light Division were fast and they could almost keep up with our horses. As we passed General Erskine and his division, I saluted but the General pointedly looked away. He was not only strange and incompetent, but he was also rude as well. I did not envy the men whom he led. Black Bob actually smiled when he saw me. "Ah, Major, tell me that we are not to be stuck out here while the battle rages elsewhere."

"Yes sir, Sir Arthur asks you to place your division behind the village and ready to support once they are attacked."

He turned to his two colonels, "Right gentlemen. Let us see if we can beat the good major back to the village!" As we rode behind the 5th I saw them forming up because in the time it had taken to reach Sir Robert,

Reynier's Corps had moved up to threaten the British left flank. I wondered what the unpredictable Erskine would do. In truth, all that he needed to do was stand as his men had the high ground and their musketry would ensure that they defeated Reynier who commanded an equally sized force. I saw that the general's division was being deployed into line and the Caçadores and the Brunswick Oels were in skirmish order. I knew that they had at least one rifle company but they were inferior to our own rifles.

By the time I reached General Wellesley, the French were much closer and I saw that there were two columns each of six or seven battalions. They would outnumber the men led by Colonel Williams. As I reached them Sir Arthur was leading his staff from the village to a vantage point on a hill behind it. He was not afraid of the French nor did he fear for his life but Sir Arthur needed to see the whole battle and to react to it.

I waved to the Colonel as I passed him, "Good luck, sir!"

"We will give them a warm welcome, Major Matthews!"

Once on the hill, I saw the French as they approached the almost dry Don Casas River. The artillery opened up but we had too few guns to carve lines through the enemy and the columns kept coming. Lieutenant Mountshaft shouted, "Sir, I can see red uniforms amongst the French!"

Sighing Sir Arthur said, "Educate him, Matthews, I have better things to do!"

I said, to the Licutenant, "They are Bonaparte's allies. They are the Hanoverian legion. The Emperor has a polyglot army, Lieutenant."

The rifles in the village began to take their toll of the officers and sergeants as they ploughed across the dry river bed and approached the village. I could see that the 2,000 men stationed there would have to face more than twice their number. Soon the smoke from the fighting obscured the village but we could hear the screams of the dying and the French officers as they exhorted their men to fight for their Emperor. When the first column began to falter, I saw an aide ride to the second column. General Ferey was committing more men to the attack.

Sir Arthur kept flicking his glass to view the French right but Reynier appeared to be holding his position. On the French left, the ominously placed French cavalry waited. Marshal Masséna appeared to be trying to bludgeon his way through the village. When casualties were carried from the village and we saw the skirmishers falling back it became obvious that the French were winning. They had sheer weight of numbers and the rifles were less effective in the close-quarter fighting of a village. I saw Sir Arthur look at his watch. It was now the early afternoon and if we lost the village before dark, we would not be able to recover it without serious loss.

"Major Matthews, be so good as to ask Sir Brent for three of his battalions and an officer to lead them. I want stout fellows. Take them into the flank of the French, eh?" He pointed to an area of dead ground to the north of the village where we would be hidden from the French and achieve some sort of surprise.

"Yes, sir."

Sharp and I spurred our horses. We only had two hundred paces to go but speed was of the essence. We dismounted and while Sharp tethered our horses I reported to the General. He nodded, "Colonel Cadogan, take the Camerons, the Warwicks and the Glasgow Light Infantry. Go with Major Matthews, Sir Arthur has a little job for you."

As I led the colonel to the waiting battalions, I told him what was intended. "I am not certain I know where this dead ground is, exactly, Major Matthews."

"My sergeant and I shall be with you, sir."

"Good fellow. Don't risk yourself; once we are there these chaps will sort out Johnny Frenchman eh?" We had reached the brigade. "71st, 79th and 24th Foot, you will follow Major Matthews and me. Fix bayonets for we are going to show the French what we can do! The 71st will lead."

Colonel Cameron of the Cameron Highlanders said, "Colonel Cadogan, my lads are handy with cold steel! Let us lead."

"They will have their day, Colonel. Now be sharp about it for the General does not wish to lose the village!"

I took out my sword as I led the column of men. It was not for bravado; it would enable the other men behind to see which direction we were taking. I held it above my head and ran; Colonel Cadogan trotted next to me. We could hear the crack of muskets and the shouts of men engaged in hand to hand combat. We could see little for the village was wreathed in musket smoke. I knew the path to take for I had observed the route before the battle had begun and, indeed, used it when I had rejoined Sir Arthur on the hill.

The defenders had been forced from the lower half of the village and I feared that we might have to endure some friendly fire and so I shouted, "Ware left! 1st Division coming in!" We hit the French to their side and rear. Colonel Cameron had not followed orders and he had raced around the bottom of the village, closer to the river. He and his Highlanders were screaming Gaelic curses as they tore into the rear of the French. The 71st were light infantry and this was their sort of terrain. Added to that they were all hard Scotsmen from one of the toughest cities in Britain. They needed no inducement to fight.

The Lines of Torres Vedras

If General Wellesley had thought that Sharp and I could just leave the column once it was engaged then he was sadly mistaken. For one thing, there was no way back through the press of men and for another, the French turned to engage us once the first musket balls from the 71st tore into them. I drew my pistol and fired into the mass of blue before holstering it and following up with a scything swing from my sword. I connected with a shako and the freshly sharpened blade drove into the skull of the French soldier who crumpled at my feet. This was a mêlée, pure and simple. There was no order and there were no rules; you killed any way that you could. We looked for blue and stabbed, bayoneted, punched and kicked. Men wrestled on the ground where they bit, gouged and stabbed to kill the enemy they fought. A bayonet came out of the gunpowder fog and missed my cheek by the width of a finger. I punched blindly with the hilt of my sword and struck a musket. Stepping forward I struck the Frenchman repeatedly in the face with my sword until he fell unconscious at my feet. A face appeared before me and I lunged. The soldier managed to turn slightly but the tip and edge ripped out his left eye and he turned, screaming, to run to the rear.

As more of the 24th joined the battle I heard English voices, calmer, replacing the screams of the Scots. "Steady boys! Keep it steady." It was why Colonel Cadogan had placed them at the rear. They were solid and dependable. The Scots were the steel with which we would break their spirit but the 24th were the iron which would hold the line.

Colonel Williams and his men had used the hiatus to reform and reorder their lines. I heard his shout above the din of battle, "Light detachment, push them! Push them!"

With pressure from two sides, the French had to give way and they were on a slope. Colonel Cameron might have disobeyed orders but they had helped to give the French but one way out and that was to the south. The Light Division was there, having followed me from the north, and they poured volley after volley into the flanks of the Frenchmen. It was too much and the thirteen battalions broke. I was with Colonel Cadogan and we surrounded a large number of Frenchmen. With muskets and rifles above them and bayonets behind them, over a hundred and twenty men surrendered.

Even as we began to assess our success Colonel Cadogan saw the body of Colonel Cameron. He had died leading his men. He shook his head for the 71st were pouring down the hill after the fleeing French. It was Talavera all over again. "Damn fools! As mad as their Colonel, God rest his soul!"

"I will fetch them back! Sharp report to the General!"

"But sir!"

"Just do it, eh, Sharp!"

I ran through the recaptured village almost tripping over the blue bodies which littered it. I saw that some of the 71st had reached the river and were crossing. There were 30,000 Frenchmen waiting for them including 4,000 cavalrymen. As I passed the Highlanders, some still fighting I shouted, "Hold here! Do not cross!"

Already those who had crossed were being subjected to musket fire and men were falling. I saw a Cameron Highlander Captain. He had just slain a French officer and had a wild look in his eyes, "Captain! Pull yourself together. That is an order! Help me get your men back before they are slaughtered!"

He seemed to see me for the first time and he nodded, "Aye, sir, sorry sir! Sergeant Major Forsyth, find the bugler and order the withdrawal."

I nodded and, with the Captain behind me, we headed for the river. As the notes of the recall rang out some of the Highlanders heard and began to make their way back. Some did not and they were killed. Then I saw a squadron of French Hussars. They were forming up and I knew what they intended, I turned to the Captain, "Have your men form three lines here. The Hussars are going to attack and we don't have enough time for a square. Quickly!"

I think that we were lucky that the Sergeant Major had survived for whilst they might not obey us, they were petrified of him. He chivvied the nearest forty men into three lines as the thirty odd horsemen sabred and slashed at the Cameronians who had been too slow to respond.

Sergeant Major Forsyth said, "Front rank, kneel! First and second ranks, present!" He looked at me and I nodded. When the horses were forty paces from us, he shouted, "Fire!" A wall of smoke filled the space where the horsemen had been and Sergeant Major Forsyth shouted, "Second rank kneel, rear rank, fire!"

The forty musket balls had done damage but some of the horsemen on the two flanks had avoided the lead and two loomed up out of the fog of war. I had my pistol in my left hand and I brought it up instinctively and fired. I did not hit the trooper but the ball went into the head of his horse and the beast crashed to the ground, trapping the man. The other trooper slashed his sword at me. I raised my pistol to block it and, as the blade broke the pistol in two, I lunged at the Hussar. His impetus drove him onto my sword. His horse kept going but he fell backwards. When the smoke cleared the survivors had retreated. I walked over to the dead horse and saw that the fall had crushed the rider. I threw away my useless pistol and took the one from the dead horseman's saddle holster. It was a finely made piece and was engraved: '*To Jean from his wife, Eloise, stay safe'*. I nodded to his body, "I will look after this fine weapon. Go to God!"

The sounds of the trumpets and bugles above us told us that the battle was over for the day. We turned and marched up the hill. The Captain said, "Thank you, Major! I know not what came over me!"

The Sergeant Major nodded, "It was the joy of battle, sir. No bad thing in small doses!"

As we neared the rest of the men who had followed Colonel Cadogan, they all began to cheer. We had not won the battle but at least we had not lost it, yet!

Chapter 15

Neither general was willing to fight a battle at night and so both sides gathered their dead and wounded from the battlefield while those who could cut hunks of meat from the three dead horses which lay on the battlefield. Hot food and especially meat were a treat; the soldier butchers knew their business and chose the choicest cuts. In terms of casualties, we had won the day. The French had lost over 700 hundred killed and wounded as well as losing 160 men taken prisoner. In contrast, we had lost but 260 killed and wounded. We were still outnumbered but, as I reported the numbers to him, I could tell that Sir Arthur was pleased but still found time to be critical. "The Light companies did well today although the men of the 71st were a little reckless!"

"Sir, they had lost their commanding officer!"

"And they have no other officers? It was a good job you were there, Matthews for, without you, we could have added another forty or more to the butcher's bill." It was as close to a compliment as I was ever going to get and I took it!

When dawn broke there was no attack and that surprised me but not General Wellesley who seemed to expect it. Just after dawn, he gathered all of his aides to his headquarters. "Today, gentlemen, you will all do as Major Matthews normally does and you will be my eyes and ears to gather information. I need to know what the French intend. Where are they moving their men and where are they mustering them? Get as close as you can without getting captured." He glared at Mountshaft and the other young aides as he added the admonition. "If the French look likely to attack today then return as quickly as you can. General Sanchez and his Spanish guerrillas will also be riding abroad and they, too, will report their findings to me. I have a clever opponent and he outnumbers me! Be about your business."

I knew that I was lucky for I had Sharp with me and, as we mounted our horses, I said, "Lieutenant Mountshaft, be careful. You know how close I have come to death and I have something which you may not have."

"What is that, sir, your Baker?"

"No, Lieutenant, it is luck, and as we all know luck can desert you at any time. Do not rely upon it!"

As we set off, I noticed movement from the French and I wondered if they were beginning an attack. If so, they would be catching Sir Arthur unawares and that was unusual. I had my pistols ready in case we ran into the enemy. The Spanish were at the village of Nave de Aver and they would be able to report any movement there. I realised that the movements I had seen were the horses of French cavalry. They were doing as we were and gathering information. I rode to Pozo Bello where the 85th, Bucks Light infantry and a battalion of Caçadores guarded the southern edge of our lines. As we rode by them, I waved. They were very exposed where they were and I would speak to them when we rode the homeward leg. Sharp and I had just passed the piquet which marked the outer boundary of their village when I saw four French cavalrymen ahead. They were Dragoons and when they saw us, they halted. Four to two were not good odds and so we reined in. I took out my glass and saw that the four were not alone. I spied the green uniforms all over the land to the south and east of us. I traversed the telescope and saw that Montbrun's Cavalry was now astride the other road from Cuidad Rodrigo to Almeida. The day before it had been astride the Fuentes road. Masséna was shifting his attack and moving men from one flank to the other under the screen of his large numbers of cavalry. It was obvious to me that he was attempting to outflank Sir Arthur. I needed to confirm that his infantry had shifted too. The cavalry could just be a feint.

"Sir, the Dragoons!"

While I had been speculating the four Dragoons had had enough of watching and they had spurred their horses towards us. We could have ridden back to the safety of Pozo Bello where there were two battalions who could cover us but I had faith in my horse and I knew that we needed to discover where the infantry battalions were gathered.

"Sharp, ride back to the General and tell him that the French cavalry brigades are gathered close to Pozo Bello. They are trying to outflank us."

"Sir, the Dragoons!"

As I had been talking, they had closed to within two hundred paces. "Sharp, ride!"

When we split up, we confused them and they slowed, albeit briefly. Whoever led them must have decided that I was the easier target as I was not riding towards a British battalion and they let Sharp go. I opened Donna's legs and she maintained the lead that I already had. I heard the pop of a musket and almost laughed for there was no way that a musket fired from the back of a moving horse could hit me, more importantly, the rider had no weapon to use until he stopped and reloaded. I concentrated on looking to the French on my right. I was looking beyond the horses and their troopers. Where were the infantry? As I neared the road to Fuentes some French cavalry mounted and rode down the road towards me too. As they did so I saw the infantry. There was a Corps, at least, behind the cavalry. I could now take the news back to Sir Arthur.

There was just one problem, the cavalry who had mounted were coming to take me prisoner and I could not turn to head down the Fuentes road as Reynier's corps was there. My only chance was to ride back the way I had come and that meant passing the four Dragoons.

I did the unexpected. I stopped Donna and taking my Baker leaned on her neck. The four Dragoons were just one hundred and fifty paces from me. Two more Dragoons fired at me as I squeezed the trigger and hit a Dragoon. Dropping the Baker, I spurred Donna who leapt as though stung. I drew a pistol and galloped towards the three remaining Dragoons. They drew their swords. We were closing together at great speed. I levelled the pistol but did not fire. I waited until I was twenty paces from the first Dragoon who had raised his sword to slash at me. He was confident for behind him his two comrades could get to my other side. I knew that was what they would do. I fired my pistol and then drew my sword. The Dragoon was hit in the face and he would have known little about it. I managed to block the sabre thrust and by flicking my wrist disarmed him. The last Dragoon was so surprised by the turn of events that when I lunged at him, he almost forgot to parry. When he did, he just drove my sword down and my blade cut through his stirrup leather. He tumbled from his horse. I turned and, waving a flamboyant salute, shouted in French, "Thank you, gentlemen, the compliments of the 11th Light Dragoons!" It was not just bravado it was a piece of misdirection. They would report to their general that a Major of the 11th Light Dragoons was on the battlefield. When the French scouts returned, they would assume we had one more regiment than we had.

I reined in Donna close to Pozo Bello as there was little point in hurting her. The Bucks Light Infantry had witnessed the encounter and as I walked my horse along the road they cheered. I suppose that being so exposed they would relish any victory over the French no matter how small.

I gave my report in writing and then rejoined Sharp. The other aides had all returned including an ebullient Lieutenant Mountshaft. We discussed what we had found. I think I was the only one who was able to draw on all that the others said and realise what Masséna intended. The fact that Reynier's Corps had dug in suggested to me that Marshal Masséna had not finished with Fuentes de Oñoro. We would have to defend that village as well as preparing for an outflanking manoeuvre from the south. I was about to retire when a subaltern from the Scots Guards came for me and I was summoned to Sir Arthur.

He had with him Stapleton Cotton, Sir Robert Crauford and Sir Brent Spencer. "Matthews, you write a good report and as it concurs with my thinking, I thought you might as well hear my plans."

"Sir."

"I intend to put Houston's 7th Division behind Pozzo Bello and have the cavalry for support." I saw Stapleton Cotton nod. "Craufard, your chaps will be behind the 7th and our last line of defence will be the 1st Division. I intend to put the 71st, 79th and 24th in Fuentes de Oñoro and have Colonel's William's detachment as a reserve. I need to be flexible. Now if the battle is anything like yesterday then there will be confusion. You three gentlemen need to know my mind so that you can act as I would. I do not want to lose either the Light Division nor the cavalry. I want them pulled back in good order so that our line extends west from Fuentes de Oñoro. General Houston would be here but he is busy setting up a defence for Pozo Bello. Major Matthews, you will be the grease that makes this work. You will be attached to the cavalry; from what I have seen you are a damned good horseman and quick thinking. You and your Sergeant can report back to me and plug any holes which appear. For this battle, I am giving you the temporary rank of Lieutenant Colonel. After the battle, you will, of course, revert to Major. You will use your authority only in extreme emergency; understand?"

"Sir!"

"Now get to your units. It is Marshal Masséna who will begin this battle and he thinks to keep me on my toes. With your help, gentlemen, we shall humbug him!"

I left with Sir Stapleton Cotton. "It is a pity that the 11th Light Dragoons are not here. They are a damned fine regiment."

"As you can imagine, sir, I agree with you. I am neither fish nor fowl and find myself attached here there and everywhere."

"That is because you have made yourself indispensable to his lordship."

"Me sir?"

"Who else below the rank of general knows his plans? It is a privilege and you should take it as a compliment. Who do you wish to ride with on the morrow?"

"I know the 14th best, sir."

"Good. We will be in position before dawn."

"Of course, sir."

I made certain that we were with the 14th shortly after midnight. They made a great fuss over my new rank but I pointed out to them that it was purely temporary and only to help me give orders. I wanted the regiment to be sharp for Masséna had attacked the Light Division at night and he had also done so at Bussaco; he might not wait for daylight. General Slade led the cavalry towards Pozo Bello. When we stopped, I realised how thin was our line. The four brigades stretched for two miles. We were just an early warning system for we could not stop over 4000 cavalrymen. That it would be cavalry which attacked was obvious to me. There would be infantry who would attack but this was not Bussaco. This was perfect country for horsemen. We were further away from Pozo Bello but we were in a good position to see, as dawn broke, the whole of the thin cavalry line. To my horror, we suddenly heard, as the sun rose, firing from Pozo Bello and the guerrilla cavalry hurtled past us racing for the Côa. Our right flank had fled and that put the rest of the line in jeopardy. I heard the trumpets from the King's German Legion and the Hussars as they sounded the charge.

General Slade shouted, "Stand to and prepare carbines." I nudged my horse closer to him. "What is going on, Matthews?"

"The Spanish are good soldiers when they have the element of surprise on their side but when the shoe is on the other foot, they are less reliable. I would say the French attacked. Sir, with your permission Sharp and I, will ride to Pozo Bello and try to get you some reliable information."

"Good man!"

"Sharp!"

We galloped towards the sound of the guns. I could see the 85th and the Caçadores streaming from the village and the wood. They were pursued by voltigeurs. Then I saw the French cavalry riding towards them. It was at that moment that General Arentschild led his two brigades towards the French cavalry. Some of the 95th were coming to the aid of the two fleeing battalions which were still trying to pull back in good order. "Sharp, ride and tell General Slade that he needs to bring the Horse Artillery and support the 85th and the Portuguese or they will be slaughtered." I knew that it might already be too late.

"Sir!"

I galloped towards the Germans and I drew my Baker as I did so. I heard the charge sounded and joined the German troopers as they galloped towards the French Dragoons. This would not be a charge where we met at full speed. We would hit at little more than a trot. Sabring fleeing infantry slowed down the French horsemen while General Arentschild had been assessing the threat as he led his brigades. The King's German Legion and the British Hussars were good and we were facing the least effective of the French horsemen. Even so, it would be a hard fight for we were outnumbered. I fired my Baker at almost point-blank range and threw a Dragoon from his saddle. I drew a pistol and fired at the Dragoon next to him. As he, too, fell from the saddle, I heard the German next to me laugh but as I did not understand his comment I could not reply. I drew my sword and it clattered into the steel of a Dragoon's sword. It must have been poorly made for it shattered.

The trumpet sounded to withdraw for the French were busy pursuing the Spanish cavalry and the men who had fled towards the river, and we were in danger of becoming isolated. The withdrawal was easier said than done. I used another pistol to create a diversion and the blast and smoke made the Dragoons who were close to me stop. I heard the French trumpets ordering the cavalry to reform. I turned and joined the German trooper. As we rode, he spoke to me in English. It was halting but it was better than my German. "You are one they call, Mad Major! Your gun, it is good. I will get one!"

I nodded, "It packs a punch!"

"Punch?"

"It is powerful!"

"Ja, it is!"

I saw General Slade forming up the 1st Dragoons and the 14th. The 1st Dragoons was a regiment of heavy cavalry and the equal of any French unit except for the Imperial Guard or the Carabiners. General Arentschild stopped to speak with General Slade and the four brigades reformed to face the French. The 85th and the Caçadores had managed, somehow, to reach the rest of the 7th Division which had advanced to help them. Our brigade of cavalry had done well. The 7th Division were still vulnerable to an attack but at least we had two guns of Bull's Battery with us. I saw a rider coming from the hill behind Fuentes. It was Lieutenant Mountshaft. He reined in next to General Houston and after speaking to him he galloped to the two cavalry generals. I spurred Donna to join them.

As I began to reload my weapons I caught the end of the conversation, "When the 7th begin to move back to safety then Sir Arthur wishes you to stop the French from pursuing them until they reach the rocks."

General Slade snorted, "That will be a neat trick!"

He was right but I could see that the rocks and slightly higher ground were close enough for the Division to manage. I could see the Light Division marching to support them. We just had to buy time.

General Slade said, "We will advance and engage the French. We will use the regiments with carbines to help the other squadrons withdraw. When I give the command then we withdraw by squadrons."

A German Major shouted, "They are forming up, sir!"

"Form line! Lieutenant Ramsay, if you could annoy the French then that would help. Bugler sound the charge!"

I saw Lieutenant Mountshaft hesitate, "Lieutenant, back to the General. You are his eyes and ears this day!" I wheeled Donna as I watched Sergeant Sharp leaving the Light Division to come to join us. He would have to catch up as we needed every horseman we could get. There were 1500 of us taking on 4000 men! I spurred Donna and joined Captain Wilson and his troop. They were the nearest I had to friends and when you went to battle friends were always an advantage.

I saw Troop Sergeant Hale nod. He was grinning, "About time we showed these Froggies who is better, sir!"

The 14th Light Dragoons all had their carbines at the ready and I took pride in that for until I had led their patrols, they had not even thought of using them. They were hung, like my Baker, on a sling attached to the swivel belt but they were ready to be used. The French Dragoons who charged at us were equally keen to show their mettle. General Slade obviously knew of the skills of the 14th and he shouted, "1st Dragoons, slow. The 14th will advance and fire on command!" I cocked my Baker as I rode forward. The green-coated French Dragoons were just fifty paces from us when General Slade roared, "The 14th will halt." We all stopped. "Fire and draw swords!"

As we fired a wall of smoke appeared before us and I dropped my Baker as the General shouted, "1st Dragoons, charge!"

The carbine balls had thinned the ranks of the French horsemen and unhorsed riders. The British Dragoons managed to charge into their lines and we, after drawing our swords, followed them. We struck the French cavalry and they fell back. There were more coming but they would have to negotiate their own dead and wounded. Colonel Oakley shouted, "Alternate squadrons will retire 200 paces and reload!"

When Captain Wilson's troop did not move, I knew that we would get to reload next. As we advanced to spar with the Dragoons, I saw Captain Knipe lead his squadron to attack a battery which was unlimbering. The infantry brigades were not out of artillery range yet and it was a brave charge but I knew how good French horse artillery was and as we fenced with the French Dragoons the cannons belched and I saw poor Captain Knipe and his horse blown to pieces. His men avenged him and sabred the gunners. When they came under fire from French infantry the survivors retired. It had been costly but the guns were silenced and other men lived because of the sacrifice of Captain Knipe.

"The 14th will retire!"

I slashed across the face of a French Dragoon who lowered his head and caught him on his helmet. It stunned him and allowed me to join Captain Wilson and his troopers as we headed back to the rest of the regiment. They had reloaded and had left gaps for us to ride through. As we did so I saw them raise their carbines. We stopped two hundred paces behind our comrades and turned to reload. As half our regiment opened fire I saw, to my horror, that Lieutenant Ramsay and his guns had unlimbered and were now in danger of being taken. We could not afford to lose any guns. I spurred Donna and rode obliquely across the front of the cavalry.

The gunners had limbered the gun but were having to fight off the French Dragoons. Donna was fast and, it seemed, I was the only one who had seen their dilemma. Then, as I heard hooves behind me, I saw Sergeant Sharp, "Sorry I am late, sir, I had an altercation with a Dragoon!" I saw that he had a sabre cut to his face.

"Better late than never!"

I still had my sword drawn and we galloped into the mêlée. It was hard to see the gunners but anything in green was a target and my sword swept into the back of a Dragoon who spread his arms as he fell from the saddle. My sword had sliced through his uniform, flesh and I had felt it scrape bone. I whirled Donna and my sword to create a space around us. Sharp had not fired his Baker and he did so at the perfect moment. It threw one Dragoon to the ground. I sheathed my sword and drew two pistols. I fired them at the Dragoons as Lieutenant Ramsay, who was commanding Captain Bull's battery at the time, had finally managed to man his horses and he shouted, "Ride like the devil is behind you, boys!" I holstered my pistols and drew my sword again.

Riding next to the lead horse of one of the guns we ploughed through Dragoons. It seemed impossible that we would survive and yet we did. Perhaps it was the madness of it or the fact that the crazed horses looked ready to tear apart any enemy who stood in their way. Sharp and I, along with Lieutenant Ramsay and his gunners laid about us with our swords as we swept aside the French. As we neared the cavalry the troopers all gave a cheer. I saw that the 85th and the rest of the 7th Division were now safely on the slopes of a rock covered hill. It was the perfect country for Light Infantry.

We kept facing the French and Sharp and I joined a squadron of the 14th which was reloading while Ramsay took the battery to set it up in the middle of the 7th Division. I reloaded my weapons and I was aware that I was out of breath. I was getting old. We were still withdrawing but it was our turn to fire as some Chasseurs galloped at us. Our volleys were more ragged now as we had lost men and some carbines had fouled but it slowed the French and, as Ramsay's guns opened fire, we were able to retreat through the cheering 7th Division to take our place on the higher ground behind them.

I saluted General Slade, "I will report to Sir Arthur. He cannot be anything but delighted with the performance of our men."

"You are right, Matthews, and may go in some way to make up for the criticisms the cavalry have endured from him."

As we made our way through the Light Division there were cheers and shouts from those who had observed the charge. I could hear fighting around Fuentes de Oñoro and turning to my left I saw that the French cavalry had reached the 1st Division. There was a company of the Scots Guards and they formed square. We reined in for Donna had charged too many times and the climb up the slope had tired her. She was breathing heavily. Giving my horse time to recover, I watched the Guards fire volley after volley into the French Dragoons who were forced to withdraw. I was just about to carry on my way when I saw, as the French retreated, the Guards break square. As a cavalryman, I knew that was a mistake and the elite unit was suddenly charged by a second French regiment, Chasseurs. Caught in the open I saw at least sixty men fall and the Lieutenant Colonel of the regiment captured. It was a needless waste and I knew that Sir Arthur would not be happy.

Chapter 16

By the time we reached Sir Arthur, busy in conference with his senior staff, I saw that the French cavalry had retired. As Donna had demonstrated, a horse, no matter how good, needed a rest. The French attack had lasted some time and the horses would need time to recover.

The elevated position meant I could dismount and still see the battlefield. As I did so I saw Sergeant Sharp's wound, "Sharp, go and find a doctor and have your face attended to."

"Sir!" He headed for the medical orderlies who were dealing with those wounded in the fighting in the village which lay not far away. Their base was close to Sir Arthur and his generals.

I took out my telescope to view the new defensive line. In pulling back to form a huge letter L, Sir Arthur had ensured that the French could no longer outflank us for the river now protected one flank. We still held the village and there were troops north of Fuente who had yet to fire a shot. If Marshal Masséna still wished to relieve Almeida then he had to come through the line at some point.

For some reason, the French cavalry were still just standing there and it was then I realised that the Guards had not been involved. Why? Had those 1000 elite and fresh horsemen charged then there would have been little chance of any surviving. You could not form an effective square if there were lancers and I knew that they had Polish Lancers with them. I saw Lieutenant Mountshaft leading his horse towards us. He had been given instructions by Sir Arthur. He grinned as he mounted close by me, "Sir Arthur is entrusting me with tasks which are more to my liking, sir! I am to tell the artillery to move to defend the village. The French battalions are massing."

He rode away and I saw that Picton's Brigade were forming up as were the Light Division. I could see that Ferey's troops, which were just on the other side of the river from the village, were also forming up. There were more than 6000 of them and the village was just held by the 71st and 79th regiments. Sharp returned, his head heavily bandaged. He said, "Lieutenant Colonel Matthews, Sir Arthur wishes to see you." Sergeant Sharp was proud of my temporary promotion and he beamed as he used it.

I nodded and handed him Donna's reins.

When I reached the General, he was alone. He had given his orders and sent his aides to deliver them. He pointed to the east where I heard the batteries begin a duel with their French counterpart. There we could hear above the sound of firing the distinctive sound of the *pas de charge*.

The French attack had begun. "I have sent the 24th to aid their fellows but I think we might need Lieutenant Colonel Williams and his light companies and rifles. Be a good fellow and have them wait close enough to the village to offer support. Stay with them for you did a reasonable job the last time." His eyes met mine, "Try to survive, eh? I have just managed to get you so that you are half decent as an aide and I cannot be pestered to train another!"

"Yes, sir!" I ran back to Sharp. "Tether the horses. We shall be on foot."

"The Bakers?"

"Bring yours. I shall make do with my pistols."

While he did as I had asked, I quickly reloaded one of my pistols. In a perfect world, I would have put an edge onto my sword but we had no time, and when he rejoined me we ran east, towards the light companies who were formed up close to the village.

Lieutenant Colonel Williams was smoking a cigar when I arrived. He threw it away and said, "I am guessing, Matthews, that your rapid arrival means that we are to be in action again soon?"

"Yes, colonel. There are 6000 men about to attack the three battalions in the village. Sir Arthur wishes you to support the men in the village."

He nodded, "This is the reverse of the other day! It is good that we know the village." He pointed to six companies on the left of his line. "Major Cartwright commanded those but the poor chap got himself shot the other day. Would you take charge of them? They are good fellows."

"Of course, and what are my orders, Lieutenant Colonel Williams?"

"Do the same as you did the other day. We know the village and I will take the other chaps through the alleys. You take these fellows up that path you used, eh? Wait for the sound of my bugle though; wouldn't want you to attack prematurely."

Four of the companies were Scottish and they were tough men but inclined to go wild. I did not have much time for I heard the firing as General Ferey and his men began to attack the village. I stood before the men that I would lead. I saw that each had either a captain or lieutenant commanding them. The two lieutenants looked young and I guessed the officer who normally commanded them had fallen. They had lost men in the fighting and none was a full company.

"I am Lieutenant Colonel Matthews and I have been given temporary command of this detachment. When we hear the bugle, you will follow me and we will enter the village from the side where we will attack the French." I looked pointedly at the 79th and their officers. "The other day I had to follow some rash fellows down to the river where we were nearly caught by cavalry! I do not wish to repeat that with such chosen men as you. Do I make myself clear?" When I had fought for Napoleon, I had been a sergeant and I used that voice now. It worked for they all nodded. The Light Company of the 79th knew of the incident and how close their fellow Scots had come to death. "Fix bayonets for this may be bloody."

As they fixed bayonets and I drew my sword a captain of the 24th approached, "Sir, I am Captain Gilbert and I had been given command of this detachment." I wondered if he was going to complain. "I am honoured to serve with you for I have been told by the rest of the regiment of what you did on the first day!"

I lowered my voice, "Thank you, Captain, and if you would be so good as to have your company follow me. In my experience, the Warwicks are a little less wild than the Scots. We shall need their wildness but first, we have to secure the village. Now let us go."

The firing, the shouts and the screams had intensified as we made our way around the side of the village to the dead ground. Had we not held the village then this approach would have been impossible but the French could not see it and the only way they could have made life difficult was by the use of howitzers but I could only hear British guns. Unusually we had won the battle of the cannons! We had barely made the starting point when I heard the bugle of the 60th. It was the signal for us to begin.

Raising my sword, I shouted, "For Sir John Moore!" It had worked for Sir Robert and it seemed to work for me. Running, we hurtled between the buildings and I saw some Frenchmen ahead of us. The road, I could not call it a street, was wide enough for just six men and the six who ran along it were myself, Sharp, Captain Gilbert, his Sergeant and two chosen men. Three muskets and a Baker opened fire into the side of the Frenchmen when we were just ten paces from them. At that range, the balls did not stop with the first men they struck, they carried on and wounded others. The smoke almost obscured the Frenchmen but I was bringing my sword down as we struck them. My blade connected with a Frenchman's shoulder. I was not sure if he was already wounded but he fell anyway. I almost tripped over the bodies but I had the presence of mind to avoid the dead. In a fight such as this, you needed the feet of a dancer and the Light Infantry were good dancers!

The sheer weight of the men we brought forced the French to move away from us and that allowed the defenders of the village, now reinforced by the rest of Lieutenant Colonel William's detachment, to begin to reclaim the parts of the village which had been lost. As we pushed them back so the Scotsmen I led were able to bring their weapons to bear. Muskets fired and swords slashed as we fell amongst the French. I was leading this time and so I had to keep an eye on the progress we were making. We were winning but I was aware that some of the 92nd were moving too far down the village. We had to consolidate our hold on the village first.

"The 92nd will stand firm!"

A Scottish sergeant shouted, "You heard the Lieutenant Colonel. McGregor, you dozy man, that means you."

I heard the sergeant from the Kent regiment shout, "50th present! 50th fire!"

He had seen what I had not. That there was a gap in the houses and Frenchmen were advancing up it. His volley halted them in their tracks. "Lieutenant Colonel Matthews detachment will wheel left!" My old sergeant's voice worked and the six companies turned. I had seen that the Rifles under Lieutenant Colonel Williams had ploughed into the French ahead of us and we could face this new threat. "50th will advance. The rest fall in and listen for the command!" There was such a cacophony of noise that had I not used such stentorian tones I would not have been heard. I joined the Captain of the 50th and the sergeant whose quick thinking had saved us from an unwelcome attack. I drew a pistol.

The French infantry had been hurt but a young officer raised his sword and shouted, as he launched himself at us, "With me! For the Emperor!"

Raising his sword which looked to be engraved he ran forward and the nearest men followed him. I raised my pistol and when he was ten paces from me shot him in the chest. The slope he was ascending and the force of the ball knocked him into the men who followed him. The sergeant of the 50th shouted, "At them!" He led the light company to tear into the French. A fight with bayonets is never pretty for, more often than not, it is bloody wounds which are caused rather than mortal ones. Strong men can continue to fight even when bleeding from many bayonet wounds. My sword and that of the captain of the 50th were more effective and we both used them well. We slashed down above the stocks of the French into the necks of the soldiers who were below us. When the 92nd crashed through us with wild Scottish screams it proved too much and the French 6th Regiment of foot fled.

I laid my sword to the side and shouted, "No one advances beyond me!" A lieutenant from the 92nd and the captain of the 50th laid their swords alongside mine to create a walking barrier. As we reached the edge of the village I looked across to the other side of the river. The French had another attack planned but this time it was the eighteen companies of grenadiers. These were the elite of the French army before us. Wearing their bearskins, they were marching towards the river. I turned and spoke to my sergeant, "Sharp, go and tell Lieutenant Colonel

Williams that there are eighteen companies of grenadiers coming to join the attack and then inform Sir Arthur!"

"Sir!" As he passed the sergeant of the 24th I heard him say, "You watch my officer!"

"Will do, Sharpie!"

I looked at the position we held. We were at the entrance to the village and the road was relatively wide. It was twenty men wide. The ground before us sloped and it was a natural funnel where a small number of men could hold a larger group. I could see the grenadiers marching down to the dry river bed. They would reform once they had crossed. Each company was made up of the tallest and the best soldiers in the regiment. The best of those were chosen to join the Imperial Guard and so the grenadiers regarded themselves as the best regular soldiers in France. They would be hard to defeat. "Captain, have your men climb to the tops of the buildings so that they can fire down on them as they advance!"

"Sir!" Turning to his sergeant the captain of the 50th said, "Have half of the men use the roofs on this side of the road, Sergeant, and the other half over there."

I turned to the Scottish officer, "Lieutenant, I want the 92nd here in two ranks."

"Sir!"

I turned to the rest, "I want the other four companies to build a barricade halfway up this road. Use anything that you can find from the houses. You will be the bastion to which the rest of us retreat."

"Sir."

I turned to the Lieutenant. His eighty men were in two lines and their sergeant was marching along them to ensure that their weapons were all loaded. "What is your name Lieutenant?"

"Dunbar sir."

"What happened to your Captain?"

"He was wounded the other day."

"You have done well thus far but this will be the hardest fight you will ever endure. These grenadiers are the biggest and the toughest men outside of the Imperial Guard. They will expect to win and they will keep coming even if we pour lead balls into them. I need your men to fire five volleys in a minute! It can be done but it is hard. When they have fired their fifth volley they will retire and stand before the barrier which is being built. They can reload while the others support us."

He nodded, "Yes sir. We will not let you down!"

"I know, Lieutenant. Now go and tell your men what we intend. Men always behave better if they know the reasoning behind the decisions. They will find it hard to run before the French but they must."

"Sir!"

I looked up and shouted, "Captain, hold them as long as you can and then fall back to the barricade."

"Sir!"

And we waited. We did not have long to wait for the grenadier companies had reformed and were now advancing to envelop the village. The 92nd had one row of men kneeling and the other one standing. To accommodate them all the sergeant had curved the line around in a half-circle. I went to stand at the right-hand side with my back to the wall. I reloaded my spent pistol and waited with my two pistols ready. I noticed that one of them was the one I had taken from the dead French trooper.

The drums rattled as the grenadiers marched closer. They were singing as they came and their arms swung while their muskets were held flat against their bodies. They had three hundred paces to come and they were advancing as though on a parade ground. There were more than 2000 of them and they were a fearsome sight. They marched in perfect time and their faces were set and determined. Their moustaches showed their aspirations to be the Emperor's guards. The horse batteries ploughed lines in them but soon the guns would have to stop.

"Lieutenant, you will begin to fire at eighty paces."

"Sir!"

I knew that was cutting it fine but I wanted the grenadiers to be blown away by the five volleys. Eighty paces was the effective range of a Brown Bess. The grenadier companies spread out and I saw that four of the companies were heading for our small road. I kept my pistols aimed at the grenadiers as they closed with us and the *pas de charge* seemed to fill the air. I was glad these were veterans who were following me. They would not be intimidated by the drumbeat but I saw the Lieutenant licking his lips nervously. His sergeant saw it too, "Dinna worry, sir. It's just a lot of noise. When it comes to cold steel those bearskins just make a man taller and keep his head warm in winter!"

I saw the Lieutenant nodding. He raised his sword, "Present!" and eighty muskets were raised.

The grenadier companies presented their own muskets but they were not raised to fire. They merely marched with them held bayonet forward. It was rare for French units to halt before they launched an attack. Perhaps they thought that we would not fire.

"Fire!"

The Lieutenant had told the men to fire five volleys and so only the first one was fired with all the muskets belching flame and smoke at once. The French disappeared in a cloud of smoke and then came the second volley and it was almost as one. The third was a little more ragged while the fourth and fifth rippled on. I aimed my two pistols into the smoke and I fired as the sergeant shouted, "Back lads!" There were shouts and screams from the fog as Frenchmen fell but the others would carry on for they were grenadiers!

From above us came the sound of individual muskets as the 50th poured musket fire on to the remnants of the first attack. They were above the smoke and Light Infantry knew how to shoot. They picked off the most dangerous targets. I followed the 92nd back to the barricade. I saw that it filled the road from side to side and was as high as a man.

Captain Langley of the 24th shouted down, "Sir, there is a door to your left it leads through the house and emerges here. You and the 92nd can escape."

"Thank you, Captain. You heard that, 92nd?"

A voice from lower down said grimly, "We don't retreat from Froggie bastards, sir!"

"Silence in the ranks!"

The lack of animosity in the sergeant's voice told me that he agreed with the sentiments. The men were not afraid of the wall of grenadiers who still advanced up the slope. We all reloaded and awaited the grenadiers. We had hurt them and they reformed to fill the gaps caused by the 4000 musket balls we had fired. A fresh company, untouched by the volleys led the way. This time they would use the column and I saw them running up the road to charge into us. There were no bodies for them to negotiate as we had retreated up the road and the ground was clear for one hundred and odd paces but the 50th was making life hard for them.

Captain Langley shouted, "Barricade party! Present!"

The Lieutenant shouted, "92nd prepare!"

From above me, I heard, "Fire!" and forty muskets belched forth. "Switch!" I knew what was happening. The men who had fired would be replaced by those with fresh muskets.

The Lieutenant shouted, "Fire!"

Above me I heard, "Fire!" and then "Switch!"

I fired my pistols and saw the Highlanders next to me reloading. It was almost impossible to see through the fog of war but from above I heard, "Lieutenant Colonel Matthews, they are falling back!"

Even as they began to cheer, I heard the sergeant of the 92nd bellow. "Hold there, boys! Wait for the officer!"

As we reloaded the smoke began to clear and I saw twenty odd bodies before us. I saw bloodied men being helped back down the road. We had stopped them but not defeated them. I watched them reform out of range of our muskets although the 50th still made life uncomfortable for them. Then one of the sergeants of the 50th above us shouted, "Lieutenant Colonel Matthews, there are ten more battalions of fresh troops forming up. It looks like they are going to charge!"

I waved my acknowledgement, "Captain Langley be so good as to send a messenger to Sir Arthur. He might already know but it won't hurt to send him word, eh?"

"Yes, sir!"

I turned to the 92nd who had finished loading and were at the ready, "It looks like we have fresh Frenchmen coming. We are the boys eh? We can handle whatever they send!"

"Aye, sir!" They chorused and cheered.

This would be hard but I knew that the men who followed me, whilst not my own men, would fight as hard as any. We had endured muskets and bayonets and we were not done yet. A fresh attack by 6000 men who had not yet fought, whose muskets had not been fouled, whose bayonets were sharp and who were not tired, were about to attack us. I could hear, hidden by the buildings, the fighting as it continued in the rest of the village. Then, above it all, I heard the *pas de charge*. I saw a grenadier company forming up and knew that the new troops would form up behind them and use the elite company as a human battering ram. This time there would be almost four hundred men thundering up the small road and our volleys could only thin them so much.

Some of the Scots began to sing a lilting Scottish ballad. It was in Gaelic and I could not understand a word but I did not need to for it was sad and it was melancholic. The six Scottish companies all joined in and the song echoed down the road, seemingly silencing the sounds of battle for I did not hear it, just the haunting song. And then the peace was broken as the grenadiers led the charge up the road. The 50th kept a constant musket storm but it could not stop them for they were firing as individuals. When they were eighty paces from us, we fired and then fired again but it did not stop them. There were simply too many men pushing forward corpses and climbing over dying and wounded men. I fired my two pistols into the fog and, after holstering them, drew my sword. The bayonet which came for me almost did for me but I was saved by the pistol I had taken from the dead trooper. The bayonet struck the plate with the engraving and is slid off to gouge a bloody line along my side. I sawed my sword across the neck of the grenadier and bright arterial blood poured down his white waistcoat. The men on the

The Lines of Torres Vedras

barricade fired down on the grenadiers and the fresh battalions come to take the village and end the battle. We would fight to the end but it would merely slow down the inevitable; we would be beaten.

The Scotsman next to me gurgled his life away as two grenadiers bayonetted him. I lunged with my sword and tore through the throat of one of them and severed the nose of the other but it was too late for the Scot. As I pulled back my sword it ripped the throat of the grenadier with the torn nose. We were face to face with the French now. A line infantryman was before me and neither of us could use our weapons for there were men pushing behind him and I was against the barricade. I felt myself being crushed. He opened his mouth as he tried to bite off my nose. I brought up my left knee and rammed it between his legs. He screamed like a stuck pig and I drew my stiletto from my left boot. I was able to ram it under his chin and into his brain. He stood frozen, held in place by the press of men behind him. I could feel my chest begin to be crushed as more and more men pushed from behind. Men were no longer dying because no one could reach weapons. They were grappling as though in a bar room brawl. Even the 50th could no longer fire down for fear of hitting our own men and then the inevitable happened, the crudely constructed barricade gave way and we were all pushed back. I was luckier than some for I had a wall to my side. As I fell and there was space, I held up my sword and a Frenchman was impaled upon it. I saw other Frenchmen climbing over the bodies of the wounded and raising their bayonets to skewer helpless men lying on the ground.

I tried to push the dead Frenchman from me but he was too heavy. However, as I lifted him and managed to kneel on one knee a Frenchman triumphantly lunged at me with his bayonet. I manage to partially flick it away with my stiletto but, as I stood, he whipped it backwards and I felt it cut through my jacket, waistcoat, shirt and finally flesh. He looked triumphant but, as that moment, the dead Frenchman slipped from my sword and I hacked, with all of my force into the side of his head. I was aware that I was isolated and the only Scotsmen who were left were on the ground, dead or wounded. I was an officer and despite the fact that I had lost my hat was still a prime target. Four Frenchmen raced towards me with bayonets held before them. My pistols were empty and my two wounds meant I felt weak. I thought I was doomed and I wondered what Emily de Lacey would say when she read of my death in the Gazette. I would not go easily; I would die hard.

I said in French, "It always takes four Frenchmen to kill a real soldier. Come on you sons of whores! Do your worst!"

I should have died but the door which Captain Langley had told me was my escape route suddenly burst open and Sergeant Sharp and

Lieutenant Mountshaft raced out. The Baker held by Sharp sounded like a six-pounder while the pistols held by the Lieutenant sent enough smoke out to make an instant fog. Sharp had the sword bayonet on the end and the fourth Frenchman was gutted in one sweep of the razor-sharp weapon.

Lieutenant Mountshaft drew his sword, "Take him to safety, Sergeant, I have work to do. 92nd are you with me?"

"Aye, sir!" As Sharp dragged me to safety, I saw Lieutenant Mountshaft and a wounded Lieutenant Dunbar leading the remains of the light company of the 92nd hurtling into the Frenchmen who were, amazingly, falling back.

Leaning on my sergeant and fearful that I would expire before I could speak with him, I said, "Is that wise?"

"Don't worry sir, General Picton is leading his Division and it is full of Irishmen, the French are done for and are heading back across the river. We have won! Now let us get you to the sawbones! Sir Arthur was quite insistent that we fetch you back and alive!"

That was how it was in battles. You only saw the length of your rifle or your sword and sometimes not even that. We had fought our own little battle and it was General Wellesley who saw the bigger picture. As we left the house willing hands made a stretcher of some Charleville muskets and I was carried through a village which looked like a scene from hell. My waistcoat was covered in blood and I was sure that I would bleed to death before I could be tended to. When we reached the doctors the one who was waiting for me shook his head and said, "This one may be too far gone!"

Then I heard a familiar voice as Sir Arthur's head appeared above me, "Save this one doctor for he is that rarity. He is a soldier who is brave and can think! I should hate to think of him dying without knowing that we have just driven the last Frenchman from Portugal."

I opened my mouth to speak but nothing came and then blackness came upon me.

Epilogue

When I woke, I was in an ambulance with Sergeant Sharp and we were headed to Lisbon with the rest of the wounded. It had been touch and go for I had needed almost forty stitches and the doctor told me that he almost lost me but I was alive. We would be heading for England for leave until I recovered. The bumpy journey was hard and uncomfortable but the pain told me that I had survived. I was no longer Lieutenant Colonel but I had not had time to grow used to the title. It had been for less than half a day and I reverted to Major Matthews. We reached a Lisbon which was now heaving with reinforcements fresh from England and I was pleased that Sharp was able to leave our horses with Portuguese friends for there they would be safe. Our time in the city had not been wasted. I was just about able to climb down from the ambulance at the quayside but I still needed to sit while Sharp saw that our bags were safely loaded about the transport. It was while I was seated there that a familiar voice said, "Major Matthews, is that you?"

I looked up into the eyes of Sergeant Major Jones of the 11th Light Dragoons who saluted. I smiled, "It is, Sarn't Major, but I fear I cannot rise to return your salute. I am afraid I was wounded at Fuentes de Oñoro. What brings you here?"

"The regiment is here, sir. I am just coming to bring a trunk the Colonel left aboard. He will be sorry to have missed you." He laughed and pointed to the transport for Sharp was on his way back, "Like ships passing in the night, eh sir?"

"Something like that but I will return when I am fully recuperated. You will find, Sarn't Major that this is a harsh place in which to campaign."

He beamed, "Still, it will be good to have you back in the regiment. You are still the best officer we have, outside the colonel that is."

After Sir Arthur's last words to me, I was unsure if he would let me go but I said nothing and nodded.

When Sergeant Sharp returned, he snapped to attention and smiled at the Sergeant Major, "Good to see you, Sarn't Major."

"It is good to see you have got on Sharpie. You were always a good lad."

Sharp looked at me, "Sir, the Captain said to hurry. He does not wish to miss the tide."

I stood and saw the frown crease Jones' face as I grimaced, "Don't worry, Sarn't Major, it will heal and I will return."

"Well, you take your time, sir. I will tell the lads I saw you."

The Lines of Torres Vedras

My wounds prevented me from looking back and I leaned on the stick which Sharp had acquired for me. As we left Lisbon I reflected on the irony. I was leaving when my regiment arrived. Sir Arthur was right, we had secured Portugal but we still had Spain to free and my work was not yet done. I sat in the cabin which had a window through which I could see the sea and I thought of all that had happened. There had been many promotions after Fuentes de Oñoro. Both Lieutenant Dunbar and Jamie Mountshaft had been elevated and Captain Mountshaft had rejoined a regiment. He was no longer an aide. There were failures too; Major General Erskine had once again made a mess of a simple task and had allowed the French garrison of Almeida to escape. However, we now had a border and a frontier we could protect. Sir Arthur had a much bigger army and Marshal Marmont was now in command of the Army of Portugal. For a few months, at least, I could forget the war and concentrate on healing.

It was at the beginning of July that we rode into King's Lynn. We took rooms at the Duke's Head Inn and I rode alone to the rose-covered cottage which overlooked the sea. I reined in and saw Emily de Lacey picking peas. She had a broad-brimmed hat upon her head and was oblivious to me. I dismounted and walked Badger towards the garden wall. Just then a serving girl came out of the house carrying an empty trug. She squealed when she saw me and Emily snapped, "Susanna, what is wrong with you?"

The servant pointed and Emily dropped her peas and ran through the gate to throw her arms around me and to kiss me. I had been unsure of what to do when I had reached England. Now I was glad that I had taken such a bold decision. I kissed her back!

The End

Glossary

Fictional characters are in italics

Cesar Alpini- Robbie's cousin and the head of the Sicilian branch of the family
Sergeant Alan Sharp- Robbie's servant
Caçadores - Portuguese light infantry
Major Robbie (Macgregor) Matthews-illegitimate son of the *Count of Breteuil*
Colonel James Selkirk- War department and spymaster to Sir Arthur
Colpack-fur hat worn by the guards and elite companies
Crack- from the Irish 'craich', good fun, enjoyable
Crows' feet- metal spikes like a caltrop
Joe Seymour- Corporal and then Sergeant 11th Light Dragoons
Joseph Fouché- Napoleon's Chief of Police and Spy catcher
Lieutenant Commander Jonathan Teer- Commander of the Black Prince
Old moustache- French slang for a veteran
Middy- Midshipman (slang)
musketoon- Cavalry musket
Paget Carbine- Light Cavalry weapon
pichet- a small jug for wine in France
Pompey- naval slang for Portsmouth
Prefeito – Portuguese official
Roast Beef- French slang for British soldiers
Rooking- cheating a customer
Snotty- naval slang for a raw lieutenant
Tarleton Helmet- Headgear worn by light cavalry until 1812
Windage- the gap between the ball and the wall of the cannon which means the ball does not fire true.

Historical note

The 11th Light Dragoons were a real regiment. However, I have used them in a fictitious manner. They act and fight as real Light Dragoons. The battles in which they fight were real battles with real Light Dragoons present- just not the 11th.

I have used as many of the actual people from the time. Erskine was the loose cannon I describe and his death was equally bizarre. As he fell to his death from a window in Lisbon he was heard to say, on the way down, "Now why did I do that?" Marshal Masséna's mistress did accompany him in Portugal and his decision to go via Viseu probably cost him the battle of Bussaco. Lieutenant Ramsay's escape with the guns was a famous one although some accord Ramsay the captaincy. From my research he only received that promotion after the battle. The fighting in Fuentes de Oñoro was as I described. The incident at Sobral actually happened although the Marshal did not appear to be in danger! The Colonel Trant incident really happened. The French officer in charge of the artillery train was about to surrender when French cavalry appeared.

I have used Robbie Matthews to represent a number of real people. Wellington famously used officers riding good horses to scout out the French and to outrun them. I have combined them in Robbie to make a better narrative.

If the Lines of Torres Vedras had been a battle then it would have gone down as the greatest victory which he ever enjoyed. The French lost 30,000 men while the Anglo-Portuguese lost a couple of hundred. Quite a remarkable feat. I speak of Hadrian's wall in the novel but I realise that may be misleading. The Lines of Torres Vedras were continuous but the gaps between them allowed for the movement of civilians. The earth, wood and, sometimes, stone defences were there to slow down an enemy and make them suffer so many casualties that they gave up!

Sir Arthur had defeated the French marshals but the war to regain Spain was far from over. There were setbacks to come and many more British soldiers would die, notably at Badajoz and Cuidad Rodrigo. That, however, is for the future. Let us allow Major Matthews some time for peace and for him to enjoy the company of Emily.

The books I used for reference were:
- Bussaco 1810-Chartrand and Courcelle
- Fuentes de Oñoro 1811-Chartrand and Courcelle
- Napoleon's Line Chasseurs- Bukhari/MacBride

- Napoleon's War in Spain- Lachouque, Tranie, Carmigniani
- The Napoleonic Source Book- Philip Haythornthwaite,
- Wellington's Military Machine- Philip J Haythornthwaite
- The Peninsular War- Roger Parkinson
- Military Dress of the Peninsular War 1808-1814
- The History of the Napoleonic Wars-Richard Holmes
- The Lines of Torre Vedras 1809-1811-Fletcher and Younghusband
- The Greenhill Napoleonic Wars Data book- Digby Smith,
- The Napoleonic Wars Vol 1 & 2- Liliane and Fred Funcken
- The Napoleonic Wars- Michael Glover
- Talavera 1809-Chartrand and Turner
- Wellington's Regiments- Ian Fletcher.
- Wellington's Light Cavalry- Bryan Fosten
- Wellington's Heavy Cavalry- Bryan Fosten
- Wellington as Military Commander- Michael Glover

Other books by Griff Hosker

If you enjoyed reading this book, then why not read another one by the author?

Ancient History

The Sword of Cartimandua Series
(Germania and Britannia 50 A.D. – 128 A.D.)
Ulpius Felix- Roman Warrior (prequel)
The Sword of Cartimandua
The Horse Warriors
Invasion Caledonia
Roman Retreat
Revolt of the Red Witch
Druid's Gold
Trajan's Hunters
The Last Frontier
Hero of Rome
Roman Hawk
Roman Treachery
Roman Wall
Roman Courage

The Wolf Warrior series
(Britain in the late 6th Century)
Saxon Dawn
Saxon Revenge
Saxon England
Saxon Blood
Saxon Slayer
Saxon Slaughter
Saxon Bane
Saxon Fall: Rise of the Warlord
Saxon Throne
Saxon Sword

Medieval History

The Dragon Heart Series

Viking Slave
Viking Warrior
Viking Jarl
Viking Kingdom
Viking Wolf
Viking War
Viking Sword
Viking Wrath
Viking Raid
Viking Legend
Viking Vengeance
Viking Dragon
Viking Treasure
Viking Enemy
Viking Witch
Viking Blood
Viking Weregeld
Viking Storm
Viking Warband
Viking Shadow
Viking Legacy
Viking Clan
Viking Bravery

The Norman Genesis Series
Hrolf the Viking
Horseman
The Battle for a Home
Revenge of the Franks
The Land of the Northmen
Ragnvald Hrolfsson
Brothers in Blood
Lord of Rouen
Drekar in the Seine
Duke of Normandy
The Duke and the King

New World Series
Blood on the Blade
Across the Seas
The Savage Wilderness
The Bear and the Wolf

The Lines of Torres Vedras

The Vengeance Trail

The Reconquista Chronicles
Castilian Knight
El Campeador
The Lord of Valencia

The Aelfraed Series
(Britain and Byzantium 1050 A.D. - 1085 A.D.)
Housecarl
Outlaw
Varangian

The Anarchy Series England 1120-1180
English Knight
Knight of the Empress
Northern Knight
Baron of the North
Earl
King Henry's Champion
The King is Dead
Warlord of the North
Enemy at the Gate
The Fallen Crown
Warlord's War
Kingmaker
Henry II
Crusader
The Welsh Marches
Irish War
Poisonous Plots
The Princes' Revolt
Earl Marshal

Border Knight 1182-1300
Sword for Hire
Return of the Knight
Baron's War
Magna Carta

The Lines of Torres Vedras

Welsh Wars
Henry III
The Bloody Border
Baron's Crusade
Sentinel of the North
War in the West

Sir John Hawkwood Series
France and Italy 1339- 1387
Crécy: The Age of the Archer
Man At Arms

Lord Edward's Archer
Lord Edward's Archer
King in Waiting
An Archer's Crusade

Struggle for a Crown
1360- 1485
Blood on the Crown
To Murder A King
The Throne
King Henry IV
The Road to Agincourt
St Crispin's Day

Tales from the Sword

Conquistador
England and America in the 16th Century
Conquistador (Coming in 2021)

Modern History

The Napoleonic Horseman Series
Chasseur à Cheval
Napoleon's Guard
British Light Dragoon
Soldier Spy
1808: The Road to Coruña
Talavera

The Lines of Torres Vedras
Bloody Badajoz
The Road to France

The Lucky Jack American Civil War series
Rebel Raiders
Confederate Rangers
The Road to Gettysburg

The British Ace Series
1914
1915 Fokker Scourge
1916 Angels over the Somme
1917 Eagles Fall
1918 We will remember them
From Arctic Snow to Desert Sand
Wings over Persia

**Combined Operations series
1940-1945**
Commando
Raider
Behind Enemy Lines
Dieppe
Toehold in Europe
Sword Beach
Breakout
The Battle for Antwerp
King Tiger
Beyond the Rhine
Korea
Korean Winter

Other Books
Great Granny's Ghost (Aimed at 9-14-year-old young people)

For more information on all of the books then please visit the author's web site at www.griffhosker.com where there is a link to contact him or visit his Facebook page: GriffHosker at Sword Books

Printed in Great Britain
by Amazon